PRAISE FOR

"I had planned on an early night but couldn't put this book down until I finished it around 3am. Like her other books, this one features fascinating characters with a plot that mimics real life in the best way. My recommendation: it's time to read every book Tammy L Grace has written."
— *Carolyn, review of Beach Haven*

"This book is a clean, simple romance with a background story very similar to the works of Debbie Macomber. If you like Macomber's books you will like this one. A holiday tale filled with dogs, holiday fun, and the joy of giving will warm your heart.
— *Avid Mystery Reader, review of A Season for Hope: A Christmas Novella*

"This book was just as enchanting as the others. Hardships with the love of a special group of friends. I recommend the series as a must read. I loved every exciting moment. A new author for me. She's fabulous."
—*Maggie!, review of Pieces of Home: A Hometown Harbor Novel (Book 4)*

"Tammy is an amazing author, she reminds me of Debbie Macomber... Delightful, heartwarming...just down to earth."
— *Plee, review of A Promise of Home: A Hometown Harbor Novel (Book 3)*

"This was an entertaining and relaxing novel. Tammy Grace has a simple yet compelling way of drawing the reader into the lives of her characters. It was a pleasure to read a story that didn't rely on theatrical tricks, unrealistic events or steamy sex scenes to fill up the pages. Her characters and plot were strong enough to hold the reader's interest."
—*MrsQ125, review of Finding Home: A Hometown Harbor Novel (Book 1)*

"This is a beautifully written story of loss, grief, forgiveness and healing. I believe anyone could relate to the situations and feelings represented here. This is a read that will stay with you long after you've completed the book."
—*Cassidy Hop, review of Finally Home: A Hometown Harbor Novel (Book 5)*

"Killer Music is a clever and well-crafted whodunit. The vivid and colorful characters shine as the author gradually reveals their hidden secrets—an absorbing page-turning read."

PATHWAY TO LAVENDER VALLEY

SISTERS OF THE HEART BOOK 2

TAMMY L. GRACE

LONE MOUNTAIN PRESS

Pathway to Lavender Valley
Sisters of the Heart
Book 2
Tammy L. Grace

www.tammylgrace.com
Facebook: https://www.facebook.com/tammylgrace.books
Twitter: @TammyLGrace
Instagram: @authortammylgrace
Published in the United States by Lone Mountain Press, Nevada

ISBN (eBook) 978-1-945591-46-4
ISBN (Print) 978-1-945591-57-0
FIRST EDITION
Printed in the United States of America
Cover Design by Elizabeth Mackey Graphic Design

ALSO BY TAMMY L. GRACE

COOPER HARRINGTON DETECTIVE NOVELS

Killer Music

Deadly Connection

Dead Wrong

Cold Killer

HOMETOWN HARBOR SERIES

Hometown Harbor: The Beginning (Prequel Novella)

Finding Home

Home Blooms

A Promise of Home

Pieces of Home

Finally Home

Forever Home

Follow Me Home

CHRISTMAS STORIES

A Season for Hope: Christmas in Silver Falls Book 1

The Magic of the Season: Christmas in Silver Falls Book 2

Christmas in Snow Valley: A Hometown Christmas Book 1

One Unforgettable Christmas: A Hometown Christmas Book 2

Christmas Wishes: Souls Sisters at Cedar Mountain Lodge

Christmas Surprises: Soul Sisters at Cedar Mountain Lodge

Remember to subscribe to Tammy's exclusive group of readers for your gift, only available to readers on her mailing list. **Sign up at www.tammylgrace.com. Follow this link to subscribe at https:// wp.me/P9umIy-e** and you'll receive the exclusive interview she did with all the canine characters in her Hometown Harbor Series.

Follow Tammy on Facebook by liking her page. You may also follow Tammy on book retailers or at BookBub by clicking on the follow button.

For K, my bookish partner-in-crime, and her encouragement and friendship

CHAPTER ONE

Harry took one more look at the new shield that was part of her retirement gift from the Salem Police Department. It was so shiny and looked just like her old one, except for the ribbon across the top with RETIRED embossed on it.

She slipped it into the inside pouch of her handbag and took one last walk around her office. She didn't recognize her desk. It had been years since she'd seen the top of it and now it was clean and tidy. Ready for the next occupant.

She had spent the last thirty years of her life among her brothers and sisters in blue. Most of her career she'd been housed at City Hall, but the new building had opened two years ago, and she'd enjoyed the modern office and conveniences since. All their support services and crime lab facilities were under one roof. She would miss the camaraderie and their shared purpose that she always took so seriously. As she strode to the elevator, she paused. This was her life and her family, for all intents and purposes. She hoped she wasn't making a mistake.

Along with her purse, she toted a box filled with the mementoes and photos that had decorated her office. On top was the nameplate engraved with DEPUTY CHIEF HARRIET MCKENZIE. Legally, she was Harriet, but nobody had called her that for decades.

She'd timed her exit in early January, when everyone was still recovering from office Christmas parties, and opted for a sedate retirement celebration in the conference room. Cake and a sip of champagne was enough for her.

Chief Mills tried to get her to agree to a fancy send off with a dinner and a wild night of drinking that was the hallmark of most career law enforcement retirements, but she wasn't in the mood for a party.

She stood, holding her box and staring at the empty desk where Tim had spent the last several years of his career. It was just two months since her coworkers had found him slumped over his desk, dead from a massive heart attack.

Harry couldn't pry her tear-filled eyes from it. Tim had been her partner for years before they had taken different career paths, and he'd always been there for her. His absence was a big part of why she was leaving her office for the last time tonight.

She blinked away the tears and took the elevator to the parking garage. After tossing the box in the backseat of her SUV, she waited for the security gate to rise and turned onto the wet pavement.

She pulled into her driveway in less than ten minutes, and as rain continued to patter against her windshield, waited for her garage door to open. She carried her box to the door that opened to the small mudroom between the garage and her kitchen.

A furry, golden head popped through the opening of the doggy door and greeted her with a tongue-out smile. She chuckled and urged Chief back inside the room, as she unlocked the door.

His tail thwacked against her legs as he celebrated her happy return. She slipped out of her wet boots and opened the door to the kitchen, with the dark, almost copper colored golden at her heels. He had been Tim's golden retriever and much like his previous owner, never failed to bring a smile to her face.

She petted the top of his head. "Hey, Chief, you're a good boy. I bet you're ready for dinner, huh?"

Tim had divorced three years ago and brought the golden puppy into his life for company. His ex-wife had moved away and his two kids were grown, so Harry had helped him co-parent the dog since Chief was a puppy. When Tim died, Harry didn't think twice about adopting Chief.

His manners weren't the best. Tim had fully embraced bachelorhood and wasn't much for housekeeping or making Chief toe the line. Living at Harry's house, the dog had a rude awakening, but Harry was making great progress with him.

His eyebrows lifted at the mention of a meal and he followed her while she added food to his bowl.

While he ate, she turned on her electric kettle and added a tea bag to a cup. She wandered to her bedroom and slipped into some warm pajamas and her favorite slippers, then on the way back to the kitchen, detoured into the living room and lit the wood she had stacked in the fireplace. She was in the habit of preparing it in the morning or afternoon, since when she got home she was too tired, and yet loved the warmth of it in the winter.

With the fire taking hold, she started back toward the kitchen, when her eye drifted to the pile of mail on the floor in front of her door. She chuckled when she saw a few teeth marks in a couple of envelopes and counted her lucky stars the mail wasn't shredded.

Her house was vintage, built in the 1940's, and the mail in her neighborhood bordering Bush Park was delivered through the slot in the door. She had worked hard to teach Chief to leave the mail alone, but he must have found a few pieces irresistible. She bent to pick up the envelopes and junk mail that were scattered across the shiny wooden floor, then carried them with her into the kitchen. Chief stared at her with eyes that begged for a walk as she added hot water to her cup.

"Sorry, bud. Not tonight." She led him through the dining room, where she deposited the stack of mail, then to the sunroom and out the door into the backyard. Back in the kitchen, she gathered her tea and carried it to the sliding glass door to keep an eye on Chief.

He was going to be wet, and she wanted to avoid muddy paws, if at all possible. With a quick trot, he made his way back from the grass and across the concrete patio to the door. She held a towel and he lifted his paws, letting her dry each one. Progress.

Over the last two months, they'd developed this routine. She was almost sure Tim had never wiped the dog's paws before letting him inside, but she didn't need the hassle of cleaning her floors more than she already did.

Chief had resigned himself to the degrading task and waited as she reached for his last paw to clean. As soon as she was done, he rushed into the house and straight to the living room.

They had gotten into the same pattern since Chief had come to live with her, and as much as she resisted letting him snuggle next to her on her leather couch, that's what happened each evening. He even shared her bed. Harry figured Chief was mourning Tim and she wanted to comfort him as much as possible, so caved after only one night of making him stay on the floor.

Though Chief might have had trouble adjusting to the rules of the house, he didn't have any trouble adjusting to Harry. She had seen him almost daily and she adored him. From the look in his gentle eyes, where he waited for her, curled atop the buttery soft blanket that protected her leather couch, the feeling was mutual.

After putting the dirty towel in the laundry room, Harry carried her tea and the stack of mail she had ignored over the last few days and plopped next to him, flicking on the television for background noise.

Chief rested his head against her and sighed. She slid her hand over his soft fur and patted his head. "No more work for me, Chief. Can you believe I'm retired? That means more playtime for you."

He thumped his tail against the blanket.

She fortified herself with a sip from her cup, then began sorting through the envelopes. Most of it was junk, but she frowned when she picked up a thick envelope and saw the return address from a lawyer in Lavender Valley.

She opened the flap and slid out the contents. As she read the first lines, Harry gasped and brought her hand to her chest. "Oh, no. Not Jewel."

Chief lifted his head and inched closer to her.

She scanned the information from the attorney and reached for a tissue from the end table. Harry had intended to take a drive down to see Jewel in the coming weeks. Now, it was too late.

Within the papers from the attorney, letting Harry know Jewel had named her executor, there was a flowered address book and another envelope. The lump in Harry's throat grew bigger when she recognized the scrawl of Jewel's handwriting and her own name on it.

She took a deep breath and opened the letter, dated just over a week ago, on Christmas Day.

Dear Harry,

I should have discussed all this with you long before now, but time has a way of fooling us. It's the one thing we never have enough of and in the end the only thing we want.

I've been declining for the last few months and I know my time is near. I only wish I could have seen you one more time. Don't grieve for me, dear one. I've had the most wonderful life and know where I'm going. It's almost fifteen years since I lost Chuck and I'm looking forward to seeing him soon.

I hate to burden you, but from our last chat, got the feeling you were giving retirement some serious consideration, especially after Tim's death. With that in mind, I decided to name you my executor. Along with that, comes some special instructions.

Over the years, I've kept in touch with many of the children who lived with us, but in addition to you, there are four women with whom I've maintained a close connection. My wish is for you to find all of them and bring them back to the farm.

None of you lived at the farm at the same time, but I think you'll be good for each other. You all have different strengths and talents, and together nothing can stop you.

I am leaving the five of you the property and all my earthly possessions with the hope that you will find what you need here. It was once a haven for each of you and I think it can be again.

My only stipulation is that all five of you must spend a full season together at the farm, participating in the Lavender Festival again, and reinvigorating my animal rescue and sanctuary. Come the holidays, each of you can make a choice, to stay or go. If none of you want to stay and keep the farm, you may sell it and split the proceeds, equally.

If anyone doesn't return to the farm or leaves before the season is over, she forfeits her rights to any proceeds. Mr. Simpson knows all the legal mumbo jumbo, but that's my simple take.

My hope is that at least one of you finds a calling to stay and make Lavender Valley Farm her permanent home. I'd like nothing more than to see what Chuck and I started, so long ago, continue and thrive.

Most important to me, I want you to have my most treasured possession. My sweet girl, Hope. Please love her and give her a happy and safe life. She was my best friend and with me through some of the worst times of my life. These last few months haven't been easy and she never wavered.

I trust you to do what is right and just, Harry. You always did, and I have no doubt you will now.

I've included my address book with the most current contact information I have for each of the ladies. Georgia lives in the Boise area, Olivia in Spokane, Micki is outside of Seattle, and Lydia is a bit of a nomad. I'm sure with your resources, you'll be able to find her.

Each of you has your own story and when the time is right, I trust you will all share yours with each other. Suffice it to say, I believe you're all at a point in your lives where you need your sisters.

My neighbor's ranch is run by his son, Clay, now. He's a couple years older than you. I'm sure you remember the Nolan Ranch. His number is in the front of my address book and he's been taking care of things at the farm. We also have a business arrangement, and my lawyer has included those documents for you. Clay leases pasture from me for his angus cows.

Mr. Simpson, my lawyer, can explain everything and he is very trustworthy, as was his father, who was our lawyer before him. I have plenty of money in the bank to get you through the next year and if I know the five of you, I suspect you'll be able to be even more successful than Chuck or I ever dreamed of.

More than anything, I hope you all find a sense of belonging and love, like you did all those years ago. Although you're not related, I often think of the five of you as sisters of the heart. Know each of you will always have a piece of mine.

Please pass along my love and best wishes to all of them and my thanks for bringing me so much happiness. There is no greater joy than to know I had a small part in shaping each of your lives. You are all wonderful, talented, and loved.

With all my love,

Jewel

Harry read the letter again and shook her head. "Oh, Jewel, what have you done?"

CHAPTER TWO

After a fitful night's sleep, Harry woke to more rain falling from an overcast sky. No surprise for a January day in Salem. She glanced over and saw Chief, snuggled up with this tiny green puppy blanket that he slept with each night and Tim's old slipper under his head. Tim gave it to Chief when he brought him home as a puppy and Harry figured it comforted the big dog. He tended to carry it around and take naps with it. Despite it ragged appearance, it must still hold Tim's scent.

Chief enjoyed his breakfast while she drank a leisurely cup of tea. When she bundled up, Chief saw his leash in her hand and spun in circles.

"I know, sweet boy. You missed our walk yesterday. From now on, no excuses. We can walk whenever we want."

She attached his leash, and they made their way out the front door and down the sidewalk to the park. Harry's waterproof jacket and hood kept the rain away, but by the time they made a loop, Chief was soaked. At least his top layer was wet. She'd learned how dense and oily his coat was after their first walk in the rain.

With each step, Harry's mind wandered to Jewel and the farm and what she was going to do. It's not like she had much choice. The lawyer's letter did say she could decline the executorship, but she would never consider disappointing Jewel. If she wanted Harry overseeing things, she'd be there.

The tricky part would be convincing four others to join her. Would they all be able to commit a year of their lives to this fanciful idea of Jewel's?

Now that Harry was retired, she could go anywhere, so making the trip down to Lavender Valley was easy. Staying for the rest of the year would be the hard part. She followed the sidewalk back to her house.

What was she going to do about her house? She couldn't leave it empty for a year. She took such loving care of it, and the thought of renting it made her stomach churn. Maybe she could find someone at her old office looking for a place. She hoped to find a single person or a couple without kids. She couldn't bear the thought of her wood floors and antique glass door knobs being subjected to the harsh treatment a houseful of kids could deliver.

She was getting ahead of herself. There was every possibility none of the other women would want to come to Lavender Valley for a year. Chances were, they had families and couldn't just uproot them. The first order of business was to find them all and have that conversation.

Technically, Harry wasn't retired until the end of the month. She was burning her vacation time that exceeded the maximum allowed for a payout. She could spend a few hours at the office and see what she could learn about these four women. She had an excellent relationship with the guys in tech services, and they had ways of bypassing the police databases and scouring social media to find all sorts of information.

As soon as they got home, Harry towel dried Chief, much to his delight. He loved nothing more than sprawling across the patio and indulging Harry as she rubbed him dry. He even turned from side to side when she asked, relishing the attention, and gave the occasional nip at the edge of the towel.

With him as dry as he was going to get, she guided him inside and while he stretched out in front of the fireplace, she jumped in the shower. She was drying her hair when her thoughts drifted to Jewel.

The woman she thought of as a mother always had a way of guiding those in her care, and as much as Harry questioned her current method, she couldn't fault her proven results. She hoped Jewel knew what she was doing when she came up with this idea.

The woman had uncanny timing. Over the years, when Harry needed a little boost, she often received a letter from Jewel. Her words never failed to lift her spirits or impart the exact bit of wisdom that Harry needed to hear. And now Harry suspected Jewel knew more than she divulged.

With her hair fixed and a bit of makeup on, Harry added a jacket over her sweater and jeans, and slipped Chief's harness over his head. He stood quiet and still as she snapped the clips closed. He knew he was going to work.

Tim often brought him to work, and Chief had adapted to office life, snuggling in the bed next to Tim's desk and napping most of the day away. Harry couldn't resist indulging him in one last visit.

She loaded him into her SUV and they set off for downtown.

They parked in the visitor area, and Chief strutted through the door at Harry's side. Everyone knew Chief and Harry and showered them with greetings on their way to the technical services department.

While Harry gave the names of the four women to her favorite techie, Trevor, Chief was busy shaking the others down for treats. Harry reiterated that she wasn't looking for anything related to a case or a criminal issue, but knew Trevor could search online and find what she needed to know faster than she could ever hope to.

She pointed at Lydia's name. "She's going to be the toughest to locate."

He promised to check things out on his personal time, and guessed he'd have something for her in the next day. He sent Harry on her way with a wave and Chief with a beef flavored treat.

Next on Harry's list was a stop by Jolene's office. She was in charge of the administrative services and always had her ear to the ground. Some might call it gossip but Harry liked to think of it as intelligence gathering. Jolene knew everything that was happening. If anyone knew of a potential candidate to rent Harry's house for a year, it would be Jolene.

Jolene wasn't at her desk, but a steaming cup of coffee with a ring of bright red lipstick on the rim suggested she wouldn't be long. Harry slipped into a chair and gave Chief the command to lie down next to her.

He happily complied. Jolene always had treats and he knew he'd be rewarded for good behavior.

A few minutes later, Jolene came through the door, carrying a donut on a napkin. "Harry, what brings you by? Aren't you supposed to be retired?"

Harry laughed. "Yes, but officially at the end of the month. I'm here because I need your help."

Jolene smiled and nodded, her dyed red hair bouncing atop her shoulders. "Of course, you do. Everyone needs Jolene's help. What can I do you for?"

"I'm looking for a renter for my house, and thought you might know of someone reliable who's looking. I'll be gone for a year. I'd prefer a single woman—"

"What? You're leaving for a year?" Jolene interrupted. "That's one long holiday!"

Harry quickly explained where she was going and why, then steered the conversation back to finding the perfect renter. A single woman, with no pets, though she would consider bending the pet rule, but her house was in excellent condition and she wanted to keep it that way. The idea of a bachelor who never cleaned things and left beer bottle rings everywhere made her cringe. She was painting with a broad stereotypical brush, she knew, but didn't care. Her house was like her baby.

In between bites of a maple donut, Jolene scribbled notes on a pad. "Oh, that's a great neighborhood and furnished. That's even better. Let me give it some thought. We've had some new hires, so there might be somebody in that group that's looking for a house."

She asked about the monthly rate and other costs, and added them to her list. "Okay, Harry, I'll do some checking and be in touch." Jolene swiveled in her chair and opened a small container. She took out a bone shaped treat and wiggled her brows at Chief. "Can he have a treat?"

Like Harry could say no now? "Sure, just make him sit for you."

Chief performed like a champ and took the treat with a gentle mouth, earning a smile and scratch to his ears.

Harry stood. "Thanks, Jolene. Just call my cell if you get anywhere."

"You got it, Harry. I'll talk to you soon."

Harry led Chief down the hallway, and after stopping for more pets and greetings, they finally made their way outside to Harry's car. The rain hadn't let up, so she had to wipe Chief's paws before putting him in the backseat.

As she drove home, Harry couldn't help but think of Jewel. The woman who had healed her heart and helped her navigate her teen years was gone. Regret filled her mind as tears dripped from her brown eyes.

Harry's career often brought her to the depths of humanity. She had seen the worst of the worst, the destruction of lives, families torn apart and changed forever in the wake of horrible violence. Jewel was the soft place she could always count on when things got to be too much.

As much as Jewel enjoyed letters, Harry had taken to calling her, often when she was driving home after work. For Harry, it was a wonderful way to transition from work to home. Jewel was a great listener, and without Harry saying a word about her cases or the cruelty she had witnessed, Jewel had a way of knowing what Harry needed to hear.

Usually, it was something entertaining about her animals or life at the farm. Sometimes, it was a funny bit of gossip from town, other times it was a touching story from church. She always made Harry feel better, and a short conversation with her was all Harry needed to bolster her spirits.

On more than one occasion, Jewel had hinted that Harry might be happier if she found a partner in life. A good and honest man. The problem was, being a cop, and especially a high-ranking one, wasn't conducive to family life. Over her years, Harry witnessed countless coworkers go through the pain of a divorce, or even worse, saw the aftermath of them coming home to an empty house with a note from their spouse saying they couldn't take it anymore.

It was a lonely life, but a rewarding one. What Harry gave up on the personal front, she more than made up for in her ability to bring justice to the victims. She worked tirelessly for them.

In her early years as an officer, she had dated, usually guys affiliated with the police in some way. A few lawyers, a firefighter, even some paramedics and a doctor had captured her romantic attention, but none of them panned out. Most of them were looking for a woman who would stay home, keep house, and raise a family. That wasn't in Harry's plan.

Once promoted, Harry had given up on the idea of dating and remained laser focused on her work. She boasted the highest clearance rate in the history of the department and enjoyed imparting her wisdom to the up-and-coming detectives. She was never bored and had more work than she would ever be able to complete.

She worked early, late, and weekends and when she was home, more often than not, had a few case files next to her. She had a small circle of friends, most of them through her work. That circle got even smaller once she was promoted. She didn't want even a hint of favoritism spoken about her and walled herself off from everyone she supervised.

She wasn't a huge fan of hanging out with the others at her same rank. Most of them were older, male, and had families. Other than her career-long friendship with Tim, Harry led a rather solitary life and never gave it much thought, until now.

Maybe Jewel's idea to spend a year at the farm wasn't so outrageous after all. Harry had nowhere to be and no obligations. For once in her life, she didn't have a plan or a goal. All she knew was she didn't want to die at her desk.

After fixing a late breakfast and sharing her scrambled eggs with Chief, she thought of Hope. Jewel's compassion for animals had been passed to Harry. She remembered how sad Chief had been when Tim died and couldn't get the image of a forlorn dog, pining for Jewel, out of her mind.

Harry was friends with a family down the street. He was a fireman and they still had a daughter living at home, who Harry had employed to watch her house the last time she'd been gone for a few days. She could ask her to housesit and take off in the morning.

She sat at the dining room table and nursed a cup of coffee while she stared into the living room. Chief was sacked out on his bed, the old slipper next to him. There was no doubt he was worn out from their morning excursion and his incessant begging.

Her eyes cut to the flowered address book and she opened it to the first page. There, in Jewel's handwriting, she saw a list of locals with their phone numbers. At the top was Clay Nolan.

Before she could change her mind, Harry punched in his number on her cell phone.

He answered on the second ring. "Nolan Ranch, Clay here."

"Hi Clay, my name is Harry McKenzie. I stayed with Chuck and Jewel on their farm when I was growing up."

"Hey, Harry. Jewel told me her plans. Well, at least part of them. She said you'd probably be calling once she passed away. She was a special lady and I'm going to miss her. My condolences to you, ma'am."

Harry's nose wrinkled. The dreaded ma'am. That meant she was officially old.

"Thank you. I'm going to miss her too. I'm calling about Hope, her dog."

"Oh, yes, she's a sweet girl. I've got her over at my place for now."

"Good, I was worried about her more than anything. I just received the information from Jewel's lawyer, so I'm getting organized and will be driving down to Lavender Valley in the coming days. I thought I might need to come right away for Hope."

"Take your time. She's fine and friends with my dog, Maverick. She'll be in good hands until you get here. I'm keeping an eye on Jewel's place, too. Making sure the alpacas and donkeys are fed, along with the chickens. Just let me know when and I'll meet you over there."

Clay's deep voice and reassurance calmed her, and his mention of the animals brought back memories of getting up early to feed and help with the farm chores. She wasn't going to let Jewel down, but hoped some of the others would also feel the need to return to the farm. She couldn't imagine trying to take care of things by herself.

"I'm going to call her lawyer next and hopefully be down there next week. I just need to get things sorted here." She paused. "It's a bit of a shock."

"I understand, believe me. My dad passed away just two years ago, and filling his boots has been hard. Jewel was a sweetheart. Anything you need, just call me. I've been helping her out for several years and know the place like my own."

"You don't know what a relief that is, Clay. I'm not sure what I'm getting into, but I want to honor Jewel's wishes."

"Give me a call when you figure out your schedule. Looking forward to seeing you, Harry."

She thanked him again, disconnected, and leaned back in her chair. Now if only Jolene would come through with a suitable renter, she could do this.

The prospect of a new adventure in her old stomping grounds excited Harry. It also sent a shiver of fear through her. Jewel had reminded her more than once that being brave didn't mean you weren't afraid. It just meant doing something despite your fears.

Harry had faced down harder things than this before. She only wished she had more time to think this through.

CHAPTER THREE

Harry wasn't on social media and didn't have a platform anywhere. At work, she relied on her technical support team to navigate all things social media and had, on occasion, been assigned a fake profile when working a case, but she knew just enough to be dangerous.

When she read the email from Trevor with the links to the social media accounts of the ladies, her eyes focused on the one for Lydia. She clicked it and was met with a screen letting her know she had to sign up to view Lydia's account.

She glared at the screen and muttered. Harry believed social media was responsible for the decline of humanity and had vowed never to be part of it. She certainly didn't want to use her real name. She pondered for a few minutes and came up with something she thought would work. After tapping the keyboard and clicking the verification email, she smiled.

Her new account in the name of Harry M. Austin, a nod to Jewel and Chuck, was born. She added a profile picture, using a recent one of Chief and opted to leave off all her personal information.

With that done, the overlords granted her access to see Lydia's information. She scrolled through and didn't see any recent activity and her profile was locked down and open only to her connections. All that effort wasted to get no information.

Harry read the rest of Trevor's email. He verified the addresses for all the other ladies and said that Lydia's last known address was General Delivery in Yakima, Washington. He added that she was a chef at an upscale restaurant associated with a winery.

In addition to the contact information, he provided the verified birthdates for all the women and a few notes. From his research, Harry learned that Georgia's husband had died a few months before, and Olivia's son had also passed away recently. Micki had lost her husband years ago and had two children in college. Lydia had never married.

Harry typed in the restaurant name and made a note of their phone number. They were only open for dinner, so she'd wait to call.

The other women, with the exception of Georgia had social media accounts, but they were also locked down, except for a few posts and photos that didn't divulge much.

Taking a cue from Jewel, Harry rifled through her desk drawer until she found a box of stationery. It had been a gift from Jewel and she had only used it to send letters to Lavender Valley.

Harry labored at her desk as she drafted a rough copy of the letter she intended to send to each of the women, save Lydia. She made sure to mention Jewel's wishes and her thoughts that they needed each other. Along with sharing the sad news, Harry wrote a bit about herself, letting them know she was newly retired from law enforcement and that if they had any questions about her identity, they could contact the Salem Police Department.

After revising the draft a few times, she was happy and proceeded to use the good stationery and write to each of them. She didn't want them to think this was a scam, so included her cell phone number, along with her old business card, letting them know she'd be at Lavender Valley Farm in a few days and was looking forward to hearing from them soon and learning their decision.

She read over the letters one more time, before sealing them in envelopes and applying stamps.

By the time she finished, it was late afternoon. She grabbed Chief's leash and slipped into her jacket and boots. The rain had turned to a light drizzle, and Chief pranced next to her as they made their way down the sidewalk and across the footbridge over a small creek to the post office.

It was less than a ten-minute walk and the perfect way to clear her head. She dropped the lavender colored envelopes into the slot and let out a long breath, then saw the display of address change forms and slipped one in her pocket. "I hope Jewel knows what she's doing." She glanced down at Chief, sitting next to her, and saw the hint of a smile.

Harry took that as a good sign and instead of going straight home, stopped by Basil and Cork, the Italian place she loved. After all her work today, she rewarded herself with a carb-laden pasta dish and their delicious garlic bread in a takeout box.

Once home, she dried off Chief and fed him before settling in with her tasty dinner. As she savored the meal, she was reminded that her days of walking a few blocks to find a wonderful restaurant or going shopping would be over, once she was living back in Lavender Valley.

Medford was less than ten miles away, but in downtown Lavender Valley she would only find the essentials. On the flip side, she loved the quiet and peaceful farm, with the creek and little lake.

It's what Jewel wanted and after dedicating her life to others in need, it was the least Harry could do. She could take a year and honor the woman she credited with helping her find her way in life. Salem would be here waiting when she returned.

As she ate the last bite of pasta, she glanced at the clock. The restaurant in Yakima had opened over an hour ago. She popped the last bit of buttery bread into her mouth and took her plate to the kitchen, then picked up her phone.

A woman answered her call with a cheerful greeting.

"I'm looking for Lydia Morrow, your chef. I'm hoping to speak with her or at least get her a message to call me back. It's rather urgent."

The woman's tone changed. Harry had years of experience listening to and observing witnesses, and she could pick up on wariness when she heard it. The woman let Harry know Lydia was busy in the kitchen, but she would pass on a message to her.

"My name is Harry McKenzie. I'm the Deputy Chief of Investigations with the Salem Police Department in Oregon. I'm officially retiring at the end of the month and out of the office, but can leave my cell phone number with you. Please have Lydia call me and if she has any concerns, she can verify who I am by calling the department." She rattled off the number to her division.

"I understand, Ms. McKenzie. I'll make sure Lydia gets your message." The caution in her voice was gone.

Harry didn't like to use her position, but in this case

thought it important to lend credence to her request, and since she was technically still employed, she justified it.

After she disconnected, Harry started a fire and changed into her pajamas. She made herself a cup of tea and snuggled into the corner of the couch, with Chief next to her, his nose inside the old slipper. She wanted to savor every moment in her house.

When she made the decision to retire, she promised to spend more time at home and enjoy the space she had spent so much time creating. A trip to the coast had even crossed her mind. Now, a different path was calling her. One that would lead her back to her roots in Lavender Valley.

For the first time in a long time, Harry slept late. Last night she'd stayed up past midnight, watching an Australian series she'd discovered called *My Life is Murder*, and kept telling herself just one more episode. Before she knew it, midnight came and went. The main character in the show was a retired police detective who elected to spend her retirement baking bread. Her old boss kept showing up asking for her help, pulling her into cases he needed help solving.

Harry connected with the main character and the clever writing. The idea of baking bread in retirement didn't hold much appeal, but she wondered if her old boss would be showing up at Lavender Valley Farm to ask for her help to solve any cases. The idea made her chuckle.

After a morning walk with Chief, Harry showered and made some toast while she scanned her emails. She saw one from Jolene that included a string of happy face emojis.

She smiled as she read the contents. One of the evidence

clerks, Cora, was recently divorced and looking for a house. She needed to rent something until she could save up enough for a down payment and was interested in Harry's place. No kids, no pets.

Harry didn't socialize with her, but knew Cora to be responsible and accurate, and the fact that she was on her own appealed to Harry's need for someone that would be gentle with her house and furnishings. She put in a call to Cora's work extension and left a message to set up a time for her to come and tour the house.

Things were starting to gel.

Harry's eyes focused on a framed photo of Jewel and Chuck with Harry between them. It had been taken when they came to the Iris Festival, and a glance at their happy smiles warmed Harry's heart. She ran her finger along the edge of the silver frame. "I have a feeling you're orchestrating all of this, Jewel."

The call to the lawyer was still on her list, so she tapped in the number and the receptionist put her through to Mr. Simpson.

His warm voice was full of concern, and he assured her he would make time to meet with her whenever she arrived in Lavender Valley. Jewel had arranged for everything, and he would help her navigate the legalities.

Harry's shoulders relaxed as she listened to his slow, easy manner. She set up an appointment for the following week, giving herself plenty of time to get there.

She fixed another cup of tea and while Chief took his morning nap, Harry starting packing for the farm.

She emptied her drawers and closet and placed her clothes into suitcases, then transferred her police uniforms and most of her suits to the spare bedroom, opting to take only three, just in case she had to go somewhere that warranted it.

She scanned the bookshelves, her eyes drawn to the Sue Grafton books Jewel had given her so long ago. She had kept them alongside all the other mysteries she had collected over the years.

Now, she could read books on her tablet and chose to do that when away from home. She needed to take her laptop, tablet, and cell phone, plus all the chargers for them. She added all her toiletries to a tote bag, and took a few pairs of shoes and boots out to her SUV.

She added a variety of jackets and raincoats to the back of the SUV and then wandered through the house, looking for anything else she might need to take with her. Harry was not a collector and not much of a shopper. She spent all of her time working or sleeping and her home reflected that in the minimalist vibe. There was little clutter, and not being one to cook much, her cabinets held only the basics.

She spied her photo albums and added those, plus the framed photos in the built-in bookcase surrounding the fireplace and took the time to wrap them in bubble wrap before adding them to a box.

Harry toted that box to her SUV and was shutting the back of it when her cell phone rang. It was Cora, who sounded excited about the house. She wanted to stop by as soon as she got off work later in the afternoon.

"I'll be home and see you then," said Harry before disconnecting the call. She checked the time and realized it was well past the lunch hour. Inside, she opened the fridge to find only condiments and something in a takeout container she couldn't identify. One apple remained in the crisper and she took it out and washed it.

She ate lunch at her desk most days and grabbed something for dinner on her way home. She shouldn't be surprised to find her fridge bare.

She opened the freezer, hoping for a forgotten treasure. A package of English muffins was her reward.

She defrosted two of them in the microwave, toasted them and added peanut butter, one of the few foods she always had in her pantry, along with a squeeze of honey. Paired with slices of apple, it made for a satisfactory lunch.

While she ate, she checked her cell phone again, hoping to see a call from Yakima, but her call log didn't show any missed calls. She penned a letter to Lydia, writing what she had said to the others from memory. She addressed it to the restaurant in Yakima, hoping it would find her and prod her to make contact. She also included Mr. Simpson's name and the number in Lavender Valley, to add to the legitimacy.

Maybe Lydia was checking her out before she returned the call, but from her experience and the caution in the woman's voice who answered the phone, Harry got the feeling she was hiding from something or someone.

She finished her lunch, and after leaving out enough of Chief's food and treats to get him through the next few days, added his supplies to the back of her SUV. She'd wait until she was ready to leave to add his bed, toys and the old blanket and slipper.

As she inventoried his things, she realized he had more possessions than she did. She pulled out the bag of coffee beans she liked, along with her grinder, the boxes of tea she loved, and her electric kettle. She would use them until she left, but place them on the counter, so she wouldn't forget to take them with her. That was all she needed to take with her from the kitchen.

She opted to take Chief for a late afternoon walk before

Cora was due. As she made her way along the pathway of Bush Park, she soaked in the beauty of the stately trees. She would miss this. The park had drawn her to this neighborhood, and even before Chief came on the scene, Harry had tried to get in a daily walk.

She'd have twenty acres to walk on the farm, but wouldn't have the groomed grounds and nice pathways. She hadn't been to visit the farm in some time and was anxious to see how it looked now. With Jewel not able to do as much, Harry imagined it would need some tender loving care.

As she walked, she realized she would need to have some sort of rental agreement with Cora. Harry pulled out her phone and hit the button for a local realtor she knew. He promised to email her a template that he used. She quickened her pace to get home, so she could read it before Cora arrived.

She gave Chief an early dinner, and afterward, he stretched out in the sunroom, while she scanned the rental agreement. It spelled out all the details she could think of and she filled in the blanks for her name, the property address, and the monthly rent, then realized she'd have to contact her utilities to have them transferred to Cora, if they both decided to go ahead.

She still had a landline phone, which was only because of her work. She could disconnect it, and she had cut the cord to cable TV long ago, but would need to transfer her Internet service. So many things to do, but she felt confident she could make it happen as she added each chore to the list.

While she waited for Cora, she put in the request to cancel her landline, then called her yard service to let them know she'd be renting her house but wanted them to continue their service.

Her cleaning lady was the other thing she needed to

address. She only came monthly and was totally trustworthy. Harry would feel better if she kept coming, as she didn't want to lose her and be looking for a replacement when she came back next year. She made a note to stipulate that with Cora. Harry would cover the costs, so she shouldn't have a problem.

As she reviewed the list, the doorbell rang. Chief jumped up from his nap and raced toward the door. Harry enticed him back to his bed and told him stay before she opened it.

Cora greeted her with a warm smile, and as she followed Harry through the house, it only widened. "This is a fabulous house. When Jolene told me about it, I felt like it was meant to be."

Harry pointed out the closet in the extra bedroom. "I need to keep some things here, so this closet is off-limits, as in it's full of clothes and items I emptied out of the master." Harry paused, then added, "I may come back a few times over the year if I need to take care of anything." They wandered back to the living room and Harry offered Cora tea or coffee.

"No, I'm fine. I'm really excited and if you need to come back to town, you're welcome to stay here, anytime. I'm on my own so it would be no problem. Jolene said all your furnishings stay and that I could have the place for a year." She mentioned the monthly rent and Harry nodded.

"That would be great, and I don't expect to be here much, but I'll let you know if I have to make a trip. All the furnishings stay. For you, I'm willing to waive the last month of rent requirement. I also have a cleaning lady and would like her to continue. She comes in once a month on the first Friday, so she was just here. I'll cover the costs."

"Wow, that would be fabulous."

"I'm most concerned with keeping the house clean and

my furniture in good shape. No pets, no smoking, and my preference is that you wear slippers to keep the floors in good condition. There's a place in the mudroom to keep your street shoes."

Cora nodded. "Understood. I don't have a problem with any of that. I'm neat and clean, so I promise your house will stay pristine. If there are any issues, I'll call you right away."

Harry looked at her notes. "I've got a yard service and they'll continue to mow and weed, but you'll need to keep an eye on the planters and pots in the back yard."

"Sounds terrific. I don't need to think about it. I want the house. I'd love it here and am desperate to find a place quickly."

Harry glanced at her laptop. "I've got a rental agreement ready to go. I'll just put an end date of January first next year and if things change, let me know. I'll email it to you tonight and you can check it over. You'll have to get the utilities put in your name, and then I think you're good to go. I plan to leave Friday morning, so if you can meet me, I can give you the keys and we'll be set."

"That sounds perfect. I really appreciate it, Deputy Chief."

"Call me Harry. I'll be in Lavender Valley, so only about four hours away and can be here if there's an emergency."

"I'm sure everything will be great. I'm excited to live so close to the park and work. It'll be a good place for me. I can tell already."

Cora made her way to the door and turned to Harry before she opened it. "I really appreciate this. I won't let you down."

Harry smiled at her. "I'm sure you won't. It's a great place, and I hope you'll be happy here. Before you go, let's trade cell phone numbers, so we have them. I only have your work number."

Cora pulled hers out of her purse and tapped in the digits. "Perfect. I'll see you Friday morning."

Harry shut the door and leaned against it. She hated leaving her house behind, but at the same time, was excited to see what Jewel had in store for her in Lavender Valley.

CHAPTER FOUR

B y Friday at nine o'clock, with Chief in her backseat the old slipper and puppy blanket on the seat to comfort him, Harry was ready to leave for Lavender Valley. Her SUV was packed to the rooftop with everything she and Chief would need to survive the next year at the farm.

Harry even managed to squeeze in an appointment with her stylist and had gotten her hair colored and cut one last time. It seemed like each time she went, there were more silver strands in her dark hair. Her stylist worked her magic and wove in copper highlights and lowlights, making Harry feel a bit younger than her fifty years.

Cora promised to send anything she forgot and waved goodbye from the driveway as Harry pulled onto the street. She fought getting bogged down in regret as she drove by the park and turned toward Interstate 5.

She'd done much harder things than this in her life. The practical voice in her head that had guided much of her life took over. It wasn't like she was leaving forever. Lavender Valley was just a temporary detour, and without any big plans for retirement, it was an easy decision to honor Jewel's final wishes.

She hit the highway and set her cruise control, intent on getting to the farm by one o'clock. She'd placed a call to Clay last night and let him know her plans. He suggested they meet in town at the Grasshopper for lunch and then head out to the farm.

Except for a few horrible drivers and the typical traffic snarls and slowdowns near Portland, her drive was uneventful. She stopped to let Chief take a break along the Rouge River. Back on the highway, she took the exit to the two-lane tree lined road that led to Lavender Valley, and with five minutes to spare, parked a block off Main Street in front of the Grasshopper. She frowned when she noticed graffiti emblazoned on the building next door. She'd noticed the same style on the old welcome sign on the highway.

While it wasn't exactly warm, with it being in the mid-forties, the sun was shining in the clear skies. Clay had assured her she could bring Chief and sit on the outdoor porch at the restaurant.

She led Chief to the café, taking the path that led to the large porch that wrapped around the back and side of the building. Nobody was sitting outside, but as Clay promised, the Grasshopper was dog-friendly and provided heaters to keep the outdoor seating area comfortable.

It also wasn't exactly outdoors, as the café had glassed in the sides of the porch. She took a table that offered her a view down the street. Some of the trees still had their beautiful orange and red leaves on their branches. It reminded her of Chuck and Jewel always saying Lavender Valley was in the banana belt of Oregon. It normally didn't dip below freezing in the winter, had much less snow than cities in the north, and less rain than Salem and Portland.

Nestled in the Rouge River Valley, the quaint town Harry remembered from her youth hadn't changed all that much. It had some new restaurants and shops, but the same historic brick buildings, most of them a rich red or burnt orange, stood along Main Street. A bit of a western vibe still permeated the historic town, founded during the Gold Rush. The town covered several blocks surrounding Main Street before giving way to the countryside, where vineyards, orchards, ranches, and Jewel's farm were found.

As Harry focused on the flyer attached to the porch post advertising line dancing, the clomp of boots on the wooden deck caught her attention. She glanced over and saw a real live cowboy heading to her table. Well-worn boots, jeans, a deep blue flannel shirt under a worn canvas jacket, and a cowboy hat all worked to advertise Clay's arrival. Harry summed him up to be just over six-feet tall, then she forced herself to look down as he walked the last few steps. She'd spent too many years of observing people and suspects, memorizing their stats and characteristics in case she needed them later.

He removed his dark brown, felt hat, revealing a head of tousled sandy blond hair and the scruff of an early five o'clock shadow along his cheeks and chin. "You must be Harry. I'm Clay Dolan."

She recognized the deep voice from her phone calls and shook his outstretched hand. "Yes, I'm Harry, and thank you for meeting me."

He pulled out the chair next to her, and Chief lifted his head, his tail swishing across the wooden deck. Harry glanced at the dog. "This is Chief."

Clay grinned, his vivid blue eyes twinkling. He had what Harry called Paul Newman eyes. They were hard not to notice and enhanced by the color of his shirt. "He looks like a great friend for Hope and Maverick. They're both out in my truck. He's used to waiting on me and Hope is coming to terms with it."

A young woman came hurrying through the door that led to the main café, a checkered apron around her waist and two glasses of water in her hands. "Hey ya, Clay."

She set the waters down and smiled at Harry.

"Hey, Bonnie. This is Harry. She grew up around here with Jewel and is going to be staying out at the farm."

Bonnie pulled the menus from under her arm and handed one to each of them. "Nice to meet ya, Harry. Jewel was a real sweetheart. We all miss her."

"She was one in a million. I'm sure I'll be seeing quite a bit of you. This was always a favorite spot of mine when I was growing up." Harry took the menu and gave it a quick once-over.

Bonnie took out her order pad. "We serve breakfast all day, if that sounds good and our soup is chicken noodle. We've got a special chili burger today." She stood on her tiptoes and eyed Chief over the table. "I'll bring your dog a bowl of water, if you'd like."

Harry bobbed her head. "That would be great, and I'm going to go with your ham and cheddar scramble, plus I'll take your cinnamon raisin toast and a coffee, please."

Clay opted for the chili burger with fries and coffee. Bonnie collected their menus and promised to be back right away with their beverages.

Clay eased back in his chair. "I'm impressed you were able to get down here so quickly. Jewel thought the sun rose and set with you, so I know she'd be happy you're here and watching over her farm."

Harry smiled. "I think Jewel has a little too much faith in

my abilities. I'm a retired detective and the extent of my farming has been in pots on my back patio."

Clay chuckled. "Like I said, I know the place like my own and can help you with whatever you need to learn. Jewel had a heart of gold and quite the fan club here. There'll be plenty of folks that are willing to help out."

Bonnie arrived with their steaming cups of coffee and a tiny pitcher of cream.

He added a healthy splash and a long pour from the sugar shaker to his cup. She opted for nothing.

He pointed at her cup and winked. "Bonnie makes a strong pot of coffee. You might want to add a li'l something."

"I've drunk cop coffee for the last thirty years, so Bonnie doesn't scare me." She winked and took her first sip. "Strong, but I've had stronger."

"You're gonna be just fine at the farm, Harry." Clay lifted his cup to her.

Their plates arrived and after Harry spread fresh marionberry jam on her toast and Clay doctored his fries with a healthy dose of ketchup, they dug into their lunch. Chief's nose was in the air sniffing, but he behaved himself and didn't beg.

After a few bites, Clay wiped his mouth with a napkin. "You've got some breathing room before anything needs tending. Right now, Hope is the only dog at the farm. We were able to place her other rescue dogs around the valley when Jewel took a turn for the worse. She had cut way back, so there weren't that many. Her donkeys and alpacas are there and I take care of them. We did some goat trading, and I promised to send back some does and babies this spring. She sold me her horses years ago, but she had riding rights to mine whenever she wanted." Sadness filled his eyes.

Harry reached for her coffee. "I remember Chuck was the horseman."

Clay nodded. "Oh, yeah, he loved those horses. They're expensive and required more work than Jewel wanted, so we did some trading and transitioned most of the physical work over to me and my crew. Everything is in good shape now. Chuck remodeled the house, cottages, and barn when he retired and since he's been gone, we've been helping to keep up the maintenance."

"Wow, that's a relief. I honestly wasn't sure what to expect. I was at the farm the Christmas before last, but didn't inspect anything. The house was wonderful, but I admit, I've been concerned about the property and fences, not to mention the animals. I know we'll have to tend to the lavender and get it ready for the festival too."

He finished off a thick fry. "Yes, that was Jewel's favorite time of year. The festival has really grown and is quite the attraction for our little town." He reached for another fry. "Speaking of small towns, are you ready for that kind of life? You've lived in Salem since you left, right?"

She nodded. "Yeah, I know it will be an adjustment. I'm giving up some conveniences, I'm sure, but I would do anything for Jewel."

He nodded. "That takes some getting used to, for sure. As does everyone being in your business. I still remember picking up some beer and wine at Benson's and by the time I got back to the ranch, someone had called Mom to tell her I was buying booze. Mind you, I was in my late thirties."

Harry laughed. "That's too funny. You do lose that sense of anonymity you have in a larger town or city. Nobody cares, or it seems that way. On the plus side, I'm sure the neighborhood watch program is strong."

He took another sip from his cup. "You hit the nail on the

head when you mentioned caring. Lavender Valley is full of people who really do care about each other. If someone needs help, we all step up. There is a strong sense of community here that you don't often see in a city."

Bonnie refilled their coffees when she picked up their empty plates. As Clay swirled the sugar into his cup, he raised his brow at Harry. "You sure?"

She laughed and slid her cup closer. "Just a sprinkle."

He complied, then added cream to his cup.

She took a sip. "Better. So, I'm not sure if Jewel told you her entire plan, but she wants me to bring four other women back to the farm. They lived there when they were kids and she's leaving the farm to all of us, or whoever wants to spend the next year here."

Clay grinned as he stirred his coffee. "That sounds like Jewel. She loved the farm, and she often spoke about her girls and how much she loved them. Stands to reason she wants to see them reunited on her beloved land."

Harry sighed. "Honestly, I'm hoping I can convince them to come. I don't see how I can manage it without them."

"If I know Jewel, she knew what she was doing and I bet those ladies come back, just like you did." He put down his cup, reached into his jacket pocket, and pulled out a keyring, then retrieved a piece of paper from his wallet, and handed both to Harry. "That's the code to the gate to get in."

"Thanks, that must be a new addition." Harry rubbed her fingers over the pewter keyring embossed with a bunch of lavender. "I need to run by the market and pick up a few things, stop for gas, and then I'll head to the farm. Does that work for you?"

Clay reached for the check Bonnie slid across the table. "Sure does. I need to stop by the feed store and then I'll meet you out there."

Harry opened her purse, and he shook his head. "My treat. Welcome home, Harry."

Harry drove down Main Street to Benson's Food and Hardware. It was still the only market in town, and like Harry remembered, paired with a hardware store. Medford had more options, but Benson's had the basics.

She left Chief in the backseat with the windows half down and locked the doors. As she perused the aisles and loaded her basket with a few items, Harry noticed a woman in a store apron following her. When she met the woman's eyes, she stared at Harry, unflinching, and asked if she could help her find anything.

"No, thanks, I'm just getting a few things."

"You're not from around here. Just passing through, are ya?" asked the woman.

"Actually, I grew up here and am coming back." Harry extended her hand. "I'm Harry McKenzie, and I'll be taking over Jewel Austin's place. Lavender Valley Farm."

The frown on the woman's face melted and her face filled with a warm smile. "Oh, it's wonderful to meet you. Jewel was beloved. I'm so sorry she's gone." She extended her hand and added, "I'm Mona, by the way. Sorry about that. We've had a run of shoplifters lately, and when I don't recognize someone, I make it a point to let them know I'm watching."

"That's hard to believe you'd have a shoplifting problem here."

"We never used to. We're all baffled by it and seems to be worse when we get visitors in the store. We know everyone and it only happens when newcomers are here. Usually, a store full of them."

"Maybe you should meet with the police?" Harry added some oatmeal to her cart.

Mona rolled her eyes. "We've tried. Seems they're doing all they can."

The bell at the front door jingled and Mona darted away to check on her new customer.

Harry finished her shopping and as she left, waved goodbye to Mona, busy stocking a shelf. When she got out of her SUV at the gas station, she spotted a sign on the post next to the pump stating all gas had to be prepaid. Sure enough, there was no credit card slot at the gas pump.

With a huff, she hurried inside and found an older man at the counter. She handed him the card and asked for enough to fill the tank to be run on her card. "Is your card reader broken at the pump?" she asked.

He shook his head. "No, we used to just let people pump and pay, but over the last few months, we've had a ton of gas and dash hooligans, and they attached readers to the credit card thingamajig, so we just removed it and do it this way. It's a pain for everyone, but we can't afford the theft."

Harry took her card and fueled the SUV, using up every penny of her prepaid allotment. Lavender Valley had always been safe and crime free. It was hard to believe shoplifting and gas theft were problems in the small town where everyone knew everyone.

She slid behind the wheel and headed out of town. After several miles, she went through an area where all the mailboxes had been hit and were either mangled or missing from the posts that held them. That wasn't how she remembered Lavender Valley.

Within an hour of leaving the restaurant, Harry turned off the highway and stopped in front of the gate under the overhead arch fashioned from thick logs and decorated with a metal sign sporting bunches of lavender and the farm name. The keypad and intercom were installed beside it in a concrete pillar. She typed in the code, the gate swung open, and she steered her SUV down the long driveway that meandered through the fenced fields to farmhouse.

She pulled under the breezeway between the house and the garage and opened the door for Chief. He was all wiggles with his nose in high gear, sniffing all the new scents.

Memories flooded Harry's mind as she gazed behind the house at the barn, standing strong all these years later. Donkeys and alpacas wandered the pens nearest the barn. Chief was itching to get closer and check them out.

As she was debating whether to walk him around first or unload, Clay's crew cab truck lumbered into the yard. She noticed two golden snouts sticking out of the back window and could see tails wagging behind Clay.

After he parked, Clay opened the back door and the two dogs sprang from the truck, making a beeline for Chief and Harry. The smaller of the two wore a bandana around her neck covered in pink and red hearts. Tails swished and noses sniffed while the threesome got acquainted.

Harry laughed as she watched the dogs play. They were already fast friends. "Chief is interested in the donkeys and alpacas. I'm sure he's never seen either one."

"How about I help you unload and then give you and Chief a quick tour of the place?"

"That would be wonderful. Thank you." But before she moved to start unloading, Harry's eyes swept over the corrals, barn, outbuildings, cottages, and the expanse of land surrounding the farmhouse. It was just so much. She hoped she hadn't bitten off more than she could chew.

CHAPTER FIVE

When Harry walked through the door, the warmth and light that filled the farmhouse greeted her. The only things missing were Jewel's sweet smile and tender embrace. It was hard not to imagine Jewel sitting in her oversized chair, feet on the ottoman.

The soft scent of Jewel's lavender lotion still filled the air and tickled Harry's nose. She walked across the dark wooden floor and stopped at the bottom of the stairs, then a moment later, changed course. There were three bedrooms upstairs, but the master suite was off the hallway through the main living room. With her being on her own for the time being, she preferred to be downstairs. She'd take the master for now.

She made her way through the living room, crossed over the thick area rug, and stopped to gaze at the bookcase, filled with books and several framed photos. Harry suspected that she may soon be meeting four of the smiling faces in the frames.

The white shiplap walls and vaulted ceilings were the

perfect contrast to the dark floor, with the stone fireplace being a focal point in the room. Jewel's love for flowers and the coast were evident in the throw pillows, wall art, and decorative pieces that brightened the neutral palette. The French doors were open to the inviting sunroom that Chuck had incorporated in their last remodel. He'd turned the porch into an outdoor living area that offered a wonderful view of the fields and the gentle distant hills.

She continued through to the hallway with her suitcase and bag. Everything was neat as a pin, just as Jewel liked it. A beautiful quilt featuring squares of flowers with a lavender border was folded across the foot of the bed. Here again, Harry found touches of soft blues, greens, and lavender. They reminded her of the subtle colors of sea glass.

Watercolor and pencil drawings decorated the walls. There were several of the farm, along with the friendly faces of all of Jewel's golden retrievers. Her dresser held her wedding photo and another of her and Chuck at what Harry recognized as the Oregon coast.

Despite Harry's experience with tragedy and loss, her own, and that of thousands of others over her long career, she swallowed the dry lump in her throat. The reality of Jewel's absence weighed on her heart. Being here without her wasn't going to be easy.

She was beginning to doubt her choice of bedrooms when Clay came through the door carrying another bag. "I stashed your groceries in the kitchen. Where do you want the dog bed? I thought I'd put the dog food in the mudroom, where Jewel kept Hope's."

She took the tote bag he held. "Thanks, that would be great. I think the living room works for Chief's bed. It would be a waste in here, since I'm ashamed to say, I let Chief sleep in my bed."

Clay chuckled. "I'm also guilty. I used to be much stricter about things like that. Life...and Maverick wore me down. You'll have Hope and Chief up there with you, I'm sure. Hope misses Jewel." He paused and added, "Like we all do."

He turned and left to tend to the dog bed. Harry opened the closet and glanced through Jewel's sparse wardrobe. Jeans, t-shirts, sweaters, and two dresses hung on hangers, plus a pair of low heels, still in the box, and a few pairs of shoes lined up underneath the clothes.

Jewel had never been one to collect material things. She always told Harry it was more important to collect memories and moments than things. As Harry lugged her toiletries into the master bathroom, she thought of Jewel's collection of broken children and animals. She had a special gift of taking things that others thought were beyond repair and giving them new life.

She met Clay as he was coming through the kitchen. He gestured toward the box he left on the counter. "I figured you'd want your coffee and tea stuff in here." Her eyes took in the large space, which Jewel had often referred to as the heart of her home. During the remodel, Chuck opened the space between the kitchen and dining room, and along with modern stainless appliances, the white and gray granite counters gleamed.

Harry pointed at the island counter. "Everything looks like it was just cleaned and polished."

Clay held the stainless-steel dog bowl under the faucet. "I've got a cleaning lady who takes care of my place, and had her come through and spruce everything up here. It wasn't messy by any means, but needed a good dusting and cleaning. Jewel resisted getting any help, so things weren't as neat as she liked them these last months."

Harry glanced at the double ovens. "Well, all this will be

wasted on me. I'm not a cook. I'm on a first name basis with the staff at the restaurants around my house and office. I eat takeout all the time." Her eyes rested on the box. "How about a cup of coffee or tea?"

He smiled and shook his head. "No to tea. I like it iced in the summer, but never took to it hot. Jewel tried her best, but I'm a coffee guy."

"I'll put on a pot to brew and you can show me around outside while we wait for it."

"I'll meet you out front. I want to check on the hooligans and make sure their water bowl on the porch is full." He tipped his hat and was through the door before Harry could add water to the coffee pot.

She found him on the porch, surrounded by the three dogs, who were watching as he added the last bucket of water to the mini trough at the edge of the porch. He pointed at a tall outdoor faucet. "Water's right there and Jewel just kept this bucket on top of it."

She walked beside him toward the barn, and after lapping up more water, the dogs sprinted after them. At the corrals, they stopped and Clay leaned against the fence. The two donkeys meandered over to them. "This is Nutmeg and Olive. Nutmeg is the reddish one."

Harry petted them both, taking in their sweet eyes and Olive's soft gray color. "Jewel didn't have donkeys when I was here. I just remember horses."

"I have several horses at the ranch. Do you ride?"

She met his eyes. "Not in a very long time."

"Well, you're welcome to ride anytime. I've got a gentle girl named Merlot. She'd be a good one for you."

"Hmm, named after the wine, I take it?"

He grinned. "My dad has always had a horse named Whiskey. He favored naming them after liquor and Mom enjoyed wine, so she got in on the fun, too. We've carried on the tradition."

He scratched Nutmeg behind one massive ear. "Jewel took these two in after they were rescued from a neglectful owner." He gestured across the paddock to another corral. "Same with Agatha and Arnold over there. They were abandoned when their owners moved, so Jewel gave them a home."

Harry smiled as she walked over to greet the two cinnamon-colored alpacas. She couldn't get over their sweet eyes and huge eyelashes. As she stood at the fence, Clay joined her. "They can be shy. They like people and are curious, but tend to want to interact on their own terms. Jewel always said they're a bit like cats. Agatha, the one with the white patch on her neck, is friendlier than Arnold."

True to her reputation, Agatha wandered over to the fence and gazed at her new admirer. With a bat of her eyelashes, she won over Harry.

She started to put her hand up to the fence and then pulled it back. "They only have front bottom teeth, so even if they nibble, it won't hurt," said Clay.

Harry put her hand through the fence and Agatha bopped it with her nose, which only made Harry long to rub the top of the alpaca's fuzzy head. Somehow, she resisted, knowing Agatha might find it threatening until they got to know each other better. Regardless, she was convinced they were the cutest animals she had ever seen.

Clay motioned her toward the barn. "I'll show you their feed. It's kept in the barn and we've been putting them inside the barn at night. Without anyone here, I wanted to make sure they were safe."

Harry frowned. "Safe from...predators or humans?"

Clay shrugged. "Both, actually."

Harry followed him and watched as he unlatched the barn doors. The sweet smell of hay mingled with the earthy aroma of dirt and animals. With the scent came memories of Harry's youth and helping with the horses.

The clean stalls stood ready for the animals. Clay pointed at the far end of the barn past the row of stalls. "That's the grass hay for the alpacas, and across the way is the straw for the donkeys. I'll show you how much to feed them. I give the donkeys a bit of hay once a week, but straw is their main staple. In the spring, the alpacas can graze in the pasture."

He walked over to a pallet stacked with bags. "That's the chicken feed. It's cheaper to get as much feed as you can house once or twice a year. For the hay, Jewel gets it from Wyatt, who leases one of her fields and farms it for hay. In addition to her lease income, she gets the hay for her animals. You'll have to buy the barley straw for the donkeys."

Harry regretted not bringing a notepad with her.

He led the way to the other end of the barn and another large set of swinging doors, chained with a lock. He pointed at the golf cart and a UTV with a small bed on the back of it parked in the area nearest the doors. "These are good for hauling things around the property. Jewel always had that golf cart packed with dogs and liked to take them for a ride in the evening."

It wasn't hard to picture. Harry smiled at the thought and the memory of Jewel's caring way with animals, especially her beloved rescue dogs.

Chuck's old Chevrolet truck was parked next to them, the yellow paint faded and patchy with a bit of rust showing through the 1955 body. "Wow, that's a blast from the past."

Clay walked to it and put his hand on the fender. "Chuck loved this old truck and Jewel could never bear to get rid of it. Still runs, too." The old Lavender Valley Farm lettering was barely visible on the doors.

After leaving the barn, Clay led her to the other side where the chickens were busy strutting around their enclosure. "Jewel kept these around for fresh eggs." He pointed at the hen house. "You can check for eggs each morning. They don't lay as much in the winter. They're pretty simple to care for, just fill their feeder and make sure they have clean water. They're trained to roost in the henhouse at night, so just lock the door when you know they're in there. That keeps them safe from all sorts of critters."

He led her around the barn to another water spigot and explained how the hose was set up to reach to the troughs in the corrals. "Tyler will be back before the end of the month." He pointed to the bunkhouse down from the barn. "He stays onsite and can handle all the chores and more."

"Does Jewel pay him?"

He shook his head. "No, he's on my payroll and still works at the ranch, but just takes care of the morning and evening chores around here, and overnights to help keep an eye on things. It's all part of the business arrangement Jewel and I had."

As they walked, Clay explained the irrigation water would start around April and run through the summer, then promised to show her the ropes and give her a tour of the outlying property in the coming days.

Next, they wandered to the two cottages on the property. Harry followed him through the first door, instantly surprised at the remodeled space. She hadn't been in the cottages since she lived there, and then they had been used as sheds for crafts and planting supplies. Now, there was a small kitchen with a sink, counter, microwave, and mini-fridge, that opened into a living area, where another door opened onto a small porch. A short hallway led to the bedroom and bathroom. All the furnishings were covered with sheets. "It just needs a good dusting and cleaning, but someone could actually live here," she said, impressed. "It's cozy, but nice."

Clay nodded. "Chuck remodeled them after he retired. At one time they were talking about renting them out during the festival, but ultimately didn't do it."

She followed him outside. He pointed at the cottage next door. "It's basically the same, but Jewel stashed some things for the festival in it, so it's full of boxes and supplies."

With the sun near the horizon, he showed her how to lead the donkeys and alpacas into the barn and settle them in their stalls. Once they were tucked away, Harry helped herd the chickens into the henhouse and the automatic door on the coop came down and locked in place. "It's got a sensor so it stays closed all night and opens in the morning, or you can set a timer." He showed her the programmable pad mounted above it that connected to the pulley system. The larger door that Harry would use to access the eggs and for cleaning the coop had a lock on it. Clay pointed out that it used a carabiner and a cable. "Raccoons can open almost any latch, so we use this type because it requires more than one step."

Harry's eyes widened. "I had no idea they were so crafty. Sounds like they are the burglars of the animal kingdom."

He chuckled as they made their way back toward the farmhouse. The nightlights flickered to life as they walked and cast a warm glow over the corrals and barn. As Harry climbed the porch steps, Clay detoured to his truck and loaded Maverick in the backseat.

Moments later he jogged back to the porch. "I forgot to show you the driveway gate intercom system."

"And, I owe you that cup of coffee," she said.

She opened the door and the two dogs followed her. He pointed to the wall just inside the door. "This is the main control panel and you've got a little screen that will show you a picture of whoever is at the gate." He pressed a button and said, "You can talk to them using this button, and the green button opens the gate."

She nodded and moved to the kitchen counter, pouring two cups and retrieving cream and sugar for Clay. "Got it. Any other cameras on the property?"

He stirred his coffee and shook his head. "No, that's the only one. Sometimes we use trail cameras if we're having any trouble with predators or trespassers, but nothing permanent."

"Thanks for helping me get settled," said Harry. "I appreciate the time you took."

"My pleasure, and if you need anything, day or night, don't hesitate to call me." He glanced at the dogs. "They'll alert you to anything out of the ordinary."

She laughed. "I'm not sure Chief is the best guard dog, but maybe he'll blossom now that he has a farm to patrol."

"Hope's a good one. She'll let you know if there's trouble. Oh, and you'll find she loves to hold hands." Clay drained the last of his coffee. "You have a good evening, Harry. I'll come by in the morning and make sure you've got the hang of feeding."

A ripple of relief spread through her. "That would be great. I admit, it's a bit overwhelming." They made their way to door, and as Clay walked across the porch, she added, "I've already confessed I'm not much of a cook, but I can do breakfast. I'll have it ready for you tomorrow."

He turned and grinned. "I'll be here. Does six-thirty work?"

"Sure does. See you then." She waved as he drove down the driveway.

She locked the door and went through the kitchen to get the dogs' dinner ready for them. Chief was excited for dinner and sniffing at everything in the house, while Hope was much calmer and more serious. Her gentle eyes studied Harry as she moved about the space adding food to the bowls. While Chief was darker, almost red, Hope was a true golden color that so many associated with the happy breed.

Along with their difference in color, Harry noted Chief was stockier with a blockier head, while Hope's was narrow and her overall build was slimmer. She had the most expressive eyes and was intently focused on Harry.

As Harry finished prepping their bowls, she glanced down at the dog who Jewel had loved. "I know you miss your sweet Jewel." Hope's ears perked at the sound of her name. "I miss her too. She wanted me to take good care of you and I promise I will. I'm not as experienced, so you'll have to be patient."

When Harry bent down to place the bowls, Hope sat and extended her paw to Harry. Chief was already wolfing down his food, but Hope waited, staring at Harry. She reached for the paw and held it. "Aww, you are a sweet one." She glanced over at Chief, licking his bowl and eyeing the other one. "Hopefully, you can help me teach this big guy some manners." She let go of her paw and Hope stood and took a few steps to her bowl.

Harry left her to eat and coaxed Chief away to give Hope some peace while they did a quick check of the house to make sure all the doors and windows were locked.

Upstairs, she found the bedrooms as she remembered. Three of them, two with twin beds and the largest one with a double bed. The only space that had been remodeled was the bathroom. When she walked into her old bedroom, the one with the double bed, nostalgia rushed over her. The same white desk and bookcase were there, along with a comfy chair in the corner. She ran her fingers along the worn spines of the titles she remembered, pausing at her favorite Nancy Drew mysteries, then Agatha Christie, Mrs. Pollifax, and Nero Wolfe.

Harry had healed under this roof. She'd had the benefit of Jewel's love and guidance as she dealt with grief and came into her own as a young woman. Jewel had the wisdom and patience to nurture her interests and make her feel important and needed. As much as Harry had missed her grandmother when she first arrived, she'd come to love Jewel, and had felt a strong bond with her almost immediately.

She moved to check the window—the one she'd looked out of so often when she sat at the desk doing her homework. It had a lovely view of the lavender fields, which had grown from Jewel's original patch to what Harry estimated was a couple of acres.

Harry sighed as she turned out the light and headed downstairs. On the main floor, she stopped at the bookshelves Chuck had built for Jewel under the stairs. The shelves were staggered, and some were rectangular, while others were square, like a puzzle of boxes. They held a mixture of books and mementos. More framed photos of young people, who Harry could only guess had been fostered by Jewel and Chuck.

Despite talking with Jewel occasionally and seeing her in person only a handful of times over the last decade, Harry's heart was heavy with grief. Jewel had been a constant and stable influence in her life.

Harry wasn't a crier, but tears filled her eyes as she

studied the faces of the people most dear to Jewel. There was even a photo of herself, 16 years old and hugging Sparky, one of the rescue dogs. She remembered that day. Sparky had come in so scared and sad, shrinking away from humans as if terrified, and for some reason, Jewel thought Harry was the one who could get through to him. Harry, of course, not knowing Jewel very well yet, hadn't agreed. But she'd been right.

On the day the photo was taken, Sparky had run to Harry with complete trust in his eyes for the first time, and she couldn't resist kneeling down to hug him. Jewel had been quick with her camera and captured the wonderful moment, her timing impeccable, just as it usually was.

Being here, with her memories but without Jewel, was going to be one of Harry's most difficult challenges.

CHAPTER SIX

When Harry's phone alarm buzzed, it was still dark outside. She flicked the screen and blinked as it took her a few seconds to remember she was in Jewel's bedroom. After falling asleep in Jewel's chair with Hope sprawled in her lap, she turned in rather early and she and two furry roommates had slept long and hard last night. She grinned when she noticed Chief had shared his old green blanket with Hope, both of their snouts resting on it.

She padded out to the living room and let the dogs outside into the back yard off the sunroom. The yard was enclosed with a split rail fence with hog wire that separated it from Jewel's garden, where she grew veggies and berries. With Chief being new to the property, Harry didn't want to chance him getting distracted by a shiny squirrel and traipsing off across the fields.

She set coffee to brew and filled her electric kettle. While she waited, she fixed breakfast for the dogs and made her way to the sunroom door. The first, soft light of the day provided a glow on the horizon. The lavender light that hung along the dark hills and trees was breathtaking. Even without the fragrant plant blooming, it was easy to see how the valley had gotten its name.

Harry took a sip of tea and smiled, no longer worried about missing her neighborhood park. The view from the porch filled her with peace.

To her surprise, both dogs were sitting at the door waiting for her, tails wagging. Hope was a good influence on Chief. Harry thought she could rely on her to keep him out of trouble. He was never off a leash, so his newfound freedom could go either way.

After they ate their kibble laced with a few bits of fresh fruit, she took a quick shower and dressed before prepping for breakfast. She slid the pan of bacon into the oven to let it bake while she cut thick slices from the loaf of bread she had picked up, then whipped together eggs and milk. She opened cupboards until she found Jewel's bottle of vanilla and added a splash.

As she was dipping the bread in the egg mixture, a loud buzzer startled her. It took her a few moments to realize it was the front gate. She wiped her hands and hurried to the console. Sure enough, Clay sat in his truck waiting for her to admit him. She pushed the button and dashed back to the kitchen to get the French toast on the griddle.

A minute later, Hope barked. Chief tilted his head at her, then joined in the barkfest when his newfound sister hurried to the window. When Hope saw Clay's truck, the barking stopped and she wagged her tail so hard her body wiggled. Chief did the same.

Harry flipped the toast and adjusted the heat, then rushed to the front door to unlock it. She was in the midst of dipping more bread when Clay knocked on the door. She hollered out, "Come on in."

He and Maverick stepped through the door, and the dogs went into a frenzy of fur as they greeted each other. Clay took off his hat and hung it on a hat rack next to the door. "Something smells good," he said, stepping into the kitchen.

"Bacon," she said with a grin. "It's almost ready, and I made some French toast to go with it." She flipped the last slices on the griddle and put the bowl in the sink. "By the way, you don't need to ring the buzzer. I know you have the code."

He chuckled as he opened the cupboard and took out two plates. "That would be impolite. Not to mention, I carried in your gun cases and your bedside gun safe yesterday. I'm not about to surprise an armed woman."

She took the syrup she'd warmed and added it to the island, where Clay had set their plates. "Smart man," she said, with a wink.

She blotted the bacon on paper towels before adding it and the stack of French toast to the island counter. Clay had already filled his cup with coffee and retrieved the sugar and cream. He held up the coffee pot and raised his brows at her.

"Sure, thanks."

After filling her cup, Clay poured syrup over his stack of French toast, then handed the bottle to Harry and whispered. "Don't look now, but we're being watched."

She glanced over and saw the three dogs, piled together on the floor, their eyes glued to the counter, following her movements as she added bacon onto her plate. "Makes you feel guilty, right?"

He nodded. "Yeah, they're good at that, but they know better than to beg." He took a bite of bacon. "This is really good."

"I put some brown sugar and a hint of cayenne pepper on it before I baked it."

"Ah, that's the little spice I tasted. It's great." He sipped from his cup and added, "Speaking of armed women, I have a proposition for you."

Her brows arched. "Sounds intriguing and maybe dangerous."

He laughed and put down his cup. "Jewel told me about your impressive career in law enforcement. Each year, we have a competitive shoot at the ranch. It's a fun time with a big barbecue. Could I convince you to join our team?"

"That might be fun, but not sure I'm the shoo-in you think I am."

"Honestly, I would invite you regardless of your skill. It's just a fun day, and a way to get to know everybody in Lavender Valley. The whole town turns out and loves to watch the competitions, plus visit and eat. It's a three-gun shoot. Rifle, pistol, and shotgun."

She nodded as she chewed a bit of syrup-infused bread. "Sure, count me in. I don't have a shotgun, but if I can borrow one, I'm in."

"Perfect. We've got plenty of shotguns, and you'll probably find one in Chuck's old gun safe too. It's set for the first weekend in February at our ranch. We call it our Groundhog Day Celebration." He leaned back in his chair. "Full disclosure, I am hoping you'll give us an edge and surprise a few of the others who aren't privy to your history."

Her eyes widened as she grinned. "Not much time to practice. I'll need to get some more ammo."

"I have a feeling you don't need to practice, but you can get ammo at the hardware store and Ranchland carries some, too." He mopped up the remaining syrup on his plate with a large chuck of toasted bread.

She chuckled as she gathered the plates and set them in the sink. Not many people could say they buy bullets, bananas, and bolts at the same store. "We should probably get out there and tend to the animals before it gets any later, right?"

He swallowed the last of his coffee and nodded. "Yeah, they'll be itching for breakfast." He carried his cup across the kitchen. "Thanks again. It was great."

He donned his hat, and she slipped into a pair of insulated, waterproof boots she found in the mudroom. They were a bit snug but would do until she could get into town and find a pair of her own. She'd realized yesterday that her leather boots weren't the best choice for the farm.

Harry and the dogs followed Clay as he showed her how to do the morning chores, releasing the chickens, checking for eggs—she found four of them—and getting the alpacas and donkeys in their corrals and fed.

It sounded simple enough, but rather than watch, Harry insisted on doing everything herself, with Clay guiding her. By the time everything was done, it was almost eleven o'clock. She shook her head when she checked her watch.

"You'll get faster as you develop your own rhythm and way that works best." They wandered back to the barn and he pointed at the UTV. "If you're game, we could take a ride around the property, wander over to my ranch and I could show you around. You can meet my brother, Heath."

"I'd like that. I don't have anything on my agenda today. Just hoping to hear back from the other women Jewel wanted me to find. I meet with Mr. Simpson tomorrow, so imagine he'll have more details."

"He's a good guy. His dad had the only law practice in town for decades and when he died, Buck took over. Same salt of the earth kind of guy and smart. He works hard and has the respect of everyone in town."

"I figured as much. Jewel spoke highly of him, which

holds quite a bit of weight with me. She did the same for you."

He grinned, and she noticed the boyish dimple in his cheek. "Jewel was aptly named."

She couldn't argue with that one. He showed her where the keys to the vehicles were kept, in a little cubbyhole in the wall.

After unlocking the chain, Clay drove the vehicle out the doors, and together they got the dogs loaded in the back. Harry made sure the barn doors were shut, then made her way back to the house to add a hat, gloves, and a warmer jacket. She poured the rest of the coffee into a thermos, added sugar and a splash of cream, and met Clay on the running UTV, waiting in the breezeway.

Hope and Maverick, who shared the same color, but Maverick was built like Chief, seemed relaxed and like old pros at riding on the small bed of the vehicle. Chief, on the other hand, wasn't so sure, and had a hard time sitting still. Harry climbed into the passenger side and rested her hand on the side of his neck, hoping to calm him.

As Clay eased them down the pathway that wound past the barn and into the expanse of fields and pastures, Chief took his cues from the other dogs and began to settle, finally lying down between them. As he drove, Clay pointed out the white fence to his left. "That's the fence line between my ranch and the farm. The white fence ends and it changes to barbed wire and lodgepoles the rest of the way."

He drove down to where Secret Creek crossed into the farm's acreage and the small lake that formed from it. This time of year, it wasn't much more than a trickle of water, but come spring, it would be flowing.

He pointed at the pasture beyond the creek. "That's the

piece I lease from Jewel. Those are my cows out there. We move them around between pastures."

"I know nothing about cattle, but they look happy and healthy."

"Grass fed beef, and it's delicious. Jewel has some in her freezer and when you get low, just let me know. That's another part of our agreement. I furnish the farm with beef and Jewel supplies me with eggs."

Harry smiled. "Very neighborly."

Clay turned the wheel and found the dirt pathway near the fence line. "There's a gate up here we'll go through to get to my ranch."

At the gate, he started to get out of his seat, but Harry put up her hand. "I'll get it." She hurried to the gate, which was a heavy piece of wire looped over the post. She moved it and lifted the pole to allow him to drive through the space, then secured the gate behind him.

He waited for her to get settled in her seat, then continued to drive along the edge of the pasture. More cows dotted the landscape, and he kept driving, closer and closer to the rolling hills that rimmed the valley.

As he kept driving, Harry realized Clay's ranch ran all the way to those hills. He stopped at the ravine that formed a natural barrier between his land and the hills when he couldn't go further and climbed out from behind the steering wheel. "We can give the dogs a bit of a break here."

He let them out of the back, and they bounded onto the pasture. Harry sucked in a breath. "Chief does not have a reliable recall. I've been trying to work with him on it, but his previous owner wasn't the best at training him."

"Maverick and Hope have excellent recall, and chances are, he'll learn from them. One thing for sure, he'll follow their lead and won't run off on his own. Jewel liked to use her trained goldens to help educate the new rescues, and I think you'll find Hope a valuable teacher."

As she listened to his explanation, her shoulders dropped and she relaxed, watching the dogs romp with each other. She noted Chief never left the other two. She sighed. "Chief is definitely a city dog. I just don't want anything to happen to him."

"He'll be fine with Hope. She knows the farm and this ranch better than anyone. We've got an excellent vet, too. Duke Walker is his name. He takes care of all the animals around here and was especially good to Jewel with her rescues. He's out here often. I'll introduce you."

"That would be great. I forgot all about finding a vet. I haven't had Chief long. He belonged to a friend who died."

"Oh, man, I'm sorry. That's kind of you to take him. It's heartbreaking when animals lose their owners, and nobody is there for them." He grinned. "But, Jewel would have taught you all about that. So many of her rescues came from those situations."

"Tim, he was my old partner, died unexpectedly at his desk. He mentioned once that he wanted me to take care of Chief if anything ever happened to him. Just the kind of thing you say when you never expect it to happen, you know?"

Clay put his hands in his pockets as they walked along the edge of the property. "Yeah, loss is never easy, and when it's unexpected, it's even worse for those left behind." He sighed, and his eyes focused on a lump of pasture at his feet. "My wife died several years ago, and it about did me in."

Harry's hand went to her chest. "I'm so sorry. I had no idea."

He shook his head. "It was a long time ago. It was roughest on our son."

"I can imagine. That had to be difficult for you, raising him and dealing with that loss."

"We lived in Lake Oswego at the time. I was a building contractor and had my own construction company. Our son, Danny, runs it now."

"Oh, wow, I guess I assumed you've lived here all your life and worked the ranch."

He gritted his teeth. "Yeah, it's a bit of a sore subject with my brother, Heath. When Dad passed away, he left me in charge of the ranch. Heath's a great guy, kind, hardworking, and he stayed here too. We've worked through it for the most part, but I came back when Dad was ill. Dad was pretty traditional, and I'm the eldest, so it makes some sense. I think he also thought I had a better head for business."

"Do you?"

He grinned, and that dimple showed itself. "Yeah, I do. I'm more organized and methodical. Heath is a more fly-by-the-seat-of-your-pants kind of guy."

"I've always found the best teams are comprised of people who have different strengths. It's better for solving problems quickly. I imagine together, you're a force."

They walked back to the UTV and she pointed at the thermos. "Coffee, if you want some. I even put sugar and a little cream in it."

His smile went all the way up to crinkle the corner of his eyes. "Well, since you went to all that trouble, how can I pass it up?"

Steam drifted from the thermos as he poured coffee into one of the convenient cups built into the lid. He extended his hand and offered it to Harry. "One sip and you'll never go back to black."

She chuckled and took the cup, sipping while he poured

himself one. He took a long swallow and smacked his lips together. "Nectar of the gods."

"I have to admit, it's good. I acquired a taste for black just because of living on it for years. I didn't want to consume the extra calories sugar and cream added. I can gain a pound by just smelling a cookie, so knew if I got in that habit, it would be bad. As I've gotten older, it's even easier to gain weight."

He finished another sip. "I hear ya. The ranch keeps me physically active, but like you said, if I take a few days off and keep eating like usual, I can tell a big difference. Getting older has good and bad points, right?"

"We're wiser, but fatter." She finished the last bit of coffee in her cup.

Clay chuckled before he swallowed the last of his and flicked the cup over to shake out any excess. Harry did the same and Clay stacked the cups back inside the lid. "So, what about you, do you have any kids?"

Harry shook her head. "No. No husband, no kids. I was pretty much married to my job."

"I would imagine it would be tough to juggle kids with your career."

She leaned against the back of the UTV. "Yeah, they like to say women can have it all, but it's tough. I think you can have it all, it's just a matter of can you do it all well. I could have never risen in the ranks like I did if I had taken time away to have children. I don't think I would have returned to the job and put myself at risk with kids in the picture either. It's easier when it's just you and you're not impacting others."

"Do I detect a hint of regret?" he asked, before he whistled for the dogs.

She shrugged. "At the time, I don't think I regretted my choices. I loved my work and was focused on it alone. Now, though, it's like seeing your life through a different lens. It's why I'm here now. I honestly don't know what to do with myself. I'm glad I have Chief or I'd truly feel alone."

He loaded the dogs and turned to her. "Jewel had a way of always knowing what people needed. Sometimes before they knew it themselves." He winked at her and stepped around to the driver's side.

CHAPTER SEVEN

After the rest of the tour of the Nolan Family Ranch, encompassing over three hundred acres, Harry had a new appreciation for Clay. It wasn't lost on her that he had no actual need to lease any property from Jewel. He had plenty of spare pasture for his cows. Making a deal with Jewel had been his way of helping her without making her feel like she was a charity case.

Harry didn't say anything to Clay, but added the lease arrangement to the list of items to ask Mr. Simpson about tomorrow. Clay drove past the main house where he and his brother lived, a sprawling stone and timber home. Harry was trained not to react or let her emotions show, but her mouth gaped open when Clay drove them along the paved road that led to the barn, arena, and a training racetrack.

The road curved through some trees before opening to a large expanse that allowed ample room for horse trailers and parking beside the barn. He parked the UTV and unloaded the dogs. Harry followed him into the large building that boasted the same style as the home with lots of stone and dark wood. It was more beautiful and cleaner than most houses she had visited.

The sweet smells of hay, grass, and leather filled the air, and Clay's boots echoed off the smooth pavers that made up the wide middle walkway between the stalls. Unlike Jewel's barn with a dirt floor, this one was modern, with lots of concrete, and clean as a whistle. Clay walked along the front of the stalls and introduced her to Tequila, Whiskey, Jack, Merlot, Margarita, and Cabernet. The horses were shiny and majestic and more than a little curious about the visitors in their midst. Chief was a little skittish, but with encouragement from Hope and Maverick, managed to step closer to each of the stalls and look up at the horses.

Harry had never seen a horse up close until she'd lived at Jewel's. That same feeling she remembered came over her as she stroked Merlot, a lovely chestnut mare. There was something almost magical about the appeal of a horse, and Harry felt that little flutter of infatuation as she ran her hand over Merlot's neck. Clay was right; she was gentle.

"From that smile on your face, I reckon you might be up for a ride someday soon. Merlot's a sweet one."

Harry continued to pet her and smiled. "I think I can be convinced. I've always wanted a horse, ever since I read *Black Beauty* and *National Velvet*."

Clay explained his dad had raised horses years ago. He'd built the huge house and barn during the boom when he was making a substantial amount of money from both the horse and cattle business.

"I was hoping to introduce you to Heath today too, but his truck is gone," Clay said, as they continued on their way through the barn. Clay wanted to introduce her to Heath, but his truck wasn't where it was usually parked and Clay suspected he'd gone into town.

"I look forward to meeting him another time," Harry replied. Outside again, Clay pointed out the quarters for the ranch hands, which also matched the style of the main house, although smaller and simpler in design.

They got into the UTV and drove back toward the house, which to Harry seemed to sprawl on forever. She was sure it had to be at least ten thousand square feet. The gorgeous landscaping at the back of the house sloped down to a large pond, and was dotted with patio spaces.

"I'd love to give you a tour of the house too," Clay offered.

"I'd love that, but another time. I want to get back to the farm with lots of time left to do the evening chores." She chuckled. "It's probably going to take me as long as it did this morning." He sped along the dirt road, now flanked by pastures with the same pristine white fencing that she recognized from Jewel's driveway. He stopped at the large gate, similar to Jewel's, and waited for the sensor to react and swing open.

When they got back to the farm, Clay put the UTV back in the barn and returned the keys to the cubbyhole. "Do you want me to help you get the animals back in the barn before I take off?"

Harry shook her head. "Nah, I need the practice. Thanks for the tour today. It was great to see everything and get a feel for it. Your ranch is fabulous."

"I enjoyed having you along." He walked toward his truck and loaded Maverick in the backseat. "I'll find a time when Heath will be home and have you over for dinner and a tour of the house. You could even get in some practice with the shotgun. Oh, and don't forget I owe you a ride on Merlot."

She grinned. "That would be great. My calendar is wide open at the moment."

He took out his phone and tapped on his screen.

Moments later her phone chimed. He slipped his phone back in his pocket. "I just texted you the gate code to the ranch. When you come to visit, feel free to just come on in. No need to call ahead or ring the intercom. We're used to lots of coming and going."

"I'll commit it to memory." She tapped the cab as he climbed into the driver's seat. "Thanks again for today. I had fun."

"You have a good evening, Harry. We'll see you soon."

He drove away with a wave, and Harry went about her evening chores. It took her much longer than it would take him, but she finished within an hour and climbed the steps to the porch with a sense of accomplishment, the dogs by her side.

Hope and Chief went straight to the mudroom and stared at their bowls. They'd had a big day and were more than ready for dinner. Once they were fed, they sprawled across the floor in the living room.

Harry started a fire that she suspected Clay had thoughtfully laid in anticipation of her arrival. With the flames licking the kindling, she took the already prepared lasagna she'd picked up the day she arrived in town and put it in the oven to bake, then turned on the kettle.

After brewing a cup of tea, she added a log to the roaring fire and settled onto the couch. She found the remote for the flat screen television that was mounted to the wall, and tapped through the menu, loading the apps she liked and logging in with her information.

The timer buzzed in the middle of an episode of the addictive mystery series she'd started back home in Salem, and she fixed her plate and brought it to the couch. Before starting her show again, Harry eyed her laptop bag sitting in the corner. She longed to set it up, but needed the wireless password. That and a few other things were on her list for tomorrow's meeting.

A few episodes later, Harry could hardly keep her eyes open. Hope was snuggled close with her head on Harry's lap and Chief was next to his new friend. The dogs seemed to be just as tired, and dragged themselves off the couch to follow her to the bedroom.

Finally in bed, she hoped she'd get to sleep quickly, and knew without a doubt that she was going to have to change a few of her habits. Morning came early on the farm.

Monday, after chores and a quick breakfast of toast and tea, Harry took a shower and put on a suit. She wasn't sure what to expect from Mr. Simpson, but wanted to make a good impression. She felt most at home in her signature navy blue pants and matching jacket, which hid the gun she always wore at her side, and that suit plus the same outfit in black had been her uniforms of choice over the last almost twenty years of her career.

Despite her retirement, she still carried her sidearm; being alone out in the middle of nowhere, it provided peace of mind. She also felt naked without it.

She closed off the doggy door and promised the two furry friends, currently lounging with each other on the kitchen floor, that she'd be back soon, then grabbed her notebook and purse, and headed to town.

With time to spare, she stopped into Winding River Coffee, craving a chai latte. Waiting for the man in front of her to finish his order, she noticed the window on the side street that intersected Main had been broken. Whoever had been sweeping it up had abandoned the broom in the corner, along with a dustpan where tiny pieces of broken glass glinted.

When she gave her name to the friendly barista, the young woman smiled and glanced at the other woman behind the counter. "We thought that must be you. We don't get many women named Harry. You're out at Jewel's place, right?"

Harry nodded. "That's right. I'm Harry McKenzie. Nice to meet you."

The young girl set her cup to the side and beamed. "I'm Lisa." She pointed at the other woman who was busy making her drink. "This is my sister, Laurie. This is our shop."

Laurie, the eldest of the two siblings, smiled and brought the steaming latte to the counter. "You'll have to forgive us. We get excited when we have someone new move to town. Bonnie over at the Grasshopper said you came in with Clay, and then when we saw him, he said you were taking over the farm. We all loved Jewel, so it's nice to have someone at her place."

"Thank you." Harry took out her credit card.

Laurie waved her away. "No, this one is on the house. Welcome to Lavender Valley."

"Oh, that's so sweet of you, but not necessary."

"Just come back and see us again."

"You can count on it." Harry pointed at the window. "What happened there?"

Laurie's smile disappeared and her forehead creased. "This is the second time this month. Some hooligans broke it last night. At least they didn't get into the store, but what a mess. Not to mention the expense."

"Do you have cameras that might have captured the event?"

Laurie shook her head. "No. I guess that's something I might have to look into. We've never had these problems until recently."

"Hopefully, the police will catch the culprit." Harry noticed the large rocks at the base of the trees that lined Main Street. Nothing like ready-made window smashers at the disposal of anyone who wanted to cause a bit of chaos.

Laurie rolled her eyes. "I wouldn't hold my breath. We've all been dealing with this kind of stuff for the last few months. My friend even had her car broken into at her house."

"I'm sorry to hear that." Harry took her first sip from her cup. "This is delicious. Thanks again, and I'll be sure to come back again. I hope your day gets better."

Laurie smiled. "You have a great day, Harry. Real nice to meet ya." Lisa was waiting on a customer but waved at Harry as she stepped toward the door.

Harry drove two blocks across Main to the old two-story house on the corner, where Mr. Simpson's law office was located. She opened the leaded glass door to find a grey-haired woman at the reception desk.

The woman glanced up from her computer screen and greeted Harry with a warm smile. "You must be Ms. McKenzie?"

"Yes, please call me Harry." She extended her hand to the woman.

"I'm Sylvia. I was going to offer you a coffee, but it looks like you've brought your own," she said. "Let me just buzz in and let Mr. Simpson know you're here."

Moments later, a man who looked to be about 45 years old, with black hair and green eyes beneath heavy brows, greeted her with a smile and a handshake. She needn't have dressed up as he was wearing a plaid shirt, dark jeans, boots, and a sport coat, with no tie. "Ms. McKenzie, Harry, right? Jewel said you liked to be called Harry. I'm Buck Simpson. Come on in."

He led her through the hallway to the double doors that opened into a large office, with a view of the lush backyard. Harry pointed at a plaque with his name beside the door. "I see your name is Oscar."

He smiled as he slid behind his desk. "Yes, named after my dad, who was Oscar. It got pretty complicated, so I've been Buck as long as I can remember, but legally and on official documents, I use Oscar. Much like you and Harriet, I imagine."

She took a seat. "Yes, I was named for my great-grandmother. Not the most popular name for a young girl, I might add. Not that Harry is much better, but it beat the alternative and sort of stuck. It has served me well." She studied his wide smile and easy-going manner as he explained he'd worked for his dad since graduating law school some twenty years ago and took over the practice when his dad retired.

Buck opened a thick file and handed her a packet of paperwork. "This is your copy of Jewel's will. I'll just dive in and go over the provisions, and if you have a question, just interrupt me."

Harry flipped a page on her notebook, ready to take notes.

He reviewed the provisions about finding the other four women and inviting them back to the farm. Harry nodded. "I've sent all of them letters, but haven't heard back yet."

He made a note in the file. "Jewel knew her time was limited and hoped to have all of the women back at the farm for the start of the season, which is March or April, depending on weather. As long as those who want to be part of this are at the farm by the end of April, they meet the requirements, and they would have to stay through the entire season. She really wanted all of you to spend Christmas at the farm too, but the end of October will suffice."

Harry scribbled on her pad. "Honestly, I'm hoping somebody shows up before April. I can handle the basics, but it would be nice to have some help."

He chuckled and turned back to his folder. "Jewel asked me to handle the finances, to ease your burden a bit. You can just submit any bills or invoices here to my office and I'll get them paid. I'll provide you a monthly accounting so you can monitor things." He passed a spreadsheet to her. "Here's the current status of her accounts."

He continued to review each portion of Jewel's last wishes. "Jewel requested that she be cremated, and that's been done. She stipulated that if desired, you and the others could coordinate a celebration of her life at a time and place of your choosing. She wants her ashes and Chuck's scattered together on the farm, by the lake. His ashes are in her closet, top shelf."

He reminded Harry that Jewel wanted her dog and animal rescue program restored, and that the Lavender Festival was most important to her. She wanted the women to feel free to put their own mark on the farm and do things differently, but more than anything she wanted the farm to live on and continue.

Buck stepped to a table and retrieved a box, hefted it to his desk, and lifted the lid. He took out three thick binders, which comprised the history of the farm, Jewel's notes about planting her garden, the lavender, taking care of the chickens and other animals, and her beloved dogs. She had kept calendars each year that told the story of irrigating, planting, and harvesting, along with other noteworthy events, including a separate journal about her rescue program.

A smaller box contained Jewel's personal journals. As Harry thumbed through them, she realized Jewel recorded her impressions of each child that arrived at the farm. She wrote about their needs and her dreams for them, and included the dates when they had arrived, their growth and experiences, and the last entry when they left her care. Harry was curious to find her own entries and learn what Jewel thought of her the first time they met.

She opened another journal and smelled the lavender scent that always accompanied Jewel. It was bittersweet to inhale her signature scent, see her things, her handwriting, and her life's work reduced to the contents of a box.

Buck put a hand on her shoulder. "We all loved Jewel. Knowing her, having her in your life, it was a special gift."

Harry bit her lip, her words sticking in her dry throat. She nodded and kept perusing the pages, as she reached for her latte.

Buck added, "I put you on the farm account, so you can just charge any supplies you need at Ranchland, Benson's, the feed store, or the fuel farm. There's a storage tank on the premises that gets refilled periodically."

Harry put the binders back in the box and glanced at her notepad. "I need the wireless password."

Buck flipped a page in the folder. "Oh, yes. I've got that and the email password for the farm, so you'll need to check on that, especially as it gets closer to the festival." He passed a typed page to her.

She checked off that item, and added, "The other thing I wondered is about the lease with Clay Nolan. It seems like he wouldn't need to lease any land, and I figured he was just being kind and helping Jewel out."

Buck's grin deepened. "As Jewel warned me, you're smart as a whip. Clay and his family have always been wonderful to Jewel and Chuck, and when he passed away, they really stepped up their efforts. It's something you can revisit in the future. It's a very small monetary amount, as most of what the agreement calls for is trading manpower to assist with chores and some feed supply. Things all stay the same for this first year."

Harry nodded. "Got it. We'll just play it by ear and see what happens. Clay has been great about showing me the ropes."

"He's a great guy. Totally trustworthy and his word is golden."

She blew out a breath. "Okay then, I guess that's it."

"If you need anything at all, just call." Buck scribbled on the back of his business card. "I added my cell number, and I'm at your disposal."

She tucked it into her purse. "Thanks, Buck. I appreciate all your help. I'm not sure how this is going to work, but for Jewel, I'm willing to try."

He took hold of the heavy box and followed her out of the office to the street, where he put it in the back of her SUV. "Jewel knew she could count on you, Harry. She was convinced the five of you needed each other, and wanted you to get to know one another. Believe me, I tried to suggest a less complicated approach, but she was adamant."

Harry laughed. "Jewel has never steered me wrong, so I'm going to keep on trusting her. Thanks again." She shook his hand and climbed into the driver's seat.

"Oh," she said, "one more odd question. I talked to a few shopkeepers, and they were all talking about vandalism, graffiti, shoplifting, and that kind of petty crime. When I was here, there was zero crime. Do you know what's going on?"

He sighed and frowned. "People are pretty upset about it. We've got a small police department, with usually just two officers on duty, so it's always tough to cover the whole town and keep an eye on everything, but something has changed over the last six months. Everyone is trying to take steps to curb it, but the short answer is, I'm not sure what's going on. At first, we figured it was just mischievous kids, but stealing gas and a rise in burglaries when school is in session points to something else."

Harry's forehead creased. "It's a shame. Hopefully, they get to the bottom of it soon. From what I understand, the sheriff handles the county while most of the crimes are taking place in town, under the jurisdiction of the police chief. Is that right?"

Buck bobbed his head. "Right. The sheriff's department is over in Central Point, but they cover the rural areas of the county, and the police handle the town of Lavender Valley. Most of the crimes are within the city limits."

"That's interesting," said Harry. "You would think criminals would be more apt to target the rural areas where less people would see them." She started the ignition and waved. "Thanks again for your help. I'll be in touch, I'm sure."

She took the long way around the block and drove all the way down Main Street, paying attention to the graffiti. Harry might be retired, but couldn't stem her curiosity at a mystery begging to be solved.

CHAPTER EIGHT

She made another loop down Main Street, in case there were any signs of graffiti or other vandalism she had missed. Downtown was confined to four square blocks bordered by Main Street and Oregon Street, with Oak and Birch completing the business district.

The majority of the shops faced Main Street, which if followed, turned into the highway that led to and from Lavender Valley. She pulled into a spot in front of Winding River Coffee and walked the downtown corridor, looking for any cameras that might be in the area.

Spotting none on the business properties, she scoped out banks and ATM units, which often picked up criminals who didn't realize some of the cameras recorded far beyond the person at the machine. She took note of the locations, scribbling on her notepad.

As she suspected, none of the vandalism was in view of any of the cameras. The banks or ATM units were at one end of Main Street as it curved, just past the business area, and she didn't see any sign of problems at the businesses facing the cameras.

The coffee shop was in a two-story building on the corner of Main and Birch. The same block housed a kitchen supply store and a women's clothing shop, along with a yarn and fabric store. Harry glanced up and wondered what was in the second story of the building. Above her, a narrow balcony went around the entire perimeter of the second floor.

She climbed behind the wheel of her SUV and drove a few blocks away from Main Street to the police station. It was on property behind the community center, in a house, and would have been mistaken for one if not for the sign out front lettered with POLICE.

She grabbed her handbag and walked up the wooden ramp that led to the main door. The homey feel continued on the inside, where the smell of coffee filled the air. A woman looked up from her computer screen and smiled at Harry. "How can we help you?"

"I was hoping to talk with Chief Phillips. I'm soon to be retired from the Salem PD, and just wanted to stop in and introduce myself. Just a quick courtesy call, really."

The woman rose from her desk and approached the long counter that served to separate her from the visiting public. "He's just in his office. Come on through." She opened the half door built into the end of the counter.

"I'm Sally, by the way," she said, leading Harry down a hallway, past a small kitchen and breakroom.

"I'm Harry McKenzie. Great to meet you, Sally."

Sally led her to an office that was once a bedroom and rapped her knuckles on the open door. "Chief, this is Harry McKenzie from Salem PD. She's just paying a courtesy call."

The gray-haired man with a bit of a paunch, eased

himself out of his chair, the leather from his gun belt squeaking. He smiled and extended his hand across his desk. "Pleased to meet you. Harry, did you say?"

She stepped forward and shook his hand. "That's right, sir. Harriet officially, but everybody calls me Harry. I'm moving into Jewel's place, Lavender Valley Farm."

At the mention of Jewel's name, his face softened and he smiled deeper. Knowing her was like having a master key to every place in town. "Aww, we all loved Jewel."

He gestured for Harry to take a seat and she sunk into the well-worn cushioned chair in front of his desk. "I grew up here on the farm, with Jewel and Chuck, and her last wishes were for me to take over her farm for the next year, along with some other women who grew up there."

He asked her about her work in Salem and his brows rose when she divulged her rank as Deputy Chief. "Very impressive. Honestly, you look too young to be retired, but we're always happy to have a fellow officer in town."

"I started young and by using some of my accrued time, was able to buy the last few months I needed to get in thirty years for retirement. I loved my work, but was looking for a change." She chuckled and added, "Jewel's last wishes just happened to coincide with that."

They chatted a bit more, and he told her about the department, which consisted of himself, four officers, and Sally. Understaffed was an understatement.

Sally came through the door with a carafe of steaming coffee and an empty mug. "Would you like coffee?" she asked Harry. "This is black, but I can bring some sugar and creamer if you use it." '

"Black is perfect. Thank you." Harry took a sip of the dark brew as Sally filled Chief Phillip's cup. It tasted just like the coffee she had enjoyed for the last thirty years. A roaster should look into creating a police blend.

After listening to Chief Phillips talk more about the department, Harry set her cup down. "I've only been in town a few days, but noticed some vandalism and graffiti that wasn't prevalent when I lived here. The shopkeepers say it's a recent development. Do you have any ideas?"

He leaned back in his chair and blew out a long breath. "We haven't been able to make much progress. If we had more personnel, we could increase our coverage, but we've basically got one officer on graveyard and one on-call for extra help. Normally, it works, but we've had more than our share of petty crime over these last months. We're trying to enlist the help of neighbors and residents. The budget just doesn't allow more, and the mayor won't budge on giving us an increase."

Harry quizzed him on the dates and times of the activity. The more she probed and jotted notes on her pad, she saw a pattern associated with the crimes that correlated to none of the crimes taking place within the purview of the ATM cameras. As she asked more questions and he tapped his keyboard, it became clear the officer on duty was distracted by other calls during most of the vandalism events, including cars being broken into in residential areas.

A variety of long-time residents would call in reports of prowlers or disturbances, like loud yelling in the street, which pulled the officer to another area of town. The officer would investigate and find nothing, only to discover later that a crime took place elsewhere at that time.

Chief Phillips shook his head, his cheeks red. "I should have seen that myself."

Harry glossed over his embarrassment with a wave of her hand. "It's easy to miss if you're not looking for something suspicious. Lavender Valley has enjoyed a relatively crime-free existence, so it's not something that would naturally come to mind."

She took another sip from her cup and stood. "Well, I best get going. I just wanted to introduce myself and let you know you had a fellow officer as a new resident, plus I do carry all the time, and next year when it's time to certify, I hope I can do that through your department."

He stood and led her down the hallway. "Sure thing, and we appreciate you coming in to say hello. Hopefully, we'll get a handle on these nuisance crimes. I know the merchants have had enough of it. I appreciate your help, Harry."

She said her goodbyes, and headed out to her SUV. She made a quick stop at the far end of Main where she went in search of boots at Ranchland. She found a pair of insulated rubber boots that fit her feet, along with a field jacket that could take more of a beating than the jackets she'd brought with her, and a new pair of gloves.

She drove back to the coffee shop. Inside, she spotted Laurie sitting at a table near the service counter. The place was empty and Harry made her way over.

"Hey, Harry, back so soon?"

She grinned and took the chair across from Laurie. "I was thinking about the vandalism problem, and thought the second story above you would offer a good view for a camera."

Laurie arched her brows. "Oh, yeah, you're right."

"I've got a little experience with surveillance. I thought I might be able to borrow some trail cameras and get them set up, see if we can catch the people doing this." Harry dug her phone out of her purse and tapped the screen and then turned it to show Laurie. "These are a good choice if you decide to put your own cameras in. They work well, and you can manage and monitor them on your phone. Not too expensive, either."

Laurie took the phone and scrolled through the information. "Not as much as I thought they'd be. Heck, I spent almost that much getting the window fixed."

Harry nodded. "Exactly. I could help you set them up, if you decide to get them. In the meantime, like I said, I could borrow some and install them. Could I take a look upstairs?"

"Sure, that sounds great. I'm the only one here right now, but could give you the key. We just use it for storage. It's not divided, so each of the merchants just has an area up there. We didn't want the expense of putting in walls and all that." She went over to the cash register, took out a key on a hot pink elastic ring, and handed it to Harry. "You mentioned experience with surveillance. Are you a cop?"

Harry smiled as she palmed the key. "Retired, but let's keep that between the two of us. I'm just trying to help and don't want to step on anybody's toes."

Laurie sighed. "If you ask me, some toes need squashing. All of us have talked to the police and we understand they're a small force and don't have the staff or budget, so we talked to Mayor Crawford and got nowhere. She acted like it was just the cost of doing business."

"I'll take a look upstairs and see if I can borrow what we need to get us some coverage. Just don't say anything. We don't need the bad guys knowing what we're up to." Harry lowered her voice, "In fact, don't even tell Lisa. Just the two of us, okay? The less people who know, the better chance we have of catching them."

Laurie nodded, her face serious. "Understood. Lisa is a little too chatty, I know. She covers the early shift on Monday, and she's off the rest of the day, so it's a great time to check things out." She pointed out the stairway and left Harry to explore.

Windows flanked all four sides of the large space upstairs. Supplies and boxes were stacked in neat rows within each space, marked off with brightly colored tape and separated by shelving. Harry made her way to the windows above Main Street, and then checked Fir Street, Birch Street, and Second Street. The elevated space offered a good view of all of them.

If she could get the cameras attached to the wooden rails on the old balcony, it would be ideal. Harry found another set of stairs at the opposite end of the building, where the fabric shop was located. However, she wanted to keep her sleuthing under the radar and preferred not to involve any other merchants at the moment, so she made her way back downstairs and waited for Laurie to finish with her customer. Laurie greeted her with a quizzical look.

"I'm going to see if I can round up some trail cameras and if I can, will get them installed upstairs. I'll give you a call when I know more and then will just need access, preferably after hours, so I can get it accomplished without anyone noticing."

Laurie took one of her coffee reward cards from the counter and wrote on it. "Here's my cell number. Just call me and let me know. I can meet you down here. I just live about a mile away."

Harry handed her back the key. "Sounds good. I'll be in touch as soon as I get things together."

"I'm going to research the cameras, and if I can swing it, I'll get them ordered later in the year, so we have a permanent solution. Winter is always slow, so I need to check my finances first."

"Understood," said Harry. "I'll call you later this week."

Laurie wouldn't let Harry leave without a complimentary coffee. Harry tried to refuse, but eventually gave in and accepted a small black coffee to go.

That little buzz of excitement that coursed through her veins whenever she was on a new case had her mind humming. That and all the coffee she'd consumed.

It wasn't anywhere near the level of cases she normally worked, but still the satisfaction of working to catch the culprits who were impacting the good people of Lavender Valley in such a negative way, piqued her inquisitive spirit. She had an idea and all she needed was a little help from Clay.

CHAPTER NINE

When Harry got home, she changed into jeans and a sweater, lit a fire, and curled up on the couch while she waited for Clay to reply to her text. It took her longer than she expected to set up her laptop and tablet, and to transfer her cable service and Internet to her new address.

With her electronic life sorted, she scrolled through her emails, dumping all the junk. She smiled when she saw an email from Buck. He had sent along an electronic copy of Jewel's will and a spreadsheet with the financial information.

After a quick bite to eat, Harry retrieved a stack of Jewel's journals from the box Buck had given her and snuggled under a soft throw blanket, the dogs resting at her feet.

Despite years of witnessing heinous crimes and reading murder reports, tears filled her eyes as she read Jewel's entries in her journals. In those pages, Harry saw for herself the dozens of children that had come through Jewel's door. It was one thing to know about them, but to see them through Jewel's eyes and written in her own hand was something else. She sifted through them all until she found the four women she had been asked to invite to join her. Each of them was heartbreaking.

When Harry lost her parents, it was difficult, but she was very young and her grandmother had swooped in and saved her, raising her and loving her. Losing her grandma had been more impactful, since she had been the only mother Harry actually remembered.

Compared to the others, Harry had been lucky. She hadn't been neglected or abused. She had only been alone and heartbroken. Jewel had given her a place to belong and the support she needed to heal. She had done much more for the other four young girls, who came with deep wounds.

As she sipped tea and read more about each one of them, her curiosity grew, as did her desire to meet them. She wanted to know what had become of their lives. Jewel believed they needed each other, and in Harry's experience, Jewel was rarely wrong.

The chime of her phone interrupted her reading. She plucked it from the side table. The time on the screen made her do a double take. It was past time to get her evening chores done. She hit the green button "Hey, Clay."

"Sorry, I was out at the far end of the ranch today working on fences and didn't look at my phone until I just got home."

"No problem. I have a favor to ask, but I need to get out and get my chores done before it gets dark. If you are up to coming over to chat tonight, I could offer you some leftover lasagna. It's safe, I got it at the market."

He chuckled. "Sounds perfect. I've got to do a few things here, but I'll be over in about an hour."

"Sounds great. See you then."

Harry slipped into her new boots and jacket and ushered the dogs outside for their evening routine. Arnold and

Agatha weren't impressed with her new wardrobe, but having boots that fit made her life easier.

With the barn buttoned up and the chickens safely in their house, she and the dogs made their way back to the porch. Like she had watched Jewel and Chuck do countless times, she knocked the dirt and mud off her boots along the edge of the porch and took them off before entering through the mudroom door.

She made sure the dogs' paws were clean before letting them in and feeding them dinner.

After washing her hands, she popped the lasagna into the oven to reheat and added butter and garlic to the partial loaf of bread that remained on the counter. Searching the fridge, looking for something to offer as a side dish, she wished she'd picked up the makings for a salad. Luckily, when she scoured the pantry, she found a nice supply of Jewel's canned veggies from her garden.

She opted for the green beans and went about getting a skillet and gathering olive oil, garlic, lemon pepper, and salt. While she was sauteing them, the intercom system alerted her to the gate opening.

As she added the green beans to the pan, the inviting aroma filled the air. Moments before Clay's headlights flashed across the front of the house, Chief and Hope stood by the door and barked to let her know someone was out front.

She slid the green beans into a serving bowl and set it on the island counter before answering the knock on her door. Maverick darted through the opening, making a dash for Chief and Hope. Clay, looking fresh from the shower, stepped inside and took off his hat. He held out a bottle of wine. "I figured red with lasagna, right?"

She took it and laughed. "I'm the last person to ask about wine. I'm not much of a drinker."

He slipped out of his coat and hung it on a hook near the hat rack. "I know just enough to be dangerous. My mom was the wine expert in our family. Heath and I aren't big on wine either and have barely made a dent in the stock in the wine cellar at the house. I always try and give it away, like tonight." He winked, then petted the dogs before getting them to gather together on Chief's dog bed in the living room.

He returned to the kitchen, where Harry was pulling the lasagna and bread from the oven. "Mom was always pushing for us to grow some grapes at the ranch. Dad wasn't keen on the idea and indulged her with a wine cellar instead. He quipped it would be cheaper."

Harry chuckled as she got plates and cutlery, and Clay opened the bottle and poured two glasses of wine.

"So," Clay said, digging his fork into the bubbling cheese atop the lasagna. "You need a favor?"

"You mentioned trail cameras and I was wondering if you would let me borrow them." She went on to explain her idea of installing them on the second story of the coffee shop building to catch any vandals in the act, and then turning the evidence over to Chief Phillips.

"Full disclosure," she said, reaching for a piece of bread. "I would need your help to install them. I don't have any tools, although, there are probably some in the barn or garage."

"I'm at your service and happy to help." He grinned and reached for his wine glass, holding it up to clink to hers.

She indulged him and took a small sip. "It's not bad."

A deep laugh erupted from his smiling mouth. "This was one of my mom's favorites. I think it runs close to a hundred bucks a bottle."

Harry shrugged. "I told you, I'm a numpty when it comes to wine."

He frowned. "Numpty. That's a new one."

She grinned "I watch way too much British programming. It's a cute way of saying moron."

"I like it, and it sounds nicer than moron."

As they ate, she told him about her day, visiting the police department and exploring the buildings downtown. "Chief Phillips seems like a nice enough guy. Not a ball of fire, by any means, but he was embarrassed when he realized his officers had been lured to other calls during the vandalism and theft events. He says he's asked the mayor for help, but she hasn't been forthcoming."

She finished her last bite. "What's your take on Mayor Crawford?"

"I haven't had many dealings with her directly. She's got a real estate company with offices here, Medford, and a couple other towns. I just hear snippets here and there, and none of the business owners are very complimentary. We had a long-time mayor who retired, and Crawford was a bit of a newcomer, but had the support of some of the most vocal city council members. Also, the other guy running in the election didn't do himself any favors. He got in trouble for not paying his taxes and that tanked his campaign."

"That's not a good look. If Chief Phillips and the business owners say she hasn't been very helpful or sympathetic, it sounds like she's not well equipped for small town leadership."

He shrugged. "I think we've had a steady guy at the helm for a long time, so we're a bit spoiled." He put his fork down.

"That lasagna was good. Thanks for dinner. So, what day were you thinking to install the cameras?"

"Well, I'd like to get them up before the weekend for sure. I think six would be ideal. Depending on the coverage, we might be able to go with only four. Maybe get them in on Thursday so we can test them and make sure everything works."

"That works for me, and I've got like a dozen of them, so whatever you need. Mine are cellular based, so they feed to my cell phone using the network. The locations I usually put them in are too far away from the house for a wireless connection, so we'll need to monitor on my cell phone."

"Oh, I'm used to dealing with wireless systems, though more in a residential setting. I guess I'll need to borrow your phone, too." She started clearing their plates. "I was going to stay above the coffee shop overnight, or maybe talk to Buck and see if I can stay in his office, more out of the way and less noticeable. That would also give me another line of sight from the other side of the street. I'm trying to do this without alerting anybody and inadvertently tipping off the bad guys."

"That makes sense." Clay put his silverware in the dishwasher while Harry filled the kettle.

She pointed to the coffee maker. "Do you want some coffee?"

"Nah, I'm tired and don't want to jinx a good night's sleep. I've got to mend more fences tomorrow."

"I'm sorry I dragged you over here. How about I treat you to dinner at the Back Door Bistro Thursday night, and then when it's dark we can sneak upstairs and get them set up?"

"Works for me. I'll pick you up around six-ish?"

She poured water over her teabag. "Sounds great. I'll get a plan together. I think the weekend is the best chance of catching them. I just need to get a feel for things so I'm ready."

"Sounds good. I'll see you Thursday." He wandered to the living room and clicked his tongue to get Maverick's attention. "Thanks again for dinner, Harry."

He retrieved his hat and coat and set out across the porch. Harry and the two dogs watched as their new friends drove down the driveway.

She turned off the outside light and took her tea into the living room, where she got out her notepad and let the dogs up on the couch next to her. "Time for you two to settle down for the night while I work on my stakeout plan."

CHAPTER TEN

Thursday, Clay was at the door a few minutes before six o'clock. Armed with keys and alarm codes to the coffee shop, Harry left her two dogs at the door with a promise to be home soon.

She climbed into the passenger seat of his pickup, and he pointed at the backseat. "I've got all the stuff we should need, including zip ties and duct tape if things get desperate."

She glanced over and laughed, catching a whiff of the woodsy scent of his aftershave. "Oh, and you brought binoculars, too. That's great."

He grinned as he shut her door, then hurried to slide behind the wheel. "I admit, I'm a little more than excited to be part of a stakeout. It's a thrill."

Harry rolled her eyes. "I hate to break it to you, but it will probably be boring. Stakeouts involve lots of sitting, waiting, and hoping you can find a restroom where you won't be noticed."

He chuckled as he steered the truck into the downtown area. "I can see that. I'm just hoping we can catch these jerks."

"Me, too. It's hard enough for people to make ends meet without having all the extra work and expense of dealing with repairs and theft."

He parked his truck in front of the Back Door Bistro, two blocks from the building that housed the coffee shop. Before opening his door, he turned toward Harry. "You're the real deal. Like one of those superheroes driven to seek justice."

She laughed and reached for her door handle. "Well, not so sure about the superhero analogy, but I've always liked righting wrongs, standing up for victims, and putting criminals where they belong. I also believe in second chances for those that make mistakes and truly want to change. Being a cop used to be more about all that, but times have changed."

He got out and came around to her side of the truck, shutting the door after she hopped down from her seat. "I think being a cop would be one of the hardest jobs around nowadays."

She nodded. "Somehow, it's become accepted for politicians to use us as pawns to score points. One minute we're vilified and they want us defunded, and the next we don't do enough to protect people and property. With my responsibility for investigations and major crimes, I wasn't as involved with those who were in the public trenches, patrolling the streets, but morale and officer recruitment suffered throughout the ranks. That was one of the reasons I retired."

He opened the door and they stepped inside. The restaurant was a cozy space, with brick walls and lots of wood beams. The hostess greeted Clay by name and led him to a table in an alcove near the fireplace.

Like a gentleman, he moved the chair, cushioned in red velvet, away from the table to allow Harry an easy entry. He took the chair next to her and the hostess left them with menus and the promise of a waiter.

While she studied the menu, Clay didn't even give it a passing glance. "You know what you're having?" she asked.

"Steak. They buy my beef and it's always delicious."

"Alrighty then, I'll follow your lead and do a steak."

"I wouldn't steer you wrong. Their twice baked potatoes are really good, too and I love their rosemary truffle fries."

"Oh, I'm a sucker for a twice baked potato. That sounds yummy."

A staff member arrived with a basket of warm bread and filled their water glasses. Moments later, their server appeared and took their orders.

While they waited, they savored the bread and dipping oil. Instead of chatting about their upcoming sting operation, Harry quizzed Clay about the local eateries.

"For dinner, I typically like a good steak, and along with this place frequent the Ranch House. The pizza is great at Brick's and the Riverside Grille is also good for lunch or dinner. I love Daisy's and the Grasshopper for homecooked breakfast and lunch."

She tore off a piece of bread and dipped it in the herbed oil. "Do you like to cook?"

He shrugged. "I'm neutral. Usually, I'm busy with work and don't have time to cook something. I like to make chili and grill burgers or steaks and can make a roast. I can handle breakfast and make a sandwich, but anything else is a bridge too far. I like to come into town and support the local restaurants, especially since they're big supporters of the ranch."

He offered her more from the breadbasket and she held up a hand. "No, thanks. I won't be able to eat my dinner if I have more." She popped the last bite of her bread in her mouth. "Like you, I can figure out breakfast and eat whatever for lunch. I'm used to eating dinner out or at least getting takeout. In a pinch, I can make soup or something like that, but need to figure out a proper meal routine, I guess."

"My brother, Heath, likes to cook. In fact, when we can nail down a night that works, he'll make dinner for us."

The server delivered their meals, and Harry took her first bite of her filet. "Oh, my, that is the best steak I've ever eaten. It's perfect and so tender."

He smiled. "Nolan Ranch has the best beef in Oregon. And Chef John knows how to cook it."

By the time they finished the scrumptious meal and refused dessert, it was almost eight o'clock and plenty dark enough to begin their operation. Clay tried to pay the check but when Harry left the table to visit the restroom, she handled the bill.

He was still giving her a hard time about it when they walked to the truck. He drove around the corner and parked along Birch near the coffeeshop, which was closed for the evening. After hefting the large duffle bag and his toolbox from the backseat, he followed Harry to the door. She made quick work of unlocking it and silencing the alarm. The ambient glow from the under cabinet lighting behind the counter provided enough for them to make their way to the stairs.

In an effort to draw as little attention as possible, they opted to use flashlights instead of lighting up the whole upper floor of the building. With Clay's experience in installing the cameras and Harry having completed her reconnaissance of the building earlier, it didn't take them long to get a total of eight cameras mounted on the wooden balcony rails.

Once they were installed, they sat on two sturdy boxes and checked Clay's phone to make sure everything was working. After studying his phone, Clay gave her a thumbs up. "It looks good here."

"You're sure you're okay with trading phones in the evening for a few days?" Harry asked, taking his phone.

"Yep. I rarely get calls in the evening. If anyone does call, they can leave a message, or I'll have your phone and you can text me and let me know who it was."

"Same for me. Nobody should be calling me in the middle of the night though. Starting tomorrow, I'm going to spend the nights over at Buck's place. That way I'll be close enough, but not visible. When I reviewed Chief Phillips' reports, they all happened Friday to Sunday, so I feel confident that tonight will just be a dry run to make sure the cameras record."

"Sounds like a good plan and Buck is trustworthy, so he won't tell anyone." Clay reached for his toolbox and the much lighter duffle bag. "Shall we head out?"

She nodded and collected her purse, leading the way downstairs. She punched in the alarm code and locked the door, waiting to make sure it armed without a problem, then they made their way along the quiet street back to the truck.

He opened her door for Harry and slid the supplies in the backseat before settling behind the wheel. As he headed out of town, he turned to her. "If you want some help tomorrow and Saturday, I could come along and share the shift with you. That way you wouldn't have to stay awake the entire night."

She saw his smile in the glow of the dashboard lights. "Aww, that's nice of you. I've stayed up longer than that, but if you want to tag along, I wouldn't say no. It would be great to have the company."

"Cool," he said, as he pulled up to the gate at the farm and leaned out the window to punch in the code. He followed the long driveway and pulled alongside the porch. "Looks like your two buddies are waiting on you."

She laughed as she took in the sight of Hope and Chief, tails wagging, their faces filling the glass door. "Poor Maverick was all alone. I guess we should have invited him over."

"Ah, no, he was with Heath and his furry cousin. Heath has a sweet border collie, Ace. They're great buddies."

"I'm looking forward to meeting him." Clay started to get out of the truck, and she put her hand up. "No, you stay there. I'm fine getting to the door by myself. You've done more than your share helping me tonight. I appreciate it."

"I'll see you in the morning to swap phones." He touched the tip of his finger to the brim of his hat.

"Thanks, Clay. See you then."

He waited until she was inside and locked the door behind her, before turning and heading back down the driveway.

Harry petted each of the dogs, then her guilt at leaving them behind that evening prompted her to get them each a cookie from their jar on the counter. They gobbled the cookies and rushed back to stare out the door.

"Aww, I totally understand, but we'll see him tomorrow." Harry had had more fun tonight with Clay and their undercover operation than she had in a long time. As she looked at the dogs, it dawned on her, they were probably hoping to see their dog friend even more than Clay. She ruffled the fur on the top of their heads. "And we'll see Maverick, too."

CHAPTER ELEVEN

F riday morning, Clay pulled in front of the farmhouse as Harry was filling the water troughs for the donkeys and alpacas. Hope and Chief beat a path to the truck and waited, tails wagging, for Maverick to climb down from the backseat.

The three of them bounded into the field while Harry came from around the barn and greeted Clay with a wave. "Your cell phone is in the house. Coffee is on, if you want to come in for a few minutes."

"Sounds good. I'll wrangle the dogs into the backyard so we don't have to worry about them going on an adventure."

By the time Clay came through the sunroom door, Harry had exchanged her boots for slippers, washed up, and poured two cups of coffee, adding sugar and cream to his.

She nodded at his cell phone on the side table next to the chair as she handed him his cup, then took the chair on the other side of the table. A deep sigh escaped her as she gazed out large windows. "I've forgotten how peaceful and beautiful it is here. This view is one of my favorites."

He put her phone on the table between them, and picked up his. "Yep, it's part of what makes this valley so appealing. I love the hills in the distance, the river, the absolute quiet." He glanced down at his phone. "How did the cameras work?"

"Good. No action to report from last night, but they captured photos of people who tripped the motion and heat detectors. I think we're good to go for tonight."

"What time?" asked Clay.

"I think we should be in place around eight. It will be dark enough that we won't stand out, and I suspect if anything happens it will be much later."

"That makes sense. The sidewalks roll up downtown around ten or eleven on the weekends, so I agree, it will probably be after that." He reached for his coffee. "Oh, I've got binoculars and I'll bring snacks." He wiggled his brows at her.

"That is usually the best part of a stakeout. We're also getting off easy since we'll be in a house and have access to a bathroom and a kitchen. Not what you call roughing it."

He laughed and took another sip from his cup. "If you want, we could talk Heath into watching all the dogs at my place. He's going to keep an eye on Maverick for me."

"Oh, that would be great. I was already feeling guilty that they'd be stuck here alone all night. Also, I don't want them to get into trouble. Did you tell him what we're doing?"

He shook his head. "I just told him I was helping a beautiful woman with a project for the next two nights." He chuckled. "He gave me a bit of a ribbing, but didn't make much of it. We try to stay out of each other's business for the most part."

The heat rose in Harry's cheeks. Nobody had referred to her as beautiful in years, maybe decades. "If he's trustworthy, maybe we should just tell him what we're doing."

Clay gave her an impish grin, while his eyes twinkled with mischief. "Let's just keep him guessing. He can be a bit of a chatty Cathy." He pointed at the dogs. "I'll just come and pick them up after they eat their dinner tonight. We've got a nice fenced area they can go in and out of, so they'll be confined. Hope's used to it there and Chief will adapt. He'll get to meet Ace. They'll have fun."

"Okay," she said, "I just don't want to be a burden or cause any trouble."

His forehead creased. "It's no problem and Heath is great with the dogs." He took the last swallow from his cup and stood. "I better get going and get my work done. If you want, I'll pick you up with the dogs and after we drop them off, we can grab a bite to eat before we settle in at Buck's place?"

"Sure, that works for me. I'll be ready."

He retrieved his hat. "See ya then." He stepped through the door to the backyard and whistled for Maverick, who came running.

Hope and Chief followed and after using a towel to dry their paws, giving Hope's extra attention, since she loved her paws held and rubbed, she moved to the long feathers along their legs. With them as dry as possible, Harry welcomed them into the sunroom. "I bet you two are ready for a nap."

She yawned and opted to snuggle into the couch. Hope made herself comfy on Harry's lap and Chief stretched out next to them. She'd been up off and on all night, checking Clay's phone, and with the plan of being up most of tonight, she needed some rest.

After sleeping for several hours, Harry wrapped up her chores early and fed the dogs their dinner, then changed into dark jeans, a black turtleneck, and her comfy lace-up cop shoes that she always wore on the job. The television shows that depicted female detectives wearing heels always made her laugh.

She slipped on a warm coat, made sure she had a hat, scarf, and gloves, and rounded up the dogs as Clay arrived. She added the stiff, slobbered upon slipper and the green blanket along with a few other toys to the tote bag she prepped for the dogs. While she locked the door, Clay loaded the dogs in the backseat, where Maverick was waiting.

They made the short drive to the ranch, where Harry opted to wait in the truck while he took the three dogs and their tote bag into the house. She didn't want to invite questions from Heath and didn't relish the idea of lying to him.

Within a few minutes, Clay was back behind the wheel. He glanced over at her. "Chief is fine. I'm not sure he even noticed you were gone, with the excitement of meeting Ace and all the sniffing."

She looked back at the house as he steered toward the driveway. As if reading her mind, he added, "Heath said if there's a problem, he'll call, so don't worry about him. Chief will be fine. Heath is sort of like an overgrown puppy himself."

She laughed, and relaxed as they drove to town. He parked in front of Riverside Grille, a couple of blocks from where they had positioned the cameras. The place wasn't overly busy, filled with only a few couples and families out celebrating the end of a workweek at the casual eatery.

Minutes after they were seated, the server appeared to take their order. Her nametag said Sheila and she greeted Clay by name. Clay introduced Harry and gestured for her to go first.

"Oh, I'm starving. I didn't eat lunch. You go ahead and order, and I'll look at this menu a little longer."

Clay opted for the prime rib dip, which he assured her was top-notch, and also recommended the half pound cheeseburger. She joined him with the dip and chose a baked potato for her side.

As soon as the waitress left, Harry whispered, "Instead of eating lunch, I slept right through it."

Clay reached for his iced tea and grinned at her. "I confess, I also took a rather long cat nap. Trying to prepare for tonight. In my younger days, I could stay up all night and work all day and it didn't bother me, but now, I can't do it."

"Same," she said. "I've done it lots of times, but the last few years my role shifted to more of an administrative and mentoring one. I still went on some of the more exciting cases, but the boring, all-nighters went to the younger crowd."

Their food arrived and Harry dug into the warm sandwich, slathered in melted cheddar cheese. Between it and the buttery potato with a crisp, salty skin, she was in food heaven.

Clay wiped his mouth, then pointed at her plate. "How do you like it?"

"It's beyond scrumptious. You were spot on with the steak, and now this? I think you missed your calling as a foodie."

He chuckled. "I'm a basic meat and potatoes man, so pretty easy to please."

"I dug out Jewel's slow cooker and decided I could probably handle that kind of cooking. Soup, stew, and whatever else I can find online that looks easy and edible. My palate is not refined. Too many years of eating on the run, and whatever and whenever I could squeeze it in."

"When in doubt, I always opt for a steak or burger, but Heath is more adventurous and likes to try out recipes. He's good with Italian, pasta, stuff like that."

"I love Italian. There was a place by my house that I ate at often. Always takeout, but still delicious."

"If we can swing it, we'll have you over one night this week and I'll ask Heath to make Italian."

"That would be wonderful." She took the last bite of her sandwich and pushed her plate away from her. "I'm stuffed." She glanced at Clay's plate, where he still had a quarter of his sandwich left. "And I eat too fast. Hazard of the job, I'm afraid."

It didn't take him long to finish, and this time, he insisted on paying the check. "My turn," he said, swiping it before Harry could reach it.

"Thank you. It was great. I'll definitely be back." She reached for her coat, and he held it for her. As they left the restaurant, she pointed down the street. "How about a little stroll?"

"Sure," he said, offering her his arm.

She linked hers through his. "I just thought it would be good to get a lay of the land, and see if we see anything odd before we set up at our base."

They walked down Oak Street and covered the three blocks to Main, passing by Rooster's Tavern, where loud music and laughter drifted from the door. "They've got good burgers and wings," said Clay. "And cheap tacos on Tuesday, but it can get a bit rowdy on the weekends."

Across Oak, most of the businesses were closed and dark, except for a light in Daisy's Café. The closed sign hung in the window and inside, someone mopped the floor.

They turned on Main and stopped to look in the window of the Sugar Shack. The scent of sugar and cinnamon still hung in the air around the shop. The display cases were empty, and the place was dark, except for the glow of the exit light. Across Main, Brick's Pizza was busy with cars filling all the closest parking spots. They wandered down the street, where most shops were closed, their windows lit and displayed their latest offerings. The ice cream shop was open, with a couple of people at the counter. The name of the shop had changed, but Harry remembered going there with Chuck and getting double scoops of the most delicious flavors.

They stopped in front of the coffee shop and Harry gazed across Main Street at the Grasshopper, closed for the night, then looked to her left, further down Main at Benson's, which was open until ten o'clock for late night grocery and hardware needs.

As Harry surveyed the area, Clay remained quiet. She gazed up at the balcony where the cameras were and met Clay's questioning eyes. "So, what do you think?" he asked.

"Well, if I was looking to cause trouble, I'd target one of the stores off of Main along First or Second Street. Once business hours are over, there's little to no traffic on those interior streets. The cameras will cover part of Second Street but won't reach First Street."

She tugged on Clay's arm and led the way back down the block, then turned onto Pine Street, getting a feel for the businesses, most of which had large glass windows, ripe for smashing. They made their way back to Oregon Street and Cranberry Cottage, the large gift shop and antique store next to the Riverside Grille, where they had eaten dinner.

Clay nodded toward the gift shop. "May, one of the owners, is Duke's sister. He's the veterinarian I told you about. She's a great gal. She and her friend, Janet have quite the thriving business. Janet is divorced and moved here from

Portland. She was married to some guy who was big in the art scene."

Harry admired the window, filled with cozy wares with glittery snowflakes hung above, making for a perfect winter scene.

The downtown shopping area was comprised of a three-block square. Harry studied the small shops and eateries as they turned to explore the shops along the other main interior street. The pharmacy she remembered from her youth was still in the same spot and the pretty vintage bottles that had caught her eye then, still lined the shelves in the back of the shop.

Across from it, the Lavender Valley Florist was decked out in red and pink, the cold case behind the counter, lit up and filled with cheerful bouquets. Lavender Valley still held the quaint appeal of small town life.

Clay leaned closer to her. "I can see those wheels in your head turning. What are you thinking?"

She wrinkled her nose. "Just trying to get a feel for everything and put myself in the shoes of the criminal." She stopped and gazed at the buildings. "We had a case once where a guy was living above a store. He'd come down at night and steal whatever he needed. Lots of small thefts were reported, but there was no sign of a break-in. It was like this, with all the buildings connected. I had the idea to take a look upstairs and we found his little nest. He had it made. A nice warm place to stay and access to all the supplies and food he needed." They walked back to the truck, taking First Street and turning when they got to Rooster's Tavern.

Harry glanced down the street. "It makes sense the vandals would want to stay out of sight and not draw attention to themselves. On the other hand, if they can throw something through a window from a car and not risk getting out, the side streets might be their best bet. With so little information, it's hard to know."

He opened the passenger door for her, and she stepped up into the seat. He drove the same outer loop they had walked and crossed Main, parking two blocks from it on the same side as Buck's office.

Clay slid his duffle out of the backseat while Harry opened the back gate and unlocked the door, tapping in the alarm code Buck had provided.

With the beeping quieted, she held the door wider for Clay and then closed and locked it behind him. The house was quiet and dark, save for a night light plugged into the wall in the kitchen area.

They moved through the house, using the bit of moonlight shining through the windows, making their way to the staircase. Harry reached in her pocket and extracted a flashlight, then lit the way up the stairs to the room that overlooked the street.

She moved the light across the room to see pillows, blankets, and even an electric kettle, ceramic mugs, bottles of water, and packets of hot chocolate and tea bags. She chuckled. "It looks like Buck went out of his way to make us comfy."

Another night light provided a soft glow near the table with the beverage station. Clay set the duffle bag on the floor. "Seems like more of a slumber party than a stakeout."

"Right?" Harry moved the two chairs so they were closer to the French doors that opened onto a balcony and took the binoculars Clay handed her. "We've got a good view of Oak and Pine, and of course, Main Street."

He took out another pair of binoculars and a spotting scope, and slid the patio door open to step out onto the narrow balcony. "I wonder if it's any better out here."

She stood next to him, barely enough room for the two of them to extend their elbows, and positioned the scope along the same line she had viewed from inside. "I think it's fine inside. That will save us freezing out here all night."

He followed her inside and placed his hat on the coffee table. "I didn't want you thinking I was a wimp, but I'm happy to stay inside." He bent and unearthed bags of nuts, candy bars, kettle corn, cookies, apples, and a thermos of coffee from his duffle.

Her eyes widened when she flashed the light across the table, filled with goodies. "Okay, you're my favorite stakeout partner ever."

In the low light, she sensed his grin more than saw it and his deep laugh made her smile. She settled into a chair, and after grabbing a bag of chocolate covered almonds, he did the same.

"So, boss, how does this work?" He extended his hand and offered her a nut.

"Well, I think things will be quiet until everything closes, so for the next couple hours, we can just keep our eye on activities. With Rooster's closing at eleven, I would say our actual window will probably be from midnight until maybe five in the morning, at the latest."

"The Sugar Shack starts baking about three-thirty, so there will be a few people out and about by then." He popped another nut in his mouth.

"That will probably keep them away from Oak Street. Chief Phillips said the reports that served as distractions came in between one o'clock and four o'clock, so if they keep to that same pattern, that will be our window of opportunity."

"Make sense to me."

"You can take the first shift from ten to one and I'll take

one to four. If either of us is asleep and we get some action, we'll just wake the other one up, okay?"

"Sounds like a plan." Clay tossed his empty bag into the trash can.

They kept their eyes focused on the blocks across Main Street and made sure Clay's phone was within reach while they talked in hushed tones. "So, have you heard from any of the ladies Jewel wanted you to contact?" he asked.

"Not yet. Actually, I haven't received any mail. I need to stop by the post office this week and see if they are holding it. I think it takes time for a change of address to catch up, too."

Clay got up and poured himself some coffee from his thermos. "Want anything to drink?"

"I wouldn't say no to a cup a tea. Just flip that kettle on." She watched as a few cars backed out of parking spots in front of the pizza place and drove down Main.

Minutes later, Clay returned with a steaming cup and handed it to her. She took a sip. "So, you mentioned your dad passed away and you talked about your mom. Did she pass away before him?"

Clay's head bobbed slowly. "Yes, she had cancer and thought she had it whipped, but it came back with a vengeance and took her about ten years before him. I wasn't sure I would survive her loss. Especially, after watching it take my wife just three years before my mom died."

"Aww, I'm so sorry, Clay. I know what it's like to lose your parents, but for me it was so long ago and I was so young when they died, I sometimes don't remember. I'm not sure it's any easier when you're older and you've had a lifetime with them."

He turned toward her and reached across the table between them, clasping her hand. "I admire your strength at such a young age and am so sorry for your loss, especially losing both of them. Losing my mom was the hardest thing I've faced in my life. When Karen died, I thought that was my darkest day, but Mom was there for me. She was a big help and lessened that pain for me and Danny. My mom was my biggest fan, my best friend, the person who made everything right with the world, even when it wasn't. I wouldn't have made it through Karen's death without her. She was my strength. Now, I feel very alone."

She squeezed his hand, and the burn of tears seared her throat. "Believe me, I understand that feeling. I'm not sure I fully grasped Jewel's death, but knowing she was always there was a comfort and now without that...I feel adrift."

He squeezed her hand back and the two of them sat in silence, staring at the streets below. Harry didn't trust her voice. Thankful for the dim light, she willed the tears on her cheeks to evaporate. She hated showing her vulnerability, and part of her marveled at Clay's ability to show his emotions. It wasn't like her.

CHAPTER TWELVE

S aturday morning, a few minutes after five o'clock, with the sky still dark and only a few cars on Main Street, the lights of the Sugar Shack shined brightly. Harry nudged Clay from his slumber.

She whispered. "Hey, it's time to go. It was a bust."

He blinked several times and mumbled. "That's a bummer. I guess that means we're back here tonight. Let's go grab breakfast before we head back to the ranch."

They left the duffle and all their supplies and snacks in the room and headed downstairs. After Harry made sure the alarm engaged, Clay drove across Main and parked in front of the Sugar Shack.

The welcoming aroma of fried dough and sugar greeted them the moment they walked through the door. A smiling woman in an apron behind the counter waved to Clay. "Hey, Darcy," he said, eyeing the display case.

"What can I get you today, Clay?"

He gestured to Harry. "This is Harry. She's taking over Jewel's place. Harry, this is Darcy, Aimee's daughter."

"Great to meet you. I grew up here and lived with Jewel for years, so I remember your mom and this shop."

"That's wonderful that you've come back. Jewel was such a fixture in Lavender Valley. I can't imagine the Lavender Festival with her gone."

Harry nodded. "It won't be the same without her."

Clay pointed at the glass case. "What sounds good?"

Harry laughed. "I'm easy. Surprise me." She glanced over at the counter where a coffee bar invited customers to help themselves to free coffee with the purchase of a dozen donuts.

Clay sighed and said, "You better get two boxes ready. I'll let you pick them out, Darcy, as long as you make sure there are plenty of those cinnamon rolls with nuts."

She started packing two dozen donuts into the kraft boxes emblazoned with her colorful logo, and as soon as she closed their lids, she reached for two plates and added a cinnamon roll to each.

Harry took the plates to a table near the front window, as Clay paid and collected the pastry boxes.

"Heath and the rest of the gang will be so happy to see me with these." He set them to the side and slid into the chair across from Harry, then took a sip from the ceramic mug. "Mmm, perfection."

She poised her fork over the thick cinnamon roll dripping with cream cheese frosting. "This looks to be a day's worth of calories."

He took his first bite. "But worth every one of them."

After her first taste, she agreed. "I'm going to have to make myself walk to town if I want one of these. Way too tempting."

"If we get you hooked on riding horses, you'll burn up all those calories and then some."

"If the weather is nice, maybe we can shoot for Wednesday or Thursday this week. I need to recover from the weekend and do a few errands, but should be ready to try it by then."

"Sounds perfect," said Clay. "We can get in a little shotgun practice, go riding, and have dinner, courtesy of Heath."

"Only if he's up to it." She pointed at the bakery boxes. "I guess you have the perfect bribe for him."

Clay leaned across the table, a serious look in his eye, and whispered. "I have a question for you. Do cops really eat as many donuts as we're led to believe?"

Harry burst out laughing, releasing the bit of tension she held from expecting a far more sobering inquiry.

After they finished their cinnamon rolls and coffee, they drove to the ranch, where Clay dashed inside with his boxes of treats and returned with the three golden retrievers, who hurried to leap into the backseat. He handed Harry the tote bag. "I made sure the blanket and slipper are in there."

Chief and Hope couldn't quit wiggling and wagging, their tongues darting over the back of Harry's seat. "Thank you. I don't think he can sleep without them."

Clay nodded. "Our son was like that. He had a favorite little blanket he packed around."

When they pulled up to Jewel's house, Clay turned off his truck and insisted on helping Harry with her morning chores. "It'll be faster with two of us, and then you can get in and get some sleep before we start again tonight."

Harry was smart enough to know there was no point in arguing and with his help, they were finished in less than thirty minutes. She made him wait to leave until she went inside and retrieved a dozen eggs. "I meant to give you these yesterday and forgot."

He smiled and opened the passenger door, placing them on the seat and telling Maverick to leave them alone. "I'll see you tonight. Pick you up about the same time?"

"Works for me. Hopefully, we'll get some action tonight."

His eyes went wide. "Well, I'm not sure I know you that well yet, but I'm game."

She shook her head and laughed. "I think you need more sleep, my friend." He touched the brim of his hat and climbed behind the wheel.

She waved as he left, then shooed the two dogs indoors. After feeding them and letting them out for a bit, she snuggled into her pajamas for a few hours of rest before her next shift.

The dogs climbed onto her bed with her, unfazed by the idea of sleeping in the daylight. Chief had both his blanket and the slipper stuck in his mouth and dropped them next to Hope. Harry set her phone alarm for one, shut her eyes, and willed herself to ignore the bright light flowing through the bedroom windows.

She had to get some sleep or she'd be useless tonight.

After trying to quiet her mind for some shuteye for what seemed like hours, the next thing she knew, the beeping of her phone woke Harry from a deep sleep. The dogs had abandoned her at some point, and she found them lounging in the sunroom.

She let them out in the yard while she brewed herself some tea and made scrambled eggs and toast, her go-to meal no matter what time of the day it was.

After eating, she scrolled through her email with the hope of seeing something from one of the ladies. They had her email, Jewel's address, her old address, and her phone number. She hated waiting and couldn't figure out why none of them had reached out to her. Even if was to say thanks but no thanks.

Rather than drum her fingers on the table, she typed in a search for the Lavender Festival. It was Jewel's pride and joy to be part of it, and no matter what happened with the other women, Harry wasn't going to let her down.

However, her love of the scent and sight of the gorgeous waves of purple that would soon surround the house, was the extent of her experience with lavender. Harry needed to know more about the plant itself. Now, the plants were a silvery green, lacking the beautiful color she remembered from past summers.

She consulted Jewel's binder and calendars where she learned that if the winter was dry, Jewel watered the fields using the soaker hoses installed in the rows. Once the season began, she relied on irrigation to water her precious plants.

After checking out last year's festival and everything she could find online related to it and other similar events, Harry sighed. She had her work cut out for her.

She took the dogs outside for a romp around the property before tackling the afternoon chores. Harry had been chatting with Agatha and Arnold each morning and evening, enchanted by their gentle eyes, and they were beginning to trust her, approaching her when she arrived, instead of skittering away from her.

Olive and Nutmeg had warmed to her from the first day and often pressed their heads against her. In Jewel's journals she had written about donkey hugs and now Harry understood. The sweet animals never failed to make her smile.

Harry found the chickens much more difficult. They weren't friendly, and when they darted around, they often seemed to want to peck at her. She did her best to gather the eggs and get out of their way. Clay explained the chickens naturally go in the house to roost as it gets dark. When Harry tried to button things up earlier in the day, it proved to be a real struggle to wrangle them inside before they were ready.

Clay mentioned they were trained, but they treated Harry like a substitute teacher. They tested her patience, but she finally got them inside and locked the door. At her whistle, the dogs came running, and Harry rewarded them with a cookie before she took a shower and got ready for another night of surveillance.

Like clockwork, Clay turned up on time and after dropping the dogs at his house, drove Harry into town. "I thought we could try the Ranch House tonight. It's further down Main away from our little surveillance operation, just at the edge of shops as it turns to residential."

"Sure, I'm game."

"And it's my treat tonight."

"Fair enough. You called it, but next time, it's on me."

He drove to the old Victorian house with the lit sign advertising it as a restaurant. They walked through the front door and found a bar in what was once the parlor. The décor was vintage with lots of velvet, wood, and antiques.

The bartender greeted Clay by name and waved them through. "Anywhere you like, Clay. Your server will be right with you."

Clay chose a small room with only four tables, all empty. A fire crackled in the stone fireplace, and the flames reflected in the window, with the crystals from the chandelier sparkling above. A bookshelf along one wall held antique books below old landscape paintings.

"It's beautiful," Harry breathed. "I guess I was thinking more of a peanut shells and sawdust on the floor sort of place. This is quite lovely." As she admired the surroundings, her nerves got the best of her. This place seemed more like a spot for a date, not a casual dinner before a stakeout. Not that she wouldn't date Clay. She just wasn't looking for that.

"There are more rooms with tables too. This is just my favorite one."

Their server delivered waters and a basket of warm focaccia bread with butter and dipping oil before reciting a few of the specials.

Harry perused the menu, and when she looked up, met Clay's eyes. "Well, this is not what I expected. Everything sounds delicious."

"They have great food and I'm partial to their steaks." He winked and added, "The owners moved here about ten years ago, I guess. From the Seattle area. They restored this house from top to bottom."

Harry settled on the panzanella salad with wild mushroom risotto, and Clay went with the steak frites and truffle fries. "I promise to share with you. They are out of this world."

Within minutes her salad was delivered, and her eyes went wide at the huge bowl. She asked for an extra plate, so she could share it with Clay. After her first bite of the fresh flavors of the ripe tomatoes with the basil, along with the thick croutons that had soaked up the tasty vinaigrette, she declared it delicious. Clay nodded and said, "They have a greenhouse and grow their own produce."

"I think it's the best I've ever had." She slid half of the salad onto the extra plate.

When the main course arrived, Clay asked for another extra plate and shared some of his steak and the to-die-for truffle fries with her. As he stacked them on the plate, he grinned. "I don't share these with just anybody, you know. Only special friends."

He looked so happy. Did he think this was a date?

She concentrated on the fries and moaned when she tasted the first one. They were perfectly crispy on the outside and fluffy on the inside. They were obviously hand cut and the infusion of the earthiness of the truffle oil and the bit of parmesan cheese that clung to each of them made them sheer perfection. "Wow, I'm going to order those next time. I actually thought about salad and fries only, but didn't want to embarrass you."

He laughed as he cut his steak. "You'll learn I'm not easily embarrassed."

They chatted with each other throughout the meal, passing samples of their meals back and forth. Her fear of this outing being more than a friendly dinner evaporated. The setting was more romantic than she expected, but Clay was a perfect gentleman and offered nothing beyond friendly conversation.

They waved away the offer of dessert. With the bill paid, they left and headed to Buck's office, parking along the side, out of sight.

Inside, they got things ready for their evening of spying. Harry raised her eyebrows at the table full of snacks and shook her head. "I don't think I'll be snacking much tonight. I am more than stuffed."

He chuckled. "I can't promise I won't dive in. It helps me stay awake."

With things in order and the nightlight providing a soft glow in the otherwise dark room, Harry put her hands on her hips, gazing down on the street below. "Shall we take another stroll around downtown before we settle in for the night?"

"Sounds good."

She pulled her hat from her jacket pocket and pulled it over her head. "I wonder if you ought to leave your cowboy hat here, just so you're less apt to be recognized."

He nodded and placed it on the coffee table. "I've got a winter cap in my bag. I'll put that on. I rarely wear it, so it'll make for a good disguise."

He rifled through the bag and unearthed it, slipping it on his head. Downstairs, they locked up and made their way to Main Street. With their arms linked together, feigning a couple out for an evening stroll, they wandered the perimeter of the main shopping blocks.

The streets and sidewalks were busier than last night, with people making their way to eateries. Rooster's Tavern was the hot spot again, with the beat of country music flowing from the door.

Clay gestured his head in the direction of the busy establishment. "Along with cheap tacos, Rooster's has a fun Tuesday Trivia game each week. Heath and I have gone a few times. It's a calmer crowd during the week. They do line dancing on Thursdays."

She grinned and said, "Trivia is more my speed than line dancing. I've never actually done either, but trivia games sound intriguing."

"We'll have to try it one week. Rooster isn't picky about how many are on a team, so we could do it with Heath, who is like an encyclopedia when it comes to music, but we'll see if we can entice one more person to join us. Usually, the teams with four or five people have a better shot at winning."

"Makes sense. More of a knowledge base helps, I'm sure." They turned at the corner and continued down First Street, which was quiet, with the exception of the Lucky Duck Deli, in the process of closing for the night.

The ice cream store was the only busy place along Main, with the coffee shop closed. All the shops along Birch Street, except for the bistro, were closed and dark.

They took their time and looped down Pine and Fir, where no vehicles passed by and only a few were parked on the street. At the corner on Main, Clay pointed down the block toward the Grasshopper. "I forgot they're doing Saturday night dinners. We could've gone there. They do a limited menu, but it's always something good."

"I'll keep that in mind. But this week I'm determined to figure out some soups or stews to cook in the slow cooker. I'm sure Jewel has a cookbook or two. She always made some great meals."

He chuckled. "Oh, yes. I've had many a meal at her table. She was quite the caretaker. She always made a point of having us for dinner when we visited. Food has always been a form of love at our house. We could always count on a meal from Mom to celebrate something or to make us feel better. After I lost my mom, Jewel was there for us even more."

They turned the corner on Buck's street, and she leaned her shoulder against his. "I'm sorry about your mom and know exactly what you mean about Jewel. She had a gift for getting people to talk, and just her presence had a way of making me feel better. Like everything would be okay, even when things seemed hopeless."

Clay held the gate to Buck's backyard for her. "That's what made her so special. These last few years, she really did become like a second mom to me and Heath. She shared stories of my parents and talked about the early days with such fondness. She loved Lavender Valley." His voice quieted. "Her loss shook the entire community."

Harry locked the door behind them. "Jewel is proof of the butterfly effect. I'm reading her journals right now, and she had a huge influence on so many lives."

He led the way up the stairs. "Her fingerprints are all over everything good in this valley. She was one of a kind."

"And she left some big shoes to fill," said Harry. So big in fact, it might not be possible. For the first time in a long time, Harry wasn't sure of what she was getting into or if she would succeed.

CHAPTER THIRTEEN

They passed the next couple of hours watching and waiting, Harry sipping the occasional cup of tea and Clay digging into the chocolate almonds.

As the restaurants closed, the sidewalk traffic dwindled, and when Rooster's locked their door after eleven o'clock, things got even quieter. Harry curled up on the sofa to nap until her shift started at one o'clock.

She could have sworn she just closed her eyes, when a soft tap on her shoulder jostled her awake. "Hey," said Clay. "You were sleeping so soundly, I gave you an extra hour. It's two o'clock. All is quiet and no sign of any mischief."

"Oh, wow, I'm sorry. You should have booted me off the couch." She tossed the blanket aside and stood, rolling her shoulders before she took over the chair with the best view.

He eased onto the couch and within minutes, the soft sound of his snoring made Harry grin. She kept her focus on the interior blocks where she knew the cameras wouldn't detect anything.

At seven minutes after three, she watched as a car

parked along Birch Street and two figures, both with backpacks over their dark clothes and hoodies, ran down First Street. She kept her eyes trained on the action. "Clay, hey, we've got something. Can you check your camera on the corner of Birch and see what you can tell about the car parked there. Two perps just headed down First."

Clay was off the couch in a flurry of blankets. He snatched up his phone. "Looks like a Honda or Toyota to me." He joined her and trained the scope on the area of First Street.

Harry carefully opened the balcony door. Moments later the shatter of broken glass filled the air and the two people ran from the street toward the car. "Got the plate," she said, reciting the numbers and letters.

Clay tapped them into his phone.

She shut the door and said, "Let's follow them."

They rushed downstairs and Harry sprinted for Main Street, while Clay hurried to his truck. Harry watched as the car turned on Main and headed toward Benson's and the highway.

Clay picked her up at the corner, and she pointed. "Follow, but not too close." She scrolled her phone and tapped the screen.

"Hey, Chief Phillips, sorry to wake you. This is Harry McKenzie. I think I've got a line on the suspects in the vandalism." She gave him a brief summary and recited the plate number from memory. She suggested he send someone to check the businesses for damage, and she would continue to follow the suspects.

She disconnected and peered at the taillights ahead of them. "Where do you think they're headed?"

"Not Medford, they took the other turn back there.

They're heading toward Grants Pass, but there are tons of little towns between here and there."

The suspects' car maintained a normal speed and didn't drive erratically. Unlike how joyriding kids usually behaved, their calm exit led Harry to believe this wasn't their first rodeo.

Harry's phone vibrated. "Chief," she said, then listened. "Got it, we'll continue to observe, and let you know when and where they stop."

She glanced over at Clay. "The car, a Honda, is registered to a body shop in Gold Point. Address is on Union Street."

He nodded. "That's less than thirty minutes from Lavender Valley."

Harry brought the binoculars up to her eyes again. "If they actually go there, we should be there in a few minutes, right?"

"Yep. Less than ten minutes away now."

"Just hang back as far as we can. We don't want them to see us. If they turn, just keep going by them and take the next turn. We don't want to spook them."

A few minutes later, they passed by the sign welcoming them to Gold Point. Clay slowed down and increased the distance between them and the suspect vehicle.

"Good," she said. "Without the cover of other traffic, we don't want to draw attention to ourselves."

The flash of a turn indicator caught Clay's eye. "He's turning, but that's not Union."

Clay kept to the main road and turned onto Ninth Street, the street after River's Edge, where the Honda had turned. "River's Edge dead ends at the river, like all these streets along here, so they can't go anywhere unless they turn around."

He drove down the street, turned at the end, and parked away from the house at the end of the cul-de-sac.

She opened the door. "Turn your phone to silent or vibrate. and let's go see what we can see."

They made their way along the wide walkway that bordered the river to the next block, where the car had turned.

It didn't take them long to spot the blue Honda parked alongside the huge house that was closest to the river. The headlights were off, but the running lights were on. The front of the house was dark, but there was a light glowing in the back and the gate to the backyard was ajar.

Harry took note of the address and linked her arm in Clay's, leaning close enough to whisper in his ear, as they walked toward a tree. "You go get your truck and wait at the intersection to the highway. I'll walk down this street and keep my eye out in case they leave before you're ready to roll. I want to keep following them. I'll meet you at the corner and keep my cell phone connected to yours while I'm watching, so you know which way they're going."

The sound of the gate creaking and footfalls made Harry catch her breath. A person in a hoodie approached the passenger side of the car, where they stood only a few feet away. She wrapped her arms around Clay's neck and locked her lips against his. Her mind raced with what she would say if the person in the hoodie confronted them, while she tried to ignore the warmth of Clay's skin against hers and the hint of chocolate and coffee she tasted.

Keeping her lips firmly against Clay's, she shifted position to look across the walkway and scanned the area where the Honda was parked. The person in the hoodie went back through the gate and closed it.

She released Clay and whispered. "Sorry, I was afraid we were going to get caught. I think we're in the clear."

"Whew," Clay whispered with a chuckle. "Never apologize for a kiss like that one."

Thankful for the cover of darkness to hide the warmth in her cheeks, Harry laughed. "I normally don't make a habit of grabbing men and making out with them." She paused and added, "At least not until I've known them more than a couple of weeks."

"Aww, I thought I was the first."

She grinned as she took out her cell phone and called his number. He answered it and kept it in his hand while he hurried toward the street where they had parked.

Harry set out at a jog, hoping to look like an early morning jogger if anyone caught sight of her. The rest of the street was dark except for a few porch lights. She made it to the intersection with the highway, thankful for the large bush on the corner where she could hide.

A few minutes later, the purr of an engine alerted Harry. She whispered into the phone to let Clay know the status and he confirmed he was in position, parked with his lights off.

The Honda came to the corner and turned left, heading in the opposite direction toward the downtown area. She told Clay as she sprinted toward where he'd parked, then she jumped in the passenger seat. "Let's go."

Clay eased onto the highway, keeping the taillights of the Honda in view, but hanging back far enough not to draw their attention.

They turned opposite the river onto a street that led to a neighborhood filled with rundown homes and apartments. Harry studied the map she brought up on her phone. "There's a school in just a block. Pull over there and we can jog the rest of the way to keep up with them. This neighborhood isn't very big, and I don't want to spook them."

Clay pulled over to the curb and doused his lights. They hurried to the street, where they jogged to the next block. Harry pointed at the brake lights as the Honda turned right.

They kept up a quick pace and arrived at the street in time to see the Honda pull into a driveway of a duplex. They slowed their steps, and Harry focused on the pair climbing out of the car. She wasn't close enough to make out any details, but the hoods were off their heads. The driver was a male with dark hair and the other was female, with long blondish hair, glistening in the streetlights.

The two went inside the house. No lights came on in the windows.

Harry pointed across the street and Clay followed her lead. They jogged down the street, until they got close enough to make out the address on the duplex, then hurried back to Clay's truck.

Once inside, she put in a call to Chief Phillips, giving him an update and both addresses. He was in the office and she heard the tapping of a keyboard in the background.

Moments later, he let her know who owned the big house by the river and promised to do more digging into the rental duplex property. "Swing by when you get back to town."

She disconnected and turned to Clay. "You'll never guess who owns the big house by the river."

CHAPTER FOURTEEN

C lay arched his brows. "It'll be quicker if you just tell me. I'm not a great guesser."

She chuckled. "The mayor of Gold Point."

He started the ignition and drove them back toward the highway.

Harry drummed her fingers on the console.

Clay glanced over at her. "I can almost hear those gears in your head moving. What are you thinking?"

"I've got a theory, or at least the beginning of one. I need more information, though. Do you mind stopping by the police department when we get back?"

"Sure, as long as we can do breakfast. I'm starving. I'll drop you off and run over to the Grasshopper and order breakfast."

"Deal," she said, with a smile.

With the road almost to themselves, it didn't take long to get back to Lavender Valley. The Grasshopper was just opening for the day, and Harry promised to be quick and meet Clay there in a few minutes.

She opened the door to the police department and the smell of strong coffee tickled her nose. Sally's desk was empty, and Harry let herself through the open half-door at the end of the counter. Chief Phillips was at his desk.

"How's it going?" asked Harry.

His wide forehead wrinkled. "Well, the renter and driver is one Caleb Marks, who works at the body shop where the Honda is registered. He's got a record for petty crimes going back several years. The duplex he's living in is owned by CC Enterprises, which is a limited liability corporation owned by our own Mayor Crawford and her husband." He glanced down at his notepad. "Marks and his little friend spray painted the buildings and broke out the windows in the pharmacy and the florist last night. The owners are doing inventory to see if anything is missing." He sighed. "Right now, I'm reluctant to involve the police in Gold Point."

She nodded. "Yeah, I think we suspect the same thing. I'm curious about the relationship between Mayor Crawford and the mayor in Gold Point."

He nodded. "That would be Mayor Irwin. Honestly, I don't know. With Mayor Crawford's lack of interest or help to combat these nuisance and vandalism crimes, it's got me wondering."

"Exactly," said Harry. "I admit I'm a bit cynical when it comes to political animals, but my gut tells me there's more to this story. These little criminal enterprises can work their way into the police, controlled by the mayor, so it's hard to know who can be trusted, and we don't want to trip a wire by asking the wrong person."

He sighed. "I think I'm looking at surveilling Mayor Crawford and Mayor Irwin." He leaned back in his chair and stared up at the ceiling. "Won't be winning any popularity contests."

"I'm happy to help out. Maybe the Sheriff can help, too."

He nodded. "Yes, Sheriff Bill Lester. He's a good man and I trust him. I'll give him a call." He glanced at his watch. "Closer to eight o'clock."

"With me being new and unknown, I'm happy to take a shift or two to help out, if you need someone they won't recognize."

He nodded. "I appreciate it. Without you, we wouldn't have a lead at all. I'll text you later today, in case you're sleeping." He winked. "I bet you thought your graveyard days were over."

She stood and gave him her best advice, coming from her days of investigating corruption within the political minefield in Salem. It consisted of documenting everything and keeping the investigation as small as possible, along with sticking only to facts and not speculation. "Run it like the press are riding along with you. By the book. Take it to a prosecutor you can trust, not a political motivated one."

"Thanks, Harry. I'll be in touch."

She waved goodbye and hurried down the street to the Grasshopper, arriving just as Bonnie was delivering their plates. "That looks delicious," she said, eyeing her omelet topped with cheese.

Bonnie returned with the coffee pot and filled Harry's cup. "You two enjoy," she said.

Harry dug in, noticing Clay was already over half done with his breakfast and side of pancakes. "I guess you were hungry." She tilted her eyes toward his plate.

"Close to starvation," he said with a grin. "So, what did Chief Phillips have to say?"

She whispered. "Not much. I'll tell you when we leave."

It didn't take long for Clay to mop up the last of the syrup on his plate with his pancakes, then he nursed another cup of coffee while Harry finished her meal.

When it was time to go, he started to dig out his wallet. Harry wiggled her finger at him. "Nope, already got it. I owe you. More than breakfast for what we had to do last night."

He laughed. "Don't say that too loud. The rumors will be flying before we get back to the ranch. We always say the Lavender Valley information highway is way faster than fiber optics."

She shook her head and laughed as she led the way out the door.

On the drive home, Harry's eyes fluttered to stay open as she gave Clay a brief recap of what Chief Phillips learned about the working theory. "Would you be able to handle the farm for a couple of days?" she asked. "I'm going to do some surveillance for the chief and might need to be out of town tomorrow and the next day."

He nodded. "No problem. Tyler is due back tomorrow. He'll be back in the bunkhouse at the farm and has been taking care of the chores for Jewel. He can do the same for you."

"That would be great. I really appreciate the help. I'm not sure where this all will lead, but something is definitely up. There's only one reason criminal elements would be cozy with the mayor in the middle of the night. The tangential connection to our own mayor gives me pause."

"I'd say you're right that there are some shenanigans going on. Mayor Crawford has proven herself to be a failure, in my opinion. She's not well liked. The one person on the city council I know best is no fan of hers and I don't make a habit of talking about her to the others."

Harry frowned. "Has Mayor Irwin been in office a long time?"

Clay's forehead creased. "At least a couple of terms, maybe longer."

He pulled into her driveway, and stopped for the gate. "If you're okay with it, the dogs can stay at the ranch today until you're up from your nap. Heath will be around and will watch over them, plus they have acres to roam."

Harry glanced over at him. "Are you sure?"

"Positive." He opened the gate and drove through. "Just come over when you're ready for them. I'm going to catch a nap, but will be up in the early afternoon."

She opened her door, motioning for him to stay put. "You get home and get some rest, and I'll see you this afternoon."

He touched the brim of his hat and dipped his head. "See you then."

Harry left her shoes on the porch, slipped into her chore boots, and hurried to the barn. She fed and watered her four-legged friends while she chatted with them and told them about her evening before she went to the henhouse. She grabbed a basket from the back of the barn, let the chickens out for the day, and collected the eggs.

By the time she was done and inside, she could hardly keep her eyes open. She stripped out of her clothes and into her pajamas, and fell asleep before her head rested against her pillow.

———

Harry woke after two o'clock, fixed a cup of tea, scrolled her email, and hopped in the shower. She was dressed and ready to head over to the ranch when her phone chimed.

She smiled when she read the message from Clay, inviting her to dinner and assuring her Heath would still cook for them later this week, but she was welcome to join them for a simple meal tonight.

She'd had no idea what she would make for dinner and with a quick tap on the screen accepted the invitation. She noticed a voicemail on her phone when she sent the message and saw Chief Phillips had called an hour ago.

She played the message while she sipped another cup of tea. He wanted to take her up on her offer of some surveillance work. Both mayors were set to attend a meeting in Ashland that week, and he wanted her to keep an eye on the two of them outside of the formal meeting. He had the particulars and the agenda for the two-day meeting in his office, and said he'd be there until six that night.

She checked the time and sent a quick text to Clay, letting him know she'd be there by six o'clock. She buttoned up the barn and herded the chickens into their house earlier than usual. With her afternoon chores wrapped up, she locked up and climbed into her SUV.

Most of the shops on Main Street were closed for Sunday. As Harry made her way to the police department, she tried to think of something she could take to the dinner at Clay's tonight. Wine was her old standby, but with Clay's mention of their wine cellar, it wouldn't be necessary. Benson's was open. They were bound to have something.

She turned into the parking lot and darted inside the store, where she made a beeline for the bakery. A cheesecake caught her eye. "Everybody likes cheesecake," she muttered as she opted for the one that had sections of different flavors.

She paid the cashier and set the container on the floor of the passenger side, then headed for Chief Phillips' office. The front desk was deserted, and she found him behind his desk, hanging up his phone.

"Hey, Harry," he said, motioning her to a chair. "That was Sheriff Lester. He and I are keeping this one close to the vest, but he's helping dig into the details of both Mayor Crawford and Mayor Irwin. Seems there are quiet rumors that they may be more than colleagues." He wiggled his brows.

"Ah, are they both married?"

He nodded.

"Makes it even more interesting. Do you have somebody checking finances on both of them?"

"Yeah, Sheriff Lester has a contact at the state level, removed from everyone in the county."

"In my experience, these things are about money. But, now we've also added in a possible affair. Maybe I can learn more about that in Ashland."

He passed her a folder. "Here are the particulars on what we know so far. Everything we have on the two, including the cars they'll be driving. They got rooms next to each other too. We booked you a room at the venue, next to Irwin's, and used your old address in Salem, so there's no connection to Lavender Valley."

She tapped the file on the edge of the desk. "Sounds good."

He pointed to a metal case next to the doorway. "There's a kit with everything you might need. Sheriff Lester is also sending one of his detectives to the venue, Burt Silver, but he'll be undercover. He's booked in a room at the end of the hallway you're in, next to Crawford, under the name of Burt Richards. There's a sheet on him with his cell number, photo, and room number, so you recognize him."

"Got it. I'll reach out to him and set up a meet at the conference venue."

"Thanks again, Harry. Call me if you need anything or if you get some good intel."

She took the case and the folder, and left him in his office.

She made it to the ranch before six o'clock and punched in the code at Clay's gate. The long and winding driveway, lit with lights atop the white fence posts lining it, led her to the spectacular home, where she parked under the portico. On her last visit and with the vastness of the property, she'd only seen the barn and the rear of the house, but was in awe at the stunning entrance. A huge bronze statue of a stallion lit from below with soft lights, stood in the grassy area in front of the house.

She gazed in awe at the workmanship that showed the ripple of muscles and the lifelike mane and tail. After gawking a few more moments and taking in the white twinkle lights in the shrubs surrounding the entryway, she carried the cheesecake up the stone steps to the huge entrance, boasting lots of glass and double wooden doors.

Clay opened the door and greeted her with a warm smile. She extended the cheesecake to him. "I know you have a cellar full of wine, so I opted for cheesecake."

He grinned and took it. "You didn't have to bring anything. We're pretty casual around here."

Her eyes traveled the length of the high ceiling of tongue and groove wood, with huge beams traversing it, then back down to the wide wooden planks of the floor. More statues of horses graced side tables, and the stone columns from the entry were carried through into the floor to ceiling fireplace in the great room.

Clay gestured to his left. "Heath is in the kitchen. As are all the dogs, who are watching with interest for anything he might drop on the floor." He pointed at the living room, as they passed it. "This is the formal living room, but we don't use it much. I'll get this in the fridge and give you a tour."

She followed him down a short hallway and through an

archway into a massive kitchen, where an inviting and rich aroma greeted her. The stone and wood dominated the space, graced by granite counters, including two islands in the middle of the room. One was in use. A tall man, clad in jeans, a flannel shirt, and suede slippers, bent over a cutting board.

The dogs were busy munching on carrots and barely acknowledged Harry, intent on waiting for their next bite. Clay slipped the cheesecake into one of the built-in glass doored refrigerators along the wall. "Heath," he said, "Harry's here."

Heath put down his knife and wiped his hands on a towel before turning toward Harry. He shared the same striking blue eyes and easy smile as his brother. His hair was a bit darker and thicker, tousled and longer, his five o'clock shadow more pronounced, but there was no mistaking the family resemblance.

Clay clapped a hand on Heath's shoulder. "Harry, this is my little brother, Heath."

Harry extended her hand. "Wonderful to meet you. Clay raves about your cooking talents and whatever you're making smells delicious. Thanks for having me."

Heath, clad in an apron, moved closer and offered his hand. "Clay never brings any ladies home, so it's great to have you here, Harry. Tonight's dinner is nothing special. Just a stew, courtesy of my mom's recipe, but we have big plans for later in the week."

"Well, I have zero skills when it comes to cooking, so I'm grateful for whatever you make. Thank you, too, for taking care of the dogs."

Heath waved away her thanks. "No problem. We're always happy to help out a neighbor. They're great, and Ace

loves the extra company. Clay says you've got some busin
out of town, so they're going to stay with us for a couple day
this week?"

Harry stepped over to the dogs, lined up across an area
rug, watching and waiting, and gave each of them a scratch
on the head. "Yes, he was kind enough to agree to let Chief
and Hope stay. It looks like Chief is quite happy with his new
friends."

"He's a sweet one, and Clay warned me about the slipper
and blanket" said Heath, slipping the veggies off the cutting
board and into the large salad bowl. "They seem to soothe
him."

Clay pointed back toward the hallway. "I'm going to give
Harry a quick tour while we wait for dinner."

First, he pointed out the formal dining room across the
hall from the kitchen. "Heath and I usually eat at the island in
the kitchen or out on the patio, so this room doesn't get
much use."

Harry's eyes widened at the spacious room with the dark
wooden hutch filled with dishes and glassware. The huge
table with eight leather chairs, atop the thick area rug, was
both intimidating and welcoming. When her gaze went to
the large windows, Clay added, "It's hard to see this time of
evening, but that patio is my favorite place to eat, especially
in the summer. It's got a great view of the pond."

"It's beautiful," said Harry, running her hand along the
edge of the shiny table.

"Let's head down the other direction." Clay led her out of
the room and back to the great room, which she had
glimpsed when she came through the entry.

"This is another room we don't use much, unless we have
company." He wandered through the space where two

GRACE

...airs were positioned in the middle of the
... the fireplace. A large L-shaped desk filled
... space and was ringed by thickly padded
... This was the meeting space my dad used for
...g to clients and horse owners."

Two huge paintings of horses hung above the built-in bookcases behind the desk. The dark wood, leather, and heavy furniture gave off a masculine vibe. "I noticed the bronze horse outside," said Harry. "Are all the statues and paintings of the same horse?"

Clay smiled. "Dad's pride and joy was his racehorse, Whiskey Grin. He's the statue out front and in many of the works in the house, but Dad had several paintings of his favorites over the years. These two," he pointed up to the wall with the paintings, "are of Whiskey Grin. He was a descendent of Secretariat and his earnings built this place. He was a thoroughbred who won a lot of races, and then made Dad a fortune as a stud."

"He's a beauty. I don't know much about horses, but have always loved to watch them. They're so majestic."

"They're also expensive and require a ton of work." He chuckled as he made his way back to the main hallway. "But, you're right, they are beautiful and majestic." He lowered his voice, "When you're done with your side job, we'll set up a ride."

"I'd like that," she said, following him to a room where the huge flat screen television caught her eye first. Her feet sunk into the thick carpet that covered the entire floor. Leather couches, chairs, and tables were situated for optimal viewing, and one side of the room held floor-to-ceiling bookcases in the same dark wood that was favored throughout the home. A small stone hearth with a wood burning stove graced the other side of the room.

"We use this as a den and television room. It's where Heath and I spend most of our evenings."

"It's cozy and looks perfect for relaxing," she said, as she followed him to the next room, outfitted with matching bookcases built into twin archways, with a stately desk between them. Two plump, fabric chairs were in front of the desk with a matching sofa along the side, and more windows and glass doors that led to another patio.

"This is my office."

"It's so neat and clean. I don't even see a sticky note on your desk."

He laughed. "Don't open the drawers."

She noticed the wall of monitors that showed all the camera feeds from the property. "That's a nice setup."

He nodded. "I use my phone to monitor when I'm out and about, but spend much of the workday in here, so it's nice to have the larger images. If I get an alert at night, my bedroom is just next door."

He pointed at the doorway at the end of the room. "This is basically my wing of the house. It's got two master suites, so I have one and Heath has the other. Sort of mirror images of each other."

He led her out into the hallway again and to his master suite. When he opened the double doors, Harry gasped. Like the rest of the house, the room was filled with archways and rich, dark wood. To the right was a huge bathroom, with long granite counters and sinks on each side of the room, an oversized walk-in shower, and a deep jetted tub stuck into an alcove surrounded by windows.

On the left was a master closet, bigger than Harry's entire bedroom at home. Clay led her past the columns that separated the sleeping chamber, where the king-sized bed was dwarfed by the expanse of the curved room. A fainting couch and double chair with an ottoman, along with a table took up the space in front of the windows, that Clay said also had a nice view of the pond and mountains. Another flat screen television was mounted opposite the bed, and a large dresser held family photos, including one of a much younger Clay with his arm around a beautiful woman, holding a small tow-headed boy.

"This is gorgeous, Clay. I don't think I'd ever want to get up if this was my room."

"It's a bit over the top, I know. Dad went overboard when he built this place, but I'm used to it now."

"I know a few women who would sell a kidney for that closet."

Clay laughed and led the way through the doors to the hallway. "I'll show you one of the guest rooms. There are two in this section."

The hall curved, and he led her through a doorway into another large room. A king-sized bed dominated, with an armoire across from it, and a well-appointed bathroom provided everything a guest would need.

"We can show you the wine cellar after dinner, and I'll let Heath show you his side of the house." He led the way back toward the entry, where he pointed out another bathroom. "This is the closest powder room, if you need one."

Harry slipped inside to wash her hands for dinner and sniffed in the fresh citrus scent that permeated the room. It reminded her of a posh hotel, with thick towels, lovely scented soap and lotion, every surface gleaming, and one of those flameless candles that was so real, it made her look twice.

When she joined the two brothers in the kitchen, Clay gestured at the second island, with the barstool height chairs next to it. "I told Heath I didn't think you'd mind eating here, like we usually do."

"Not at all. I rarely eat at a table at home."

Heath looked up from ladling stew into bowls. "I knew I liked this lady."

Clay pulled out the middle chair for her and then poured water into their glasses. He helped Heath carry the salad, bread, and stew to the table before taking a seat next to her.

Harry bent and inhaled the steam rising from her bowl. "This smells absolutely yummy. I hope you'll share your recipe. I'm almost useless in the kitchen, but would love to try this in the slow cooker."

"Sure. I'm happy to give it to you, but taste it first and make sure you like it."

She took her first spoonful and sighed. "I love it. It's beyond delicious."

Heath smiled and dug into his own bowl. "I'll send some home with you and email you the recipe."

Clay helped himself to more bread and butter. "Duke is coming over tomorrow. That's Doc Walker, the vet we use. He comes every Monday to check on all the animals and tend to anything we need. Since Chief will be here, he'll get an introduction."

"Oh, I'm sorry to miss him, but I'll be sure to drop by next week, if that's okay?"

"Of course."

Heath offered the breadbasket to Harry. "Duke's a great guy and an awesome vet. His dad was a vet for years, and he took the reins when old Doc Walker retired."

"It's nice to live in a place with so much history and the traditions of longtime residents. It gives you a sense of belonging," said Harry.

Clay reached for his glass. "There are so many upsides to

living here. It does take a bit of time to get used to the busybodies and everyone knowing everything about you. But, to be fair, most of them see it as looking out for each other."

Heath nodded. "Neighbors helping neighbors. Lavender Valley is like one big family."

CHAPTER FIFTEEN

M onday, Harry left the chores to Tyler while she dressed in one of her signature pantsuits, choosing the purple one matched with a lavender silk blouse. She thought she looked less like a cop in the softer color. She drove the two dogs over to Clay's, and left with a wave and a promise to call Clay that night.

She made the pleasant ride to Ashland, and found the hotel and conference center bustling with activity. After parking, she quickly checked for the vehicles belonging to the mayors. Neither car was in the parking lot, so she made her way to the registration desk, hoping the request for an early check-in was granted.

The friendly woman behind the counter checked her computer, smiled, and gave Harry a key to her room, on the third floor in the main building. Harry elected to take the stairs.

She wandered the hallway, getting a feel for the layout, noting the rooms next to hers and getting an eye on Burt's room, on the other side of Mayor Crawford's.

The rooms had small balconies that offered a view of the tennis courts and behind them, dense forest. She put her toiletries in the bathroom and hung her extra blouse in the closet, then added her jeans and sweaters to the dresser drawer.

In addition to the conference for city leaders, there were a couple of other conferences happening at the hotel, which would give Harry the cover she needed. The conference would kick off with a meeting and luncheon, was scheduled to break up before the dinner hour, and would finish tomorrow afternoon.

She put the DO NOT DISTURB hanger on her door and unlocked the metal surveillance case. It had everything she was accustomed to using, including the small photo and camera recorder that could fit in the palm of her hand, earpieces and earbuds, a listening device for enhancing audio through walls, a couple digital recorders, a monoscope, binoculars, electronic trackers, and a cell phone with a thermal camera.

Her phone chimed and she saw Chief Phillips' name appear. "Hey, Chief."

"Harry, just wanted to let you know we don't have a warrant yet, so you're limited to public areas where no perceived privacy is expected. We're working on a few things and will keep you posted if we get anything to secure a warrant."

"Copy that. I'm in my room now, and didn't see either vehicle when I checked in. Burt should be here in a few minutes and we'll get a plan together."

"Sounds good. I'm with Sheriff Lester in his office for the day."

She disconnected and slipped a couple of the items she

thought she would need into her handbag. As soon as she put the metal case in the closet, her phone chimed.

"McKenzie," she said.

"Richards here. I'm in my room."

"Same. Just getting ready to head downstairs to the conference center to get eyes on them."

"Right, I found the two vehicles, still warm to the touch, and went ahead and put trackers on them. Sheriff said we had permission, since they're not personal vehicles."

"Great. If we need to meet out of sight, I saw a maintenance shed off the walking trail by the tennis courts. It's out of view for the most part, and I don't think we'd be noticed there."

"Sounds good. We'll use channel five."

"Copy that. See you downstairs."

Harry tuned the small device in her jacket pocket to channel five, popped in the earpiece and made sure her hair covered it, then grabbed her handbag and laptop bag, and headed downstairs.

The conference center was in a different building, and Harry made her way over to it, staking out a chair in the corner that would give her a good view of the entry points as the city leaders came and went.

The lobby had a registration table with prepared nametags on lanyards, and the women at the table handed them out as they greeted attendees. Harry dug out her phone and put it to her ear, feigning a call. Talking as she slow-walked by the table, she scanned the names, organized in alphabetical order, and saw both mayors' tags were still waiting to be claimed.

Before settling in, she bought a latte and a bottle of water from the coffee bar. The laptop was a prop, for the most part.

She needed to look busy and it would help. She chose a small table, opened the laptop, and connected to the guest wi-fi.

People milled around the large lobby, drinking coffee and eating croissants and decadent looking pastries and cinnamon rolls. Harry's stomach emitted a low growl as a man walked by with a breakfast sandwich. It wasn't long before Burt came through the door, dressed in a sport jacket and tie, with a laptop bag slung over his shoulder. He purchased a coffee before heading to a table at the other end of the long lobby, near the second set of doors to the meeting room.

He went to work, setting his laptop up on his table, then took out his cell phone. Moments later, hers vibrated.

She tapped her screen. *In position and have you spotted.*

She typed in. *Copy. Neither has arrived yet.*

He went back to staring at his laptop and she took a sip of her latte. As she set it on the table next to her, Mayor Crawford and Mayor Irwin stepped through the door.

She had studied their photographs, and Mayor Irwin looked the same, thinning hair, short, and sporting a bit of a paunch under his jacket. Harry wasn't prepared for the chunks of bright red in Mayor Crawford's gray hair. Maybe it was left over from the holiday season or maybe she did it to match the color of her jacket. Whatever the reason, it made it her easy to spot. The middle-aged woman was on the short and wide side, the button of her red jacket straining against her mid-section.

Both she and Mayor Irwin were beaming and smiling, like politicians on the campaign trail, greeting colleagues and shaking hands with other attendees.

They arrived at the registration table, and Harry watched as Mayor Irwin put his hand at the small of Mayor Crawford's back, urging her to go first.

After a brief conversation with the registrar, they both slipped their lanyards over their heads and stepped through the open doors of the meeting room. The agenda called for them to eat lunch in the room and be there until six o'clock.

Harry glanced around. She'd already committed the layout of the conference center to memory. The restrooms were closer to Burt, and they each had a full view of the exits, except for a backdoor out of the lounge adjacent to the café. The only other exits were on the lower level of the building leading out to the patio that ran along the back.

Today, at least, the lower level was in use by other events, so there would be no reason for the two mayors to head that way. However, over the years, Harry had learned to prepare for the unexpected, so she had a plan to cover the patio, if that happened.

After an hour or so, catering staff rolled by with carts, and the rich aroma made Harry's stomach rumble. She wished she hadn't skipped the complimentary breakfast the hotel offered her when she registered.

The appearance of food signaled they would break for lunch soon. She tapped a message to Burt letting him know she was going to grab something at the café and change her position.

By the time she had secured a sandwich and another latte and water, Burt had moved and taken over her old position. She moved to the far end, selected a different chair than Burt had used, and gobbled down her lunch.

As she finished her last bite, the meeting room doors clicked open and attendees began to emerge, heading in Harry's direction as they sought out the restrooms.

She had already inserted an earbud into her other ear to feign talking on her cell phone, and began a conversation about sales figures as she kept her eye on the crowd. She spotted Mayor Crawford first, hurrying as fast as her short legs would carry her to beat the others to the ladies' room.

Mayor Irwin chatted with another man, as they both wandered toward the restrooms.

Without interacting, they both returned to the main meeting room. Once the doors shut, Burt left his seat and took a break at the café. While he ate his burger, Harry wandered the length of the lobby, her phone to her ear most of the time.

Boredom ensued as they passed the next few hours watching the closed doors. Mayor Crawford came through them only once during the afternoon, for another visit to the ladies' room. An hour before things were due to wrap up, Burt and Harry took turns taking their laptop bags back to their rooms and changing into casual clothes. They wanted to be ready to move quickly, and didn't need the cumbersome bags on their shoulders.

The walk outside helped revive Harry, who was feeling the pain of sitting for so long. Finally, a few minutes before six o'clock, an eruption of applause signaled that the meetings were over for the day. The doors opened.

Harry was back at her original end of the lobby, leaning against a counter height table, wearing jeans and a sweater. It wasn't much of a disguise, but she trusted it would work, since none of the attendees had made eye contact with her the entire day. She had become an invisible fixture, which was her goal.

Both mayors stood in a group with four others, and Harry stepped closer to them, talking softly on her cell phone as she listened to their every word.

The group decided to go to a sister restaurant that the hotel recommended, about three miles away in downtown Ashland. Harry tapped in a text to Burt to let him know they were heading to The Kitchen so he could get there before them.

She'd gotten too close to the group to risk being seen at the restaurant but would find something nearby so she could be close if Burt needed help.

Burt, who had donned a jacket and a baseball cap, made his way out the door before the others, who were trying to decide if they had time to go to their rooms or if they should just head to dinner. Mayor Irwin and one of the other men in the group both offered to drive.

Harry waited for them to leave, and then wandered to the parking area, keeping her distance. Mayor Crawford and two others joined Mayor Irwin in his vehicle, while the other two people climbed into a white sedan with exempt plates. She made a note of the plate number in her phone and kept walking to her car, texting it to Chief Phillips.

As she climbed behind the wheel, Burt texted to let her know he was in position at the restaurant and had secured a seat at the bar near a large table with a reserved sign on it bearing the mayor's name.

Harry followed them at a discreet distance and waited for both vehicles to park before choosing a spot one row over from them, where she could observe both cars.

There was an Italian restaurant next door and a small coffee place nestled across the street from The Kitchen. Harry opted for the coffee place. It had seating along a huge window, giving her a perfect view of the restaurant door. She texted Burt and let him know where she would be and he reported the party was seated and getting ready to order.

Harry burned over an hour at the coffee place, where she had a bowl of soup and some tea while she kept a lookout. She asked for a status report from Burt, who texted that the group was enjoying drinks and dessert.

As with most of her surveillance experience, this was proving to be boring. With the two mayors being part of a larger group, she didn't expect Burt would overhear anything significant. The two were more likely to talk freely when they were alone.

Harry bought another cup of hot tea and went to her car, ready to follow the group back to the hotel or wherever they went, once they left the restaurant. Within thirty minutes, the group of six emerged and got into the vehicles.

She poked the screen of her cell phone to connect to Burt and let him know she was following both cars.

Within a few minutes, they turned into the hotel property. They parked in the sea of white sedans with exempt plates, and Harry continued further down the row and parked in the adjacent lot.

As Harry reached for her bag, her phone vibrated. It was Burt.

"Hey, I'm back at the hotel," she said. "Waiting to see if they socialize or go up to their rooms."

"Okay, I'm bringing a female officer with me, Evie. She met me at the restaurant, and we should be there in five. I'm getting nervous they're going to recognize me or you from all our time today, so wanted the extra disguise. We're going to pose as a couple if they go to the lounge or anywhere else."

"Good plan. I'll keep eyes on them and let you know where they go."

Harry disconnected and watched as the group strolled into the conference center. With all the glass along the front, she was able to see them walk past the café and disappear inside the lounge. She texted Burt to let him know and reported she would go to her room and be on standby.

He responded with a thumbs up emoji, and as she was getting out of her car, she saw him with a blonde woman, his arm around her shoulder, walking up the pathway. Harry continued to the main lobby and took the stairs to her room.

She took out her cell phone and stretched out on the bed. Chief Phillips answered on the first ring. "Hey, Harry, what's up?"

"Nothing at this point. We've watched them all day. Saw nothing out of the ordinary. Burt and another female officer are watching them now, in the lounge. As I followed them back from dinner, I had an idea. I think we can turn up the heat on these two, and get things moving, if you're willing."

She explained her idea and they batted around scenarios for a few minutes. Chief Phillips sighed. "We've been waiting on the state guys to give us more to go on, but the financials are taking longer. Seems like shell companies are involved. I think your idea has merit. Let me talk to Sheriff Lester, and I'll get back to you."

Harry turned on the television to help her stay awake, but made sure the volume was very low so she could hear any activity next door in Mayor Irwin's room. Hotel room walls were notoriously thin, and she counted on that fact to alert her to his arrival.

After an hour, her phone chimed with a text from Burt. He reported the two mayors were leaving, and it looked like they were heading to their rooms. Evie was going to follow them and report if they deviated from their assumed destination on the third floor of the main building.

Harry flicked the television off and stationed herself at the door, watching through the peephole.

Her phone vibrated and she saw Chief Phillips' name appear on the screen. She brought the phone to her ear. "I'm watching the hallway for the two of them to arrive momentarily. Can't talk long."

"The plan is in place. Expect Mayor Irwin to receive a call

within the hour, and Sheriff Lester is briefing Burt as we speak."

"Copy. I'll keep you as posted as I can." She slipped her phone into the pocket of her jeans.

The two mayors came down the hallway, arm in arm, giggling with each other. They made a point of looking down the hall both ways, before Mayor Irwin opened his door and they both went inside.

Harry stepped over to the wall, listening, but beyond a laugh or two, didn't hear any conversation. Minutes later the flush of the toilet made Harry smile. "So romantic," she whispered to nobody.

The sound of a cabinet closing and ice clanking in glasses led Harry to believe they had retrieved something from the minibar. With the chilly weather, she had no hope that they would wander out to the balcony, which would make all of this so much easier.

Without a warrant, she couldn't use any of the fancy tools in her case, so she was stuck waiting for something to happen.

After listening to some rather grotesque sounds coming from the other side of the wall, which confirmed their romantic involvement, the shrill sound of a cell phone ringing came from the room.

She recognized Mayor's Irwin's deep voice. Heavy footfalls made their way toward the balcony side of the room. Harry smiled. She knew who was on the other end of that call.

The volume of his voice increased, and Harry had no problem making out every word. "Listen here, you little punk. Don't you threaten me. You've been paid what we agreed."

Silence followed his outburst.

"Are you sure you want to jeopardize our future relationship. We have more work for you this week."

Harry's phone chimed with a text from Chief Phillips. *Warrant authorized and we are capturing the conversation on our end. Irwin is using a second phone.*

"Caleb, I really don't have time for your games. I'm not even in Gold Point right now." Irwin's voice was tense and clipped.

While she listened, she opened her laptop and plugged in the audio and recording device, placing the amplification microphone on the wall.

She held her breath, waiting for Irwin's next move.

CHAPTER SIXTEEN

Heavy footsteps sounded through the wall and Harry felt the vibration from them under her feet as she readied the audio enhancement equipment and tested the volume, listening to the boosted level that was recording. "That lowlife is threatening to turn me into the cops if I don't pay him more."

Mayor Crawford's high-pitched voice filled the air. "We can't let him get away with that. It will never end. Once you pay him more, we'll be stuck doing it forever."

"Well, what do you suggest, Chrissy? Shall we kill him?"

"Keep your voice down, you fool."

Harry smiled at the words she could hear perfectly.

Mayor Crawford continued. "We're so close now, we can't let that little scum ball ruin everything."

"You stay here, and I'll go deal with Marks." The sound of water running filled the background. "Just go back to your room, and I'll call you. It's so late already, I'm not sure if I'll be back tonight or just stay home. I can tell my wife I had an emergency at the office and came home. She won't think anything of it. She's oblivious to my comings and goings."

Mayor Crawford's voice whined. "Don't you let him ruin this for us. We've worked way too hard to lose it all now."

"I'll handle it. Trust me."

The room door shut with a clunk, and the conversation ceased.

A few minutes later, Irwin's room door opened and closed again.

Harry dialed Burt's number, and he confirmed he was waiting in his vehicle, ready to tail Irwin. "We also found out the body shop where they're meeting and Marks works is owned by Irwin's sister and her husband."

"Interesting," said Harry.

"Evie is in my room with the audio equipment. She can record anything she hears in Mayor Crawford's room." Burt disconnected after he let her know that Irwin was on the move.

Harry paced the floor of her room. She hated this part. The waiting for the op to succeed or fail. She hadn't been stuck in the field like this for a long time and the not knowing was killing her.

Predicting a late night, she fixed herself a cup of coffee, using the fancy pod machine on the counter. As she sipped, her cell phone buzzed. It was a text from Evie letting her know all was quiet in Mayor Crawford's room. Their subject was watching television.

Harry flopped across the bed and turned on her own television. Bored and antsy was not a good combination.

She watched a mindless program, then another one, and two hours later, checked her cell phone for the hundredth time. Still nothing. She tossed it on the bed, then pounced on it a moment later when it chimed.

Chief Phillips' name filled the screen. "Hey, Chief, what's the word?"

He chuckled. "The word is, Sheriff Lester took Mayor Irwin into custody. He's in the interrogation room now and we're hoping he'll turn over on Mayor Crawford. Marks was the key that picked the lock on this one. When we offered him leniency in exchange for helping us get Irwin, he jumped at the chance, as did his roommate. She corroborated all the events, and they both admitted to being paid to vandalize property and vehicles, along with enlisting a few of their friends for the shoplifting and some other nuisance crimes."

"Great news. Hopefully, Irwin will see the light and bring Mayor Crawford down with him."

"Yeah, the kids didn't have any direct contact or communication with anyone but Irwin. He mentioned Mayor Crawford to Marks when he talked about the targets being in Lavender Valley, but we need more than that. Just wanted you to know Irwin won't be coming back to Ashland tonight. I'll be in touch when we know more, and Burt is on his way back to the hotel to babysit our other suspect."

She disconnected and leaned back against the mountain of pillows she had stuffed behind her. More waiting. After she flipped through all the channels, she settled on reruns of old sitcoms.

A few minutes before two o'clock, her phone chimed, and Chief Phillips' name appeared.

"Good news," he said. "The state team was able to get some financial links, and when we confronted Irwin with it, he gave up Mayor Crawford. He says it was all her idea. Burt and Evie are getting the word now to move on Crawford and arrest her. You might as well join the fun."

The soft ping of an incoming text fluttered in her ear. "Sounds great, Chief. Talk to you soon." After disconnecting, she read the text from Burt, letting her know they were ready to apprehend the mayor and were waiting on the hotel manager with the master key.

She took her time opening her door, turning the handle slowly to minimize the loud click hotel doors always make. She stepped into the hallway to see Burt and Evie on the other side of Mayor Crawford's door. She moved into position, past Irwin's room, and stood on the opposite side of the door.

The manager came around the corner, a sheepish look in his eye as he waved the card and a few papers in front of him. "The fax came through, like you said."

Burt took the card and copy of the warrant Sheriff Lester had faxed, and asked the manager to return to his desk.

With the hallway empty and quiet, Burt used his fist to knock on the door. "Ms. Crawford. Police. We have a warrant for your arrest and we're coming in."

He swiped the card and opened the door slowly, not sure if she had put the security lock in place, but she hadn't and it swung open. Evie flipped the light switch and Mayor Crawford, her red streaked hair sprouting every which way, pushed her sleep mask from her eyes, blinking quickly with her mouth agape.

She spilled out of the slinky negligee she wore. "What, what is going on? Who are you and what are you doing?" she screamed.

Burt stepped closer to her, showed her his credentials and said, "Jackson County Sheriff's Department. We have a warrant for your arrest. Please stand and put your hands behind your back."

"This is preposterous," she spat. "Do you *know* who I am?"

"Yes, ma'am. Christina Marie Crawford and you are under arrest." He went through the Miranda warning and read off several charges including conspiracy and fraud, while Evie attempted to help her from the bed.

"I will have all your badges. Do you hear me?" she yelled.

"Ma'am, you'll need this, and some shoes," said Evie, handing her the trench coat she found hanging in the closet.

Mayor Crawford looked down at her silk gown and shook her head. "I need to get dressed."

Evie looked at the woman. "My partner can step into the hallway and the two of us," she pointed at Harry, "will stay here. You'll have to change right here, no going anywhere else.

Harry stepped to the closet and pulled out the suit Mayor Crawford had worn earlier. She brought it to the bed. "Here you go."

"I never...this is police brutality." Mayor Crawford swiped the hanger from the bed and began shimmying into her pants. Harry stood between the bed and the exit, while Evie covered the area from the bed to the balcony.

People cornered, like trapped animals, often were unpredictable, and none of them wanted to be responsible for Mayor Crawford hurting herself in an effort to escape or even jump from her balcony.

When Crawford was dressed, Harry gave the all clear to Burt, who returned and slipped the mayor's cell phone into an evidence bag, while Evie put the cuffs on their suspect.

"I need that phone, young man. I'm entitled to call my lawyer."

"You'll get your call down at the station." He nodded at Evie. "Let's move out. The marked unit is waiting downstairs."

Harry stayed behind while they escorted the irritated woman to the elevator. She didn't have to wait long before they returned with an evidence collection specialist, and they all began the task of bagging things from the room. After, they moved on and did the same in Mayor Irwin's room.

The only item of interest was a second cell phone in Mayor Crawford's purse.

When they were done, Burt and Evie collected their things from their room, and Harry transferred the metal surveillance case to Burt and signed off the evidence log for the recording she'd made. Burt extended his hand. "Thanks for all the help, Harry. Sounds like the state team will be taking the reins, since it's elected officials and corruption, but I'm sure we'll see you soon to wrap things up."

"I'm just glad we could get them tonight. I was dreading a repeat of our day yesterday. Great working with both of you."

Evie shook hands with Harry. "See ya around, Harry."

Harry watched them walk to the elevator, then turned back to her own room. Instead of packing up and driving to Lavender Valley in the dark, she crawled under the covers for a few hours of shut eye. She settled into her pillow, reliving the satisfaction of seeing that pompous woman perp walked to the elevator. If only it had been daylight, and the local news had been around to get some photos.

Harry slept until seven, then showered and toted her bag downstairs where she checked out, and then followed the other guests to the breakfast room. The meal was pretty basic; they'd obviously had a fancier menu for the conference yesterday. There wasn't a croissant, cinnamon roll, or breakfast sandwich in sight.

She made do with toast and tea, then filled a to go cup with fresh tea for her drive back to Lavender Valley. She called Chief Phillips on the way, and he told her to stop by when she got to town.

She detoured to Daisy's Café, to try their breakfast, and found friendly servers and yummy food. Since it was across the street from the Sugar Shack, she stopped by and got a box of donuts and cinnamon rolls to take to Clay and Heath to thank them for watching the dogs.

She considered a box for the police, but assumed they would already have celebratory donuts on hand, and when she walked through the door of the Lavender Valley Police Department was proven correct.

Sally beamed at her and gestured to Chief Phillips' office. "He's in and expecting you."

Harry made her way down the hall and found him behind the desk, his phone at his ear. He waved her inside and finished his conversation.

As he hung up the phone, Sally came in with a steaming cup of coffee and a box of donuts with the flap open. "Help yourself," she offered.

Harry took the coffee and said, "Oh, I just had breakfast, but thank you."

Chief Phillips bit into one of the jelly donuts he had stacked on a notepad next to his phone. "I've got good news and better news."

"I'm all ears," said Harry.

"Mayor Crawford and Mayor Irwin, after speaking with their lawyers, have decided to resign from their respective positions. They feel all of this and the investigations will be a distraction and detriment to the people they serve." He winked and took another bite.

"That sounds familiar and almost as good as wanting to spend time with their family." She laughed and added, "They probably see the writing on the wall and would rather step down than get recalled."

He nodded, then sipped his coffee. "And, the state investigators have discovered lots of financial shenanigans where Crawford was funneling money to a consultant," he used air quotes, "that turned out to be a front company for Irwin. He did the same in Gold Point."

"Political corruption 101, right?" said Harry. "They love to launder taxpayer money for their own benefit. I'm not surprised when I see it in larger places, but Lavender Valley surprises me."

He shook his head. "I think we got complacent here. Mayor Copeland served for so long and was such an upstanding man, we got in the habit of thinking everyone would be like him. Crawford had been in real estate for a long time, and when she was campaigning, she came across as reasonable, always talking about her love of our small town and all that. Then, when her main competitor got snarled up in his tax bill problem, which really wasn't that big of a deal, it was over. He was late, but so are many other residents. Anyway, Crawford really hammered him on being a poor example to lead the city and all that. It worked."

"It's an ugly business, isn't it?" Harry asked, taking another swallow from her cup. "So, the plan with all the petty crime and vandalism was what? They had to have an end game."

He pointed his finger at her. "Bingo. Irwin was sending money Crawford's way to sell us out, basically. They cooked up this idea to merge the two cities, Gold Point and Lavender Valley and in essence have us run by Gold Point. They wanted to sell it as a savings to the community, who could have better services and less employees. Crawford floated that balloon several months ago, before last summer and it went nowhere. This was their way of putting pressure on us to cave."

"So, the idea was to make things so miserable we would welcome the rescue of getting additional services by merging with Gold Point. Then, they would funnel Lavender Valley taxes to Gold Point to pay for services, and they'd use their little fake consultants to send money back and forth to each other, only at higher levels, right?"

"Pretty much, and of course Crawford would get a cushy paid position with the new merger. Political scum, if you ask me."

Harry nodded. "All too common nowadays. You always have to look deeper when politicians offer a solution, since many times they actually create the problem so they can provide the solution they want you to accept. I wouldn't be surprised if you find more rot when you start lifting up the layers of this."

"You're probably right. Seems like her types always need lower-level minions to help. The local paper is all over the story, so I expect it will be the talk of the town. Thank you for volunteering and helping us get that first lead. Without it, I'm not sure we would have ever uncovered all this stuff. I think Irwin and Crawford are going to have bigger problems than not being employed."

Harry smiled and stood. "Ms. Crawford might have to add some orange streaks in her hair. I love it when the good guys win. I think that's what I'll miss most not working. There is such satisfaction in justice and helping victims."

"I have a feeling you might find a way to make that happen here," he said with a wink.

She frowned. "Oh, I'm done with that chapter of my life. I've got a farm to run, remember?"

His desk phone buzzed and he picked it up, waving to Harry as she went through the door.

Being a cop in Lavender Valley would probably be something she would enjoy; it would be more about service than violent crime, and she was ready for a change.

But it would have to wait. She had another problem to solve now.

Time was passing, spring was coming, and soon the farm would take more time and energy than she had to give.

She had to make another push to reach out to the four women Jewel hoped would join her.

CHAPTER SEVENTEEN

With her side surveillance work done and Tyler on board to help with the chores, Harry had the time to go by the post office to see what was going on with the mail service. But first, she had donuts to deliver and dogs to retrieve. She made the drive out to the ranch and parked at the front entry, giving the statue of the horse a more thorough inspection in the daylight. It was stunning and so lifelike.

She gazed across the property taking in the sheer beauty of the pastures and rolling hills. She hadn't appreciated it when she was living with Jewel, but now the peace of the view filled her.

The box of donuts in one hand, she rang the bell. A moment later, Clay opened the door, sporting a smile. "Hey, Harry, you're here early." He pointed at the box. "I never refuse a woman with donuts. Come on in." He swung the door wide and she stepped into the impressive space. "Heath has the dogs with him, but I'll call him on the radio and see if he can swing by with them."

"No rush. I should have called first. We finished up late last night, or rather early this morning, and I just came from Chief Phillips' office."

Clay led the way to the kitchen, pulling the walkie talkie off his belt to raise Heath. After asking him to bring Hope and Chief to the house, he put the box of donuts on the counter and brought down two mugs. "Coffee?"

"Sounds great, thanks." Harry said, sliding into the seat at the island counter.

"You say you finished up?" asked Clay. "As in you caught the bad guys?"

"Yes, and I'm not sure when it will go public, but Chief Phillips said the newspaper was already on it. Mayor Crawford and Mayor Irwin were both arrested and they've resigned their positions."

He set her mug down and went back for two plates, then picked a cinnamon roll out of the box. "Weekly paper comes out tomorrow, so maybe it will be on the front page. He gestured at the box.

Harry shook her head. "No, I was starving and stopped for breakfast on my way into town." She recapped the sting operation and the plan the two leaders had to combine the two cities, with both mayors having a financial interest in doing so.

Clay shook his head. "My friend on the council never said much, but he didn't trust her. I guess he was right. What a mess."

Harry reached for her mug. "I'm sure it will rock Lavender Valley, but I think the business owners will be happy to know the vandalism and nuisance crimes were orchestrated, and that the perpetrators weren't local."

He licked a glob of icing from his lip. "I agree. It'll be nice to have an end to all of it. Not to mention the costs of repairing windows and cleaning off graffiti. It's been a hardship for some of them."

"We can collect your trail cameras, when you have time. The only thing on my list is to get to the post office sometime this week."

He grinned. "And, don't forget dinner here, plus we need to get you used to that shotgun. Does Friday work? We could do some practice shooting and that would give Heath time to get whatever he needs for dinner. Next weekend is the shoot, so we're running out of time."

"Sounds great to me. I'll pick up some ammo when I'm in town."

"I've got plenty of shells, so just get what you need for your weapons. I'll have everything set up to practice Friday. Let's say elevenish."

"I'll be here."

The sound of toenails on the wooden floors prompted Harry to turn her head. All four dogs came barreling around the corner and into the kitchen, followed by Heath.

He removed his hat. "Howdy, Harry. Are you sure you want these hooligans back?"

She chuckled as she bent to give them attention. "I've missed them, but they're probably having way more fun here."

Clay poured a cup of coffee and handed it to Heath. "Does Friday work for dinner? Harry is going to come over earlier in the day so we can practice with the shotgun and get dialed in for the shoot."

Heath took a sip and grinned. "Clay is keeping you a secret. You're our ringer."

Harry coughed and choked on the coffee. Closest to the sink, Heath filled a glass of water for her.

She took a few swallows and cleared her throat. "Thanks

and sorry about that," she croaked. "I'm a decent shot, but I doubt I'll be a ringer. I'm sure you have people that shoot all the time and are much better suited for the contest."

Clay glanced at Heath. "When we lost Dad, we lost our best shot. He brought home the trophy year after year. I'd like to get it back in the family. Sort of a way to honor him."

"We came close last year, but lost by two points. It's a three-person team, so it combines all the scores for all three members of the team," said Heath.

"I'll do my best," said Harry, "but I don't want you pinning all your hopes on me."

Clay reached across and patted her arm. "I shouldn't have even mentioned the whole trophy thing and my dad. I don't want to put extra pressure on you. We'll have a fun time, regardless of the outcome."

Harry took a small sip from her cup, testing her raw throat. "I think I better get to Benson's and stock up on ammo. I'll do some practice between now and Friday. Is it safe to set something up in the far pasture by the creek?"

Clay nodded. "Yep, just make sure there are no cattle in the field behind your target and you're good to go. I moved the cows on Jewel's pasture, so they won't be in your way. We own all the land past yours, so there's nobody else to worry about."

"Well, guys," she stood and took her mug and glass to the sink. "Thanks again for dog sitting, and I'm going to get on with practice now that things have wrapped up with Chief Phillips."

Heath's brows rose. "Aw, I knew there was something. What have you been up to?" He glanced between the two of them.

"Clay can tell you. I need to get going. I'll see you on Friday, and if there is anything I can bring, let me know."

Heath grinned and shook his head. "I've got dinner handled, but I'm not much of a baker. If you want to bring some dessert, that would be great."

"Consider it done," she said, and motioned for Chief and Hope to come to her.

The two dogs hurried to her side, and the brothers followed them to the entryway.

"Thanks again for taking care of these two," Harry said, waving as she loaded them into her SUV.

She made her way down the long driveway, but rather than turn at the farm, she continued down the road to town. She pulled in front of Benson's and leashed Hope and Chief.

Dogs were allowed in the hardware portion of the store, but not the food side. She went through the hardware entrance, selected a small cart, and let the two dogs sniff at everything, exploring as she found the ammunition section.

She scanned the shelves and loaded a few boxes of the various sizes she would need for her rifle and handguns, and added a package of targets and a portable target stand. She turned down the next aisle in search of a water bowl for the dogs, and couldn't resist letting the two of them select a couple of dog toys before she paid for her purchases.

The gentleman behind the counter overheard her tell Chief and Hope they'd have to wait in the car while she did her grocery shopping, and told her she could leave the dogs in the area he referred to as the 'dog park.' She followed his instructions to a small fenced in area near the back of the hardware store, where she found a patch of fake grass, a play tunnel, several toys, and a big bowl of water, along with all the supplies for any cleanup necessary. She opened the gate and led the two into the playground. "I'll be right back," she told them.

She dashed back to the grocery side of the store and

gathered the ingredients she remembered from Jewel's recipe book to make her stew, as well as the chicken soup Harry sometimes made when she dragged out her slow cooker for winter.

With her basket filled with veggies, broth, and meat, she scanned the prepared food counter and picked up a tray of enchiladas with rice, along with a large salad. Harry shook her head when she noticed the price. She needed to get better about making her own food, but wanted to start with the slow cooker first.

She added a few more items and found a familiar face at the cashier's counter. "Hey, Mona. How are you?"

"Hanging in there." Mona rang up the groceries and started to bag the items. "Did you hear the news that Mayor Crawford resigned?"

Harry slipped her credit card out of her wallet. "I did hear that."

"Curt, from the newspaper, was in earlier and said it's big news and will be out tomorrow." Mona's eyes danced with excitement.

"Sounds like I better read the paper tomorrow." Harry chuckled as she took her bags and wished Mona a pleasant day.

She and her dogs headed out of town and back to the farm. As she waited for the gate, Harry noticed how nice it felt not to have to handle the morning and afternoon chores. She worried about taking advantage of Clay's kindness, but was thankful for Jewel's wisdom in having Tyler's help.

She parked under the breezeway and hauled her groceries into the house, while urging the dogs to follow her with the promise of a treat, then went about making the chicken soup she often made during the winter. With everything in the slow cooker, she tidied the kitchen, then retrieved her rifle. A thermos of hot tea and some water completed her preparation for their adventure. The dogs followed her to the barn, and she loaded them into the back of the UTV, along with her gear.

Despite her warm gloves, hat, and jacket, once she got moving, Harry shivered with the chill of the wind. Thankfully, it didn't take long to reach the creek, and she drove down it a short distance before finding the perfect spot next to a tree.

She went about setting up the target stand and attaching a paper target. She selected the silhouette style she had shot at for all of her career, then double checked the pasture behind the target again and found it empty.

She loaded her sidearm, placed the box of ammunition back in the UTV, and paced off several distances, using clumps of grass and bark to mark them.

Ready to practice, she whistled for the dogs, who weren't far from where she stood. They came running. Chief was used to shooting, but she wasn't sure how Hope would respond. Being raised on the farm, she was probably used to it, but Harry didn't want to take a chance.

She made them get into the back of the UTV and told them to stay, while she donned her safety glasses and ear protection. She walked to the closest mark and focused on the target, then fired five quick rounds. The dogs were curled together and didn't seem bothered by the noise.

Harry holstered her gun and checked the target. All five shots had hit center mass in a tight pattern. She used the marking pen in her pocket to strike through each of them, so she wouldn't count them again and then moved to the next distance and fired. She finished up at the final mark, the furthest distance from the target.

She walked back to the target to examine her work. All

fifteen of her shots were grouped together, shredding the bullseye at center mass. She reloaded and did it again, this time aiming at the head.

When she was done, she inspected the target, with all fifteen shots in the colored portion of the head. She hadn't lost her touch.

Next, she chose the colorful bulls' eye targets, and attached the smaller sized paper to the stand. She had a cup of tea, then retrieved her rifle and loaded the .223 bullets into the magazine.

She didn't shoot it nearly as often as she shot her sidearms. She approached the tree and found a spot to brace her rifle, then looked through the scope and took her first shot, adjusted, and shot nine more rounds.

It was much harder to shoot accurately without a brace or a bipod, and she wasn't sure what the rules of the shoot would require. For the next ten rounds, she stood, using the sling on the rifle to help her brace her arm.

She checked the target. Her shots were in the next ring, not quite the bull's eye, but passable. That would be the hardest stance she would have to use, so she loaded another magazine and practiced again.

She then tried shooting from a kneeling position and sitting position, using her body to support the rifle. She knew sometimes that contests required shooters to use their non-dominant hand, and she practiced that way too, but was much slower. Although she managed to shoot the paper, her score with her left hand wasn't great.

She switched back to her handgun and finished off the remaining targets on the paper, hitting the bull's eye each time. She tried her handgun skills with her left hand and was happy to manage two bull's eyes out of ten.

Before she finished her session, she went back to the rifle

and her dominant hand. She always liked to finish on a positive note, and she burned through thirty rounds, hitting the center ring each time.

While she picked up her brass and put things away, she let the dogs out of the back of the UTV so they could explore and burn off some energy. With everything stowed away and clean, she took them on an extended walk along the creek before heading back to the barn.

She was locking the rear barn doors when Chief let out a low bark. She turned and saw Tyler coming through the other end of the barn. "Chief, good boy, it's okay." Hope's tail wagged as she stepped closer to the young man in a cowboy hat.

He bent to pet her. "Hey, pretty girl, how are you?"

Chief stayed close to Harry's side and relaxed, his tail swaying a bit as they got closer to Tyler, who was now rubbing Hope's belly while her back leg moved in a steady rhythm.

"Hey, Tyler, we just were out by the creek. I was going to get started on the chores and then I remembered you're here. I appreciate your help."

"No problem, Ms. McKenzie. I've been helping Jewel for a couple years now and I like it here. It's nice to be on my own, and Jewel let me fix the bunkhouse up. It's like my own place."

"I'm glad you're happy here. I was a little worried when I toured the Nolan Ranch. Their accommodations are much more modern, and I thought you might want to stay there instead."

He grinned and reached to pet Chief. "There you go, boy. You're a good man, aren't you?" Chief's tail wagged and he leaned closer to Tyler. Their friendship was born.

Tyler glanced up at Harry. "The rooms are nice, and I still

eat my meals there, but I like the quiet here and," he winked, "don't tell Clay, but the work here is a piece of cake. The horses are the top priority and there are several guys with lots of expertise there, so I get stuck with the worst jobs. Here, I get to take care of all the different animals, and I like that."

Harry acted out zipping her lips. "Your secret is safe with me. Like I said, I'm thankful to have you." She glanced at the UTV. "I just need to unload some stuff, and I'll be out of your hair."

"No problem. I want to clean out the water troughs, so I've got plenty to keep me busy, unless you need some help."

She held up her hand. "I can handle it." She glanced at the two dogs. "I'll get these two out of your way and get them some dinner."

At the mention of dinner, their ears perked and they turned to look at Harry.

Tyler left with a wave, and Harry collected her gun cases and the bag of ammunition, then trudged to the house with both dogs at her heels. The inviting scent of chicken soup welcomed them in.

By the time she had fed the dogs their dinner and put her shooting supplies away, Harry was starving. She ladled a big bowl of soup and cut off a chunk of fresh bread to go with it. She ate two bowls of the delicious soup and stored the rest of it in the fridge, knowing it would taste even better tomorrow. When she finished doing the dishes, she spread the targets she had brought in on the dining room table, and couldn't resist snapping a photo. She texted it to Clay.

Moments later, her phone chimed.

I knew you'd be a shoo-in. Dusting off the trophy shelf now.

She chuckled, took her fresh cup of tea, and prepared to

snuggle with her dogs on the couch. As she pulled the throw blanket over herself, her phone chimed again.

In the excitement of seeing your shooting skills, I forgot to say thanks, Harry. I know the contest is silly, but it really does mean the world to me. My dad would have loved you. Sweet dreams, Clay. P.S. Read the paper in the morning.

CHAPTER EIGHTEEN

After doing some laundry and munching on some toast with her tea, Harry set off for town. She pulled into the parking lot of the post office, a charming brick building with arched details over the windows.

Inside, the walls were filled with old-fashioned brass boxes with small windows. She waited in a short line for the one clerk on duty.

When she reached the counter, she explained she'd recently moved to Lavender Valley from Salem and had put in a change of address, but hadn't been receiving her mail. "I thought I'd check and see if it might be held here or if you can check into it for me."

The woman behind the counter asked for her name.

"Harry McKenzie. Well, Harriet is my legal first name."

The woman looked up from her notepad. "You're *her*?"

Harry raised her brows. "Uh, not sure what you mean, but I am Harriet McKenzie." She pulled her wallet out of her handbag and handed the woman her identification.

The woman stared at it, then smiled at Harry. "You are *that* Harry." She pulled out a folded copy of the *Lavender Valley News* from beneath the counter, opened it, and pointed at the headline. "You're the retired cop in Curt's story. The one who helped catch our crooked Mayor Crawford." She beamed and added, "I'm Veronica, by the way."

Harry scanned the story, as Veronica hollered out behind her. "Hey, everybody, the lady police detective from the newspaper is here."

Several people came from around the corner, all of them with curious faces. Before Harry knew it, she was being introduced to everyone who worked at the post office and shaking their hands. With the line of workers exhausted and the people waiting in line behind her now getting in on the action, all of them full of smiles, thanks, and kind words, Harry tried to focus Veronica on her mail issue.

Finally, she took down Harry's old address and then headed back into the far recesses of the work area, out of sight. Another employee replaced her at the counter.

Harry took the newspaper to the side to let those in line go ahead, and to skim the story, flipping to the second page to finish the article. Curt Mansfield, the editor, provided a recap of the arrests and subsequent resignations of both mayors, and quoted Chief Phillips and Sheriff Lester throughout the article. Chief Phillips credited Harry for helping solve the case with the lead on the vandals and her volunteer work.

Curt promised more information would be forthcoming as the investigation proceeded. The City Council would be holding an emergency meeting on Friday to discuss next steps.

In reality, there were only a few lines of the article that pointed to Harry, and while she'd endured her fair share of time in the limelight with the media in Salem, she had never had people on the street or in the stores recognize her or thank her. While she appreciated their intent, she wasn't a fan of attention. She preferred to enjoy the satisfaction of her accomplishments behind the scenes.

A few minutes later, Veronica emerged. "Well, I talked to the postmaster in Salem and they are doing some research. They think your mail may be held up at a one of the branch post offices, instead of the main one. He assured me they'd do everything possible to locate it and get it transferred down here by the beginning of the week. If you leave me your number, I'd be happy to call you and let you know what we find out."

Harry took in the smiling woman and wasn't anxious to give Veronica a direct line to contact her. She didn't want it shared with everyone in town. "Oh, it's not that important. I'm sure it will get sorted. I just thought it was odd. If I don't have it next week, I'll stop back in. Thank you for your help."

As Harry turned to leave, Veronica made another announcement to all the new customers who weren't there initially. "This is Harry McKenzie, the police detective from Salem that Curt wrote about in today's paper."

Harry kept smiling and accepted handshakes and hugs from the customers as she passed by them on her way to the exit.

She needed coffee.

After getting out of her SUV at Winding River Coffee, she looked up at the second story. Clay's trail cameras were gone. Inside, she stepped into the line waiting at the counter. Laurie was making drinks and Lisa was at the register.

The line moved quickly and when Lisa saw Harry, she squealed. Laurie saw her and waved.

Lisa turned back to Harry and plucked a fresh newspaper from the pile for sale. "Have you seen the newspaper?"

"Yes, I was just at the post office and saw it there."

"Wow, that is all everybody is talking about."

Harry tried to steer the conversation back to her beverage. "I'll take a chai tea latte, please."

Laurie piped up and said, "On the house. In fact, I don't think you'll have to buy your own drinks anywhere in Lavender Valley."

Harry started to object, but couldn't get a word in edgewise with Lisa yammering to the couple behind Harry in line, telling them she was the police detective mentioned in the paper.

Soon the shop was buzzing with more people and it was worse than the post office. It was as if someone had gone up and down the street, and pulled in anyone who was roaming the sidewalk. The place was packed. Harry put on a friendly smile and talked to each of the townspeople who came in to thank her.

It took her over an hour to make a graceful exit. She slid behind the wheel and drove on the side street until she hit the main highway that led to the farm, focusing on the road and not making eye contact with anyone. She wished Chief Phillips hadn't mentioned her name.

Normally, it wouldn't be a big deal, but in a town the size of Lavender Valley, news spread like the proverbial wildfire, and Harry was sure by the time she got home, every man, woman, and child in a fifty-mile radius would know all about her.

She sighed as she waited for the electric gate to swing open. She knew they meant well and appreciated their sincere kind words, but she wasn't made for the spotlight.

She smiled when she saw Hope and Chief, standing next to Tyler, who was tightening something on the barn door.

The two fluffy monsters were the only fan club members she needed.

She waved at Tyler and whistled for the dogs, who came running to meet her. She bent to rub Chief's ears. "You're a good boy." She did the same to Hope and led them into the house.

Despite it being early afternoon, Harry was exhausted. She fixed a bowl of leftover soup and took it and her copy of the newspaper to the kitchen island. She read the article again, slowly and calmly, while she ate.

It was a good article and like she thought the first time, Curt Mansfield had only mentioned her in the context of Chief Phillips' quote, which was accurate. He and Sheriff Lester praised her policework and volunteer efforts, saying how happy they were to have her join their community.

She hadn't lived in a small town in a very long time, and growing up in Lavender Valley she hadn't done anything to garner attention. She was certain the notoriety would be short-lived. There was bound to be a new story that would take over in next week's edition.

At least, her mail should be on the way soon, and then she could get back to contacting the other women.

She tidied the kitchen and opted to celebrate her newfound celebrity by taking a well-deserved nap. She situated herself into the oversized chair Jewel loved and Hope stood next to it, giving Harry her paw. "Come on up here, Hope." The dog didn't need to be told twice and crawled into Harry's lap. Chief joined them and sprawled across the ottoman. Harry was essentially in the midst of a dog sandwich. She smiled and closed her eyes.

Harry managed to keep busy at the farm, and stayed away from town for the next few days. Friday morning, she made a quick stop at the bakery and picked up a pie for dessert. They offered a free coffee to their customers and she took the small paper cup from the cashier and headed for the exit.

At a table near the door, she ran into May and Janet, the two ladies who owned Cranberry Cottage. Clay had introduced them to Harry one morning when they were outside of their gift shop, and both had seemed pleasant and friendly.

Now, they were enjoying a sweet treat before they opened their store, and waved Harry over to their table. May, with her short dark hair in a cute wispy cut, pointed at the chair next to her. "Join us, Harry. We have a little something for you at the shop and have been hoping to run into you."

"For me?" Harry frowned.

Janet, with a sandy colored cowboy hat atop her head of long, dark hair, smiled. "Just a little something to welcome you to Lavender Valley and to thank you, of course. Along with everyone else, we're so thankful you took the bull by the horns and helped bring down our crooked mayor."

"Oh, that's really not necessary. I'm happy to help." Harry took a long swallow from her cup.

May patted Harry's arm. "We insist. It's just a little gift basket, nothing extravagant and our way of saying thank you. You can just follow us over to the shop now and pick it up."

Over the last week, Harry learned it was easier to accept the kindness of a meal or coffee than to refuse it. She was accustomed to not taking any gifts, since it was strictly prohibited in law enforcement, but this was different. She didn't want to hurt anyone's feelings or make a rift in the small community. "Sure, I've been meaning to stop in and check out your shop anyway. That's very kind of you."

Both of the women beamed and hurried to finish their cinnamon rolls. Harry stashed her pie box in her car, then continued down the street with the two women.

When they unlocked the door and ushered her in, the first thing Harry noticed was the delightful aroma. The shop was filled with candles, lotions, home décor, coffees, teas, kitchen items, a smattering of hats, gloves, and scarves, and even soup and bread mixes. Everything was artfully displayed. May gestured toward an antique desk, done in black with beautiful white and pink floral accents. "Janet and I do a ton of upcycling of old furniture and items. We clean them, repaint them, and sell them."

"Wow," said Harry, admiring a vintage dresser. "You two are beyond talented."

They gave her a quick tour, pointing out the handmade goat's milk soap that was responsible for some of the welcoming scents that filled the air. Handmade candies, jellies, and other edibles were stashed throughout the displays.

May stepped behind the counter and picked up a basket, wrapped with cellophane and adorned with a shimmery ribbon. "This is for you, Harry. It's filled with some of our favorite things, and we hope you enjoy them."

Harry eyed the huge basket. "Oh, my goodness. This is really too much."

They shook their heads in unison. "Like we said, we insist," said May. "Enjoy, and then come back and visit us when you need a gift or to indulge yourself in a special treat."

Janet added, "Or just when you feel like stopping by for a visit. We've always got coffee brewed and the kettle on."

"And, we usually pop the cork on a bottle of wine in the late afternoon," said May, with a wink. "We do quite a few sip and shops, especially as the weather warms up."

Harry took the basket. "Well, thank you very much. I love your shop, and I guarantee I'll be back."

They waved goodbye as they held the door for Harry, wishing her a good weekend.

The scent of the fancy soaps filled her SUV and made for a pleasant trip home. When she got to the house, she loaded up the dogs, her rifle, and spare handgun, plus boxes of ammunition, and drove over to the Nolan Ranch.

Clay welcomed her and the dogs through the front door, and Maverick and Ace came running down the hallway to greet them. He took the bakery box she offered, and carried it toward the kitchen. "Heath is packing up some sandwiches for us. We've got everything set up in the pasture."

Harry followed Clay into the kitchen to find Heath putting sandwiches in the ice chest. "Good morning, Heath. Thanks for making lunch."

"Hey, Harry, my pleasure."

The rich aroma of tomatoes and basil drew her to the cooktop. "Something smells delicious."

"What you smell is the sauce for our dinner tonight." Heath chuckled as he gathered water bottles to put into the ice chest. "We want to feed Lavender Valley's most famous citizen well."

"Aww, don't start. I was hoping all the hubbub would have died down by now."

He smirked. "No such luck. You're still the talk of the town, and with the big emergency meeting they held this morning, I suspect things are only going to heat up."

"Really? I just got a huge gift basket from May and Janet, and was hoping that might be the last one." She gave Maverick a chin scratch.

"I talked to my buddy on the city council just a few minutes ago," said Clay. "It seems they have accepted a couple more resignations and are planning a forensic audit. It sounds like Mayor Crawford had her claws in people in public works and the accounting office, and they have resigned and are giving evidence. Mayor Crawford's champion on the council also resigned."

Harry shook her head. "It's disgusting, but I've seen it happen many times. She probably had something over them, and then used them to do her bidding with the promise of protection or money or whatever. She may have even set them up to get them on her team. Bad actors sometimes trap people, and then instead of coming clean or contacting the authorities, they're scared and manipulated and end up in bed with the culprits. Sadly, it's all too common."

Clay nodded. "Sounds like they took a playbook from our overlords in DC."

Heath chuckled. "Don't get him started on congress. We don't have that kind of time, and we want to have a good day."

"I've got everything loaded in both the UTVs," said Clay. "Can you take Maverick and Ace with you, Heath? We'll be doing good to get Hope and Chief in my rig."

"Sure thing. I'll just add the ice chest and stir the sauce, and I'll be ready to go."

Clay herded the four dogs outside and loaded Ace and Maverick into the red vehicle, as Harry loaded Chief and Hope into his blue one. He added Harry's gun cases to Heath's UTV, which had more spare room.

By the time Harry climbed into her seat, Heath had

loaded their provisions and was behind the wheel, talking the dogs into settling.

Clay led the way down the road, past the barn and stables, and along the fence line to the empty pasture they had visited when he had shown her the property. A variety of targets were set up and waiting for them.

The four dogs roamed and sniffed at every corner while the three of them unloaded and set up for practice.

Heath and Clay went about unzipping the four leather shotgun cases. "I brought our favorite guns, plus the one my mom used to use," said Clay, glancing back at Harry. "You can try them all and see which one works best for you."

He reached for the Beretta Vittoria first. "This was Mom's, and it will be the lightest." He handed it to Harry.

She liked the feel of it and admired the floral etching in the silver accents. Clay offered her the box of shells, and she walked over to the stand, where she would wait for the clay pigeon to appear.

Harry loaded two shells and snapped the shotgun closed. It had been a very long time since she shot clay pigeons. It was a different skillset than she used throughout her law enforcement career. Heath loaded the dogs into his UTV before the shooting started.

Clay stood by while she positioned herself with the majority of her weight on her front foot, knee slightly bent. She mounted the gun against her shoulder and rested the stock against her cheekbone.

She practiced the swinging arc motion she would need to follow the target. "Looks good. Just make sure your hands are relaxed. My dad used to say like you're holding a baby bird."

She loosened her grip and swung it again.

"Nice. Looks better." Clay stepped back and let her

practice a few more times. "When you're ready, just say the word. Heath is ready to run the trap."

The trap was set up to Harry's left, so at least she knew where the target would originate. She took a deep breath, relaxed, and said, "Pull."

The bright orange disc flew into the sky, and she followed it with the gun, matching the speed as best she could, and fired.

The disc fell, unscathed, to the ground.

"Darn, I missed," said Harry. She lined up again, and hollered, "pull."

Heath dispatched another target, and Harry followed it with her gun. This time she nicked the edge of it.

She removed the two spent shells and reloaded two more.

She missed again, but blasted the target with her second shot.

She continued to shoot and reload, until the entire box of twenty was gone, then took off her glasses and ear protection. "I think I've got the hang of it, and I like this gun."

Clay pointed at the other two. "Do you want to try any others?"

She wrinkled her nose and shook her head. "Nah, I think this one feels good and I'm getting dialed in with it."

Clay picked up the Browning Citori and loaded it. After twenty shots, twenty discs lay broken on the ground.

"Wow," said Harry, "looks like you're the ringer."

Clay chuckled. "Heath and I are pretty good on clay pigeons. We have more trouble with the handgun portion. We don't use them as much as we use shotguns and rifles." He trotted over to the trap to relieve Heath.

Heath used the Beretta Silver Pigeon, and did an admirable job of shooting nineteen out of twenty.

Clay rejoined them. "Shall we move to the handguns?"

He pointed to the right where target stands, each with a different bull's eye style target, stood at the ready.

Heath opened the ice chest. "I say we eat something first. I'm starving."

He brought out thick sandwiches, loaded with slices of roast chicken, plus bananas, and brownies. Clay had a thermos of coffee and hot tea at the ready, and they enjoyed a delicious meal in the crisp afternoon. The dogs were content with their bowl of water and a few cookies as they watched their humans eat.

Once lunch was over, they turned their attention to the targets. Harry had no problem shooting a perfect score with her sidearm and put all thirty rounds in the bull's eye. Heath and Clay were evenly matched, both scoring twenty-seven in the bull's eye.

Next, came the rifles. All three of them shot every target at all distances. The afternoon light began to disappear as they collected the brass and stowed their weapons.

By the time they pulled into the driveway, it was almost totally dark. Heath took off for the house to attend to his dinner preparations, and Harry stayed behind with Clay to unload things.

Harry and Clay made quick work of gathering all the gun cases and ammunition, and carrying them to the house with dogs following in their footsteps. The moment Harry stepped inside, the welcoming aroma of garlic and basil tickled her nose. Her stomach growled as she set her gear near the entry doors.

Clay motioned her to follow him down the hallway to the den. He turned on the big screen television and scrolled through some options on the remote. "I want to show you the video from last year's shoot, so you get an idea of what it's like."

He hit the play button, and Harry watched as several shooters went through the course. It reminded her of some of the training sessions she had participated in over her career. The targets were varied and included steel plates, paper, clay pigeons, and long range exploding targets.

Clay paused the video a few times to explain that the scoring was based on speed and accuracy, with penalty points awarded in seconds for faults or failure to hit or neutralize a target. "Where you can pick up time and points is in the pistol stage. If you hit the paper target in the bull's eye you only have to hit it once, or otherwise it's twice anywhere on the paper. With your skill, you could hit the paper blindfolded. It's just a matter of speed."

She watched the rest of the video and blew out a long breath. "I'll do my best, but this is a bit of a new experience."

"Luckily, we make our own rules here. Some of the pro contests, you literally run from one stage to the other and carry all your gear on you, and the time is cumulative. At least we do each stage on its own here and that way you only have to pack one weapon at a time."

Her eyes widened. "Yeah, that would take some practice for sure."

Clay gestured to the door. "I think dinner is probably close to ready."

After a quick stop at the powder room, Harry stepped into the kitchen, where Heath was adding the finishing touches to the serving dishes. She looked over his shoulder, and asked, "How are you still single? I would think you'd be beating the women off with a stick if your food is half as good as it smells."

He chuckled and lifted the pan of stuffed shells out of the oven. "It's a small town and the pickings are slim."

"I came from a much bigger place, and the pickings were

slim there, too. For me, I focused all my efforts on my career and gave up on dating and marriage long ago. I feel like that ship has sailed, but you're younger. You have more time."

"Ah, I never give up. I'm an eternal optimist. I just haven't met the right one yet. You sound like my brother. Since he lost Karen, he's put everything into Danny and this ranch."

She went about collecting plates and silverware for three, and setting them out on the granite counter. Heath directed her to the fridge to retrieve the salad bowl. After placing it on the counter, she filled their glasses with water.

Clay came through the doorway, the dogs at his heels. "I went ahead and fed these scoundrels. That way they can settle down while we eat." He pointed them toward the big rug and told them to lay down.

With the four of them lounging nearby, Clay turned his attention to the spread. "Wow, you've outdone yourself, Heath. This looks terrific."

"Mom's recipes. Hopefully, I did them justice." He pointed to the pan he had removed from the oven. "I did her creamy mushroom stuffed shells."

Clay's gaze wandered back to the penne with meat sauce. "And my favorite."

Heath added garlic bread and then took his seat. Harry loaded her plate and dug into her first bite of the creamy shells. "Oh, my gosh. This is restaurant quality, Heath. Really, it's superb."

"Well, thank you. The credit goes to my mom. She was a great cook and these are her creations."

As they ate, the conversation turned back to the upcoming shoot. Clay took another piece of garlic bread to soak up the extra sauce on his plate. "I gotta say, I'm liking our chances with Harry on the team. Even if we shot like we all shot today, we would have won last year."

Harry took a swallow of water. "I should probably practice with the shotgun again before next weekend. I shouldn't have a problem with the stationary targets, but clay pigeons flying overhead is another issue."

"Anytime," Clay said. "One of us will be around and can operate the trap for you."

Heath grinned. "You certainly don't need to practice with the handgun or rifle. That was some awesome shooting."

She waved away his compliment. "That's only because I've trained with those for so many years. It's like second nature. Muscle memory."

After eating their fill, the three of them worked together to get the dishes done and the kitchen cleaned. Heath insisted she take some of the leftovers home with her.

She laughed and said, "Okay, if you insist." She dished up servings into the plastic containers Heath unearthed from a cupboard. "I hate cooking, so am never too proud to take any leftovers."

She stacked her containers on the counter. "Oh, and don't forget I brought pie. I'm too stuffed to even consider it, but can cut some slices if you two want some."

Clay held up his hand. "Not right now. I ate way too much."

"I'll just leave it with you guys. I should be getting home."

"No need to rush off. We could watch a movie. Your choice."

Heath turned from his work at the sink. "Yeah, Harry. Stay for a movie, and then we'll be ready for pie."

She started to protest, and then realized she had nowhere she had to be and nothing she had to do. Socializing and small talk was not her forte, and her life had been devoid of both for years.

"I guess we could stay for a movie."

"Anybody want a coffee?" asked Heath.

Clay helped himself, and after getting a nod from Heath and Harry, poured two more cups. Harry noticed he and Clay drank their coffee the same way and she watched him add a tiny sprinkle of sugar to her cup.

The three of them and all four dogs wandered down the main hallway to the den, where the dogs were quick to climb onto one couch covered in blankets that was obviously reserved for them.

Harry settled into the couch in front of the large screen television and set her coffee on the side table, while Clay picked up the remote from his side of the couch. Heath stretched out in a recliner.

"We just finished the latest season of *Yellowstone*, but we're late to the game and haven't watched *Longmire*. Have you seen it?" asked Clay.

Harry shook her head. "No. I've heard good things but haven't had much time to watch things until recently."

"Does that work for you, Heath?"

"Sounds good to me."

Clay flicked the buttons on the remote, and moments later, the screen filled with the opening scene of season one.

The first episode kept Harry's attention as she focused on the small-town sheriff in Wyoming dealing with a murder and grieving the loss of his wife. She was immediately drawn into the story and the characters.

An hour later, she was hooked. Heath lowered the footrest of his recliner. "I think we need some pie before the next episode."

She started to get up, and Clay raised his hand. "No, you stay put. You're our guest." He and Heath left her with a roaring fire and the warmth of friendship, along with four passed out dogs.

She couldn't remember the last time she had enjoyed a day like today. One filled with fun activities, lots of laughter, delicious food, and the kindness of friends. Lavender Valley was growing on her.

CHAPTER NINETEEN

O ver the next week, along with falling in love with the handmade soaps from Cranberry Cottage, Harry got into a new exercise routine and without the responsibility of the morning chores, took the dogs for a long walk every mid-morning. They loved roaming the land and exploring every piece of bark and blade of grass they found, and she got to burn a few calories on their five-mile jaunt.

On Wednesday, she made a trip to the Nolan Ranch to practice with the shotgun. Clay met her at the door with a fresh copy of the new edition of the *Lavender Valley News*.

She cringed as she read the headline. Harry's role in taking down the mayor was still the top story. The city council had voted to have a special election to fill the vacancy, and in the meantime would fill the position with an interim mayor. Curt Mansfield had done some man-on-the-street polling to see who the residents thought would be a good interim mayor, and they overwhelmingly voiced their support for Harry McKenzie.

He even printed her official photo from the Salem Police

Department. She sighed and handed the paper back to Clay, who was grinning.

"Here less than a month and already our favorite celebrity," he joked.

She shook her head. "People are funny, aren't they? I mean nobody here really knows me and yet they want to put me in charge of their town? I would be a horrible mayor."

Clay frowned as he led her outside to the UTV. "Why do you say that?"

"I'm way too bossy. I don't enjoy meetings and all that nonsense. I'm all about taking action to fix a problem or find a solution, and not sitting around and yacking about it." She blew out a long breath as she buckled her seatbelt. "I guess I don't play well with others. I'm used to being in charge and I think mayors are meant to be more collaborative. Not to mention, I have to figure out how to run Jewel's farm."

They were dogless today, with Harry leaving her two at home and Heath in charge of the other two. It didn't take Harry long to burn through a box of shells, where she blasted every target thrown at her. Her form and shots were flawless.

Clay drove them back to the house, and they made arrangements to meet again on Friday for one more practice session.

Harry squeezed in a quick practice at the Nolan Ranch early Friday morning and was in awe of all the people already coming and going, setting up for Saturday's festivities. Tents, tables, chairs, the largest barbecue grill she'd ever seen, along with people scattered about the venue, installing the targets.

When she got home, she checked her mailbox and almost

fainted with delight at the appearance of two pieces of junk mail.

She'd never been so happy to see the slick postcards for deals on tax preparation and Valentine's Day flowers, both of which would soon be recycled. Harry took the two forwarded advertisements as a sign that the logjam of her mail being held up must be breaking.

It was already February and she was anxious to hear from Olivia, Lydia, Georgia, and Micki. She had to get serious about a plan without them, since it was possible, even likely, she'd be facing the farm alone.

She had skipped her morning walk, so after a quick snack, she took Hope and Chief on the loop around the property. Once back home, she lit a fire and hunkered down with Jewel's notebooks. With the lavender fields established, Harry could manage watering them and tending to them with Tyler's help.

The animal sanctuary and taking care of multiple dogs was going to be tricky to do alone. She was no expert when it came to dogs. Clay had mentioned the veterinarian, Duke Walker, and Jewel's notes referenced him often. She needed to make the time to meet him. Harry scribbled his name on her notepad of things to do.

As the afternoon disappeared, she noticed the time, and tapped in the number to the restaurant in Yakima where Lydia worked. The same woman answered the phone.

She introduced herself again. "I sent Lydia a letter in care of the restaurant and was hoping it arrived. Is it possible to get her another message?"

The woman sighed. "I've got the letter right here at my desk. I'm afraid Lydia isn't here at the moment. She needed some time off and I expect she'll be back in the next couple of weeks, but I promise I'll get it to her. I did pass on your message."

"Oh, I see. If you happen to hear from her, please let her know I'm anxious to speak with her. I don't suppose you have a contact number for her?"

"I'm sorry. I did try to phone her when your letter arrived, and her number is no longer in service."

Harry thanked her and disconnected the call.

She reached over and rubbed the top of Hope's head. "Something's weird about Lydia. Jewel had faith I could find her. I hope she's right."

Saturday morning, Harry woke to sunshine and took a short walk to loosen up for the contest. Clay and Heath had invited her to the ranch early for breakfast before the shoot and told her she could bring Hope and Chief, who could hang out with Maverick and Ace at the house.

She loaded her SUV with her gun cases and lots of ammunition, plus her range bag. She had to convince Chief to leave his slipper and blanket behind. "You're not staying the night, buddy. This is just a playdate."

It took a few minutes, but he relented and dropped them both by the door and then she added the two dogs to her cargo and headed next door.

The gate was open, and she drove to the house. The venue was set up in the pasture closest to the barn and stables to allow for easy access and parking, and the tops of the white tents stood out against the green.

Clay met her at the door to welcome her and the dogs inside. "Go on into the kitchen. We've got breakfast almost ready. I've got a quick call to make."

Harry found Heath at the cooktop. A woman with white hair was setting a stack of plates on the island, and she greeted Harry with a warm smile.

Heath turned from the pan of eggs. "Harry, this is Clara. She's our faithful and much-loved housekeeper, and is joining us for breakfast today."

Harry stepped forward and extended her hand. "Pleasure to meet you, Clara."

Clara folded the last napkin and gripped Harry's hand. "Oh, I'm thrilled to meet you. You're the talk of the town."

Harry's jaw tightened. "Well, hopefully, they will have some other news to take my place soon."

Clara's blue eyes twinkled as she met Harry's. "I wouldn't count on that. Everybody wants you to be the next mayor. They want someone they can trust, who is honest and has our best interests at heart."

Harry smiled and stepped back to let Heath deliver the pan of cheesy eggs to the island counter. Clara took a bowl of sliced fruit from the fridge.

Clay came through the doorway, and Heath put him to work getting the bacon from the oven, while he buttered a stack of warm toast.

Moments later, a young man wearing a cowboy hat appeared at the patio door. "Come on in, Hank," hollered Clay.

Hank removed his hat and nodded at Harry. "Ma'am."

"It's Harry," she said. "Nice to meet you."

As Hank shook Harry's hand, Clara rested her hand on his arm. "This is my son." She turned to meet his eyes and smiled. "This is the lady in the paper who helped get our crooked mayor arrested."

"Great to meet you," said Hank.

Clay brought the pan of bacon to the island. "We're doing

this buffet style today, so load your plate and sit anywhere you'd like. Dining room, great room, even the patio."

It was chilly, but sunny, and Harry took her plate out to the patio table to enjoy the gorgeous view.

Soon, the others joined her, with Clara pouring coffee in all the cups and adding a plate stacked with toast to the table, and Clay turning on the patio heater. As they dug into their loaded plates, they praised the cooks.

Clay turned to Clara. "Harry brought her two dogs over to stay with Maverick and Ace today, so you'll have a couple more to keep track of for us."

He met Harry's eyes across the table. "Clara and Hank will stay here at the house to keep an eye on things and assist anyone who needs anything."

Clara reached for a piece of toast. "It's always one of my favorite days, outside of our big Christmas event."

Heath laughed. "Don't rush it now, Clara. We just got done with Christmas."

Clay went inside to retrieve more coffee for everyone. As he poured Harry's, he said, "We host a little Christmas shindig each year. Horse and carriage rides, crafts, cocoa, a few contests. It's lots of fun, and a way to give back to the community, plus a little nod to our mom. She loved Christmas."

Clara reached for her warmed up coffee cup. "It's really a wonderful day, and everyone loves it."

Heath finished his last bite and looked across the table at Clara. "But today is all about the shoot, and you might want to make room for that trophy. I have a feeling we'll be bringing it back this year." He winked at Harry.

Clay slid his chair from the table. "Well, we better get to it. Harry, if you want to load your stuff into the UTV, you can ride over with me."

She nodded and gathered her plate.

Clara shook her head. "Just leave that dear. I'll take care of it, and Hank and I will watch over your dogs. You enjoy the day."

"Thank you, Clara. I appreciate that. Hopefully, they behave for you."

Harry gave Chief and Hope a thorough petting and made them promise to be good before she hurried to her vehicle to gather her gun cases and ammo. She made her way to the back of the house and added her gear to Clay's UTV.

Minutes later, they parked in a line of other four wheelers and golf carts, and hauled their bags to a tent with a huge Nolan Ranch banner across the front of it. A hot beverage service was set up at a table, and catering staff was busy putting out snacks, bottles of water, juice, and iced tea.

Padded folding chairs encircled round tables with white cloths scattered about the tent, and long tables made up the perimeter where shooters could store their gear while they took a break.

A tall man with a thick mustache, wearing a black cowboy hat and holding a clipboard, stepped into the tent. He nodded at Harry as he stepped closer to Clay and Heath. He clapped Clay on the back.

Clay turned and smiled, shaking the man's hand. After a brief conversation, Clay turned toward Harry. "Ted is our rangemaster and shoot director. This is Harry McKenzie. She joined our team this year."

Ted touched his fingers to the rim of his hat. "Ah, I've read all about you in the paper. My pleasure to meet you." He turned his clipboard toward her. "I just need you to sign the waiver." He handed her a pen.

Clay added, "Ted and his team of volunteers run the whole event, set up, scoring, safety, the works."

Harry scanned the disclaimer and waiver language, then signed her name and handed the clipboard back to Ted. "Well, I'm a newbie, but I'm looking forward to it. It should be a fun day."

Someone called Ted's name. "Duty calls, I'm afraid," he said. "Best of luck today, Harry." He tipped his hat and made his way to the tent opening, where a young man waited for him.

Moments later, Heath joined them. "I just went to the team captains' meeting. We're up seventh in the lineup."

Clay nodded. "That works. We've got twelve teams this year, so middle of the pack is a good spot."

"I'm glad we're not first," said Harry. "At least I'll have a chance to observe a few shooters."

Heath grabbed a bottle of water from the table. "We always do shotgun first, then rifle, then pistol. So, that's the order. Each team will complete the shotgun stage, and then we'll all move to the rifle range. It keeps everyone focused and safe, plus gives the spectators the opportunity to watch every event."

Harry nodded. "So, I better get my vest." Clay had loaned her a lightweight vest that held twenty-four shells, to make reloading quick and easy.

The deep voice of an announcer came through the speakers to let them know they had thirty minutes before the shoot started.

The three of them slipped into their vests, donned their eye and ear protection, and carried their shotgun cases to the staging area. When they arrived, Heath turned to Harry. "For this one, I'll go first, then you, then Clay. He's our best shooter for this stage."

Harry nodded. "Got it, and it looks like they've got two

traps, so they'll be coming from either direction. Plus, a line of clay pigeons mounted on posts."

Clay looked across the field. "And they could use both traps at once, you never know."

Harry focused her attention on the first team of three as the first shooter took his place.

He shot the line of five clay pigeons mounted on the posts, and the two observers called to let everyone know he'd hit the targets, barely chipping the last one, but that was all that was required for a hit.

Once done, the shooter moved to the stand, where he would await the trap action. A total of six clay pigeons were launched, two from each side, and two at once, crossing in front of the shooter. The shooter missed one of them.

Harry's heart beat faster. That was going to be a challenge for her.

It didn't take long for the eighteen shooters in front of them to complete the first stage, and Harry glanced at the scoreboard with the team times before they checked in with the scorers. So far, Team Ranchland was in the lead with the time to beat.

Heath took his position and made quick work of the six mounted targets, then pulled off a flawless performance getting all six of the pigeons launched from the trap.

Harry was up. Like she had practiced hundreds of times, she quieted her mind, filtered out the background noise, and became one with the shotgun. When she heard the horn blast, she picked off the six targets, reloading between, like all the shooters had before her. She waited for the first pigeon and blasted it from the sky, then obliterated the second one. After she reloaded, the next two came at the same time. She concentrated on breathing and keeping her hands relaxed, watching as the two bright orange objects moved closer together.

She swung the shotgun, aiming for the one from the left. She blew it apart and moved the gun slightly, hoping her timing was on point and resisted every ounce of her that begged to hold her breath, as she pulled the trigger for the second time.

Time stood still as she watched for her shot to hit the target.

If she missed, the penalty would decimate their score.

CHAPTER TWENTY

Harry was still moving the shotgun through the arc, when she caught a glimpse of a piece flying off the pigeon. She had nicked it before it dropped to the ground. She ejected the two shells and reached for another off her vest. The welcome shout of "hit" came from the score table, and Harry focused on reloading as quickly as she could.

With the knowledge that the worst was over and she managed to score four hits, she relaxed and waited for the next target. She took out the last two without a problem and carried the shotgun back to the staging area.

Clay stepped forward and had a clean sweep of all twelve targets. The spectators cheered and the three shooters on Team Nolan walked over to the scoring table.

Harry checked the team score first, and smiled. They were now in the lead. They had the best time and no faults.

She studied their individual scores and saw that Clay was the quickest, Heath was only one second off of Clay's, and Harry was two seconds behind him. She could live with that.

With the rush of adrenaline during her competition,

Harry felt beyond warm. She carried her bag back to the tent and gulped down a water, then stepped over to get an iced tea. As she bent to select a bottle, a hand gripped her shoulder.

"Nice job, Harry," said Clay, smiling. "Ranchland is the team that beat us last year, so we're in a good spot." He gestured to one of the empty round tables. "You've got time for a break before the rifle stage. It will probably be close to forty-five minutes. We usually take a fifteen-minute break between each stage."

She slipped into a chair and took a sip from her bottle of tea. "That should be less stressful."

A few people were milling about the tent, and several of them approached the table. Clay introduced Harry to Joe, the owner of Ranchland, and Jim, who owned the feed store. Both of them complemented her on her shooting and then heaped praise on her for her role in taking down Mayor Crawford.

She thanked them and said goodbye as Clay wandered off with them. Then, she caught a wave from the other side of the room. Laurie from Winding River Coffee hurried to her table. "Hey, Harry. Nice shooting today."

"Thanks, and it's nice to see you out of your apron."

"I'm here with my husband. He and his friends have a team. So, are you going to run for mayor? Everybody sure hopes so."

Harry laughed and shook her head. "No, I've got my hands full with Jewel's farm, and am not much of a politician."

"That's perfect. We don't need a politician. We need someone who is honest and puts Lavender Valley first."

"I agree with that. I'm sure there is someone local that fits that bill and knows the area much better than I do."

Heath interrupted them. "Hey, Harry, it's time to get our gear."

Thankful to get away from yet another conversation about the mayoral election, Harry promised she'd see Laurie at the coffee shop and joined Heath.

Heath grabbed Clay's bag and rifle as well as his own, and the two of them made their way through the crowd to the pasture designated for the rifle contest.

Clay was already there, talking with a group of people at the fence line. Heath and Harry joined him. Heath looked out across the field. "Looks like they've set it up so we walk through the course and find the targets as we go." There was a clear path for shooters, marked by bales of hay and fences, and the way it was constructed, it was difficult to see the entire course.

As the announcer's voice came through the speakers, calling for the first team to enter the staging area, Clay's visitors left. He turned to Heath and Harry. "Are we ready?"

They both nodded. "With the shotgun behind me, I'm feeling better," said Harry.

Clay grinned. "I think we're going to do great in these next two stages. We've got a great chance of winning."

Harry's jaw tensed. "Don't get too cocky, now. Anything can happen. Remember, this style is all new to me."

Heath chuckled. "All I can say is if the shotgun was your weakness, I'm feeling pretty good right now."

The starting horn blared, and the first shooter took off down the path. The plink of shots hitting steel plates drifted through the air as the man went further into the field.

Harry double checked her vest and made sure she had two full magazines ready to go. This stage of the event moved quickly, and within a few minutes, the shooter emerged from the other side of the pasture, having completed the rifle portion of the contest.

Heath wandered over to the scoring table and when he returned, he reported Team Ranchland was in the lead in the rifle portion of the competition. Once again, they were the team to beat.

This time, Clay was shooting first for their team. Harry felt a nervous flutter as Clay started out. She was next. She was used to shooting from a stationary position, but after watching last year's video, had practiced a few targets on the move. If this was more of a normal shoot, or normal for her anyway, her confidence would be much higher.

Minutes later, Clay returned from the course and headed straight for the scoring table. Harry took her position, and as soon as the loud horn blared, she took off for the first target. It was a simple bull's eye on paper, and she hit the center with one hit. Next came a set of steel plates, all bright orange and lined up in a row. She ticked off each of them.

She turned the corner and was faced with a stack of tractor tires she used as a rest to hit a target mounted to a tree trunk about a hundred yards away. She dialed in on it and hit it with one shot.

A moving windmill of steel plates was the next target. The satisfaction of hearing each shot ping off the plate boosted Harry's confidence. She wasn't sure about her time, but she was deadly accurate.

Next, she encountered the familiar silhouette targets she had shot for three decades and had no problem hitting the inner circle with one shot on each of them. She reloaded as she made her way through the path. She climbed hay bales to shoot at distant targets and used a heavy tree branch as a rest for another exploding target that was the longest, at four hundred yards.

The course ended with another section of steel plates at different distances, and when she heard the clink of the bullet hitting the last one, and the scoring monitor shout out "time," she breathed a sigh of relief and walked down the pathway to the exit.

She had no faults, but wasn't as confident on her speed.

As she made her way to the score table, Heath was getting ready to take off to meet the first target.

She checked the column for her score and saw she had beat Clay by two seconds. They were on track to beat Team Ranchland, if Heath did well.

Minutes later, Heath met them at the scoring table, shaking his head. "I blew it. I slipped on the hay bale and lost some time."

They waited for the tally sheet. After a quick glance, Heath mumbled and walked away from them. Clay pointed at the total and shook his head. "Ranchland got us on this stage, but by less than a second."

"So, we still have a chance if we beat them on this next round, right?"

Clay gritted his teeth. "Yeah, we have a chance, but Heath needs to get his head on straight. I'm going to go talk to him. I'll come find you in the tent."

Harry nodded, took her rifle and bag, and made her way to the tent for a bottle of water. While she was sitting at the table, doing her best to clear her head and relax, a tall man with a warm smile and a full head of silvery hair walked up to her. "Ms. McKenzie," he said, extending his hand. "I'm Will Hatch. A friend of Clay's and on the city council. Mind if I join you?"

She shook his hand and smiled. "He's mentioned you." She pointed at the chair next to her. "Have a seat."

He took the chair, his hand resting on a bottle of iced tea. "Nice shooting out there."

"Thanks, I'm just hoping we can do well in this next stage. I know how much the contest means to Clay and Heath."

"They're good men, like their daddy was." He took a sip from his bottle. "I'm sure you've heard all the chatter about town regarding the vacant mayor's position. The council members are looking for someone to act as our interim mayor and your name has been mentioned several times."

She held up her hand. "I'm flattered, truly, but I'm not looking for a job in politics. I'm barely retired and am just here trying to do what Jewel wanted in taking care of her place this year. I didn't do anything special, just reached out to help."

He winked at her. "Well, everybody in Lavender Valley thinks it was pretty special. I understand, and will convey your gracious response to the council members. We've got some other ideas and will get the position filled until the special election in March can take place." He shook his head. "What a mess, huh?"

She nodded. "It's rough, especially in a small town where it feels so personal."

He stood. "I can take the heat off of you for the interim job, but fair warning, our phones are ringing constantly with people in town telling us you have to run for mayor. They love you."

She chuckled. "They don't really even know me. I just stepped in and helped out because I had the time and the skillset. I'm sure you can recruit someone more suited to run."

"I'll give it a try," he said. He reached for his tea and winked at her. "Best of luck, Harry. Please pass that on to Clay and Heath. I'll be rooting for all of you."

She'd just retrieved and holstered her handgun, and was adding another magazine to her vest, when Clay and Heath approached her. They were both smiling, and Heath looked less stressed.

"Looks like you're ready," said Clay. "We just ran into Will on our way in and he said he tried to convince you to take the interim mayor's position."

She rolled her eyes. "If I hear the word mayor one more time, I swear." She snapped her head in Clay's direction. "I think *you* should take it. Everybody loves you and knows you. It's only for a couple of months. You'd be great."

He held up his hand. "No, no, I'm way too busy here at the ranch, and you've made your point. I'm just teasing you."

She sighed. "I know. I just need to focus on this next round."

Heath finished the last swallow of water from his bottle. "Right. We decided to have you go last on this stage. You're the strongest shooter."

She blew out a breath. "Nothing like a little extra pressure."

Clay put his hand on her shoulder. "Look, if we win it will be great and if we don't it'll be fine. Heath and I made way too much of the trophy. It's just a great day to honor our dad, win or lose."

The announcer called for the first team to report to the staging area. Team Nolan followed the crowd and made their way to the third and final contest. Like the rifle course, this one was set up with obstacles and pathways, so all the targets weren't visible.

Once Team Ranchland was finished, Clay and Harry wandered over to the scoring table to check their time. They were in the lead and were going to be tough to beat.

It wasn't long before they were called to the staging area,

and Heath, with his hand resting on his holster, took off at the sound of the horn.

The plunk of bullets hitting steel and the sound of shots fired echoed throughout the property. Minutes later, Heath came through the archway of hay bales that marked the end of the course.

He met Clay's eyes and shrugged. Clay was set and ready at the starting line.

Harry focused on breathing and relaxing while she waited for him to finish. Not wanting the extra pressure, she didn't look at the times. This should be the easiest stage for her. She had shot tens of thousands of rounds through her handgun, and it was almost an extension of herself. She could do this.

She was called to the starting point, and at the signal, took off to meet her first target.

Silhouettes were up first, and she took out two on each side of the trail with one shot each, center mass. Next came a few steel plates close to the trail, and then a much longer shot. The satisfying ping of the bullet against the plate sent Harry rushing to the next target. She zeroed in on the bull's eye, hitting each with one shot.

Three more silhouettes at greater distances went down as easily as the first ones. She was in the zone and was confident in her rhythm. She reloaded as she ran to the last leg of the course.

It consisted of pop-up targets that appeared as she walked the pathway. It reminded her of her shoot-don't shoot training days. The course ended with another moving set of steel plates. When the last plate pinged, she heard the coveted "time" shouted from one of the observers and holstered her gun.

With a bit of trepidation, she walked over to the score

table. Heath and Clay were already there, waiting for the results.

As she stepped closer, the announcer's voice pierced the air. "Folks, can we have your attention for just a moment. We need the last shooter, Harry McKenzie, to bring her handgun and step over to the judges' table please."

Harry frowned. No other shooters had been asked to report to the judges' table. Her high spirits began to falter.

Clay pointed to the other side of the pasture, where a small tent stood over several tables and chairs. "What's going on?" she asked.

He shrugged. "I don't know."

As she made her way across the grass, she replayed the course in her mind. Had she made a mistake or done something wrong? She didn't think so.

Her heart beat faster as she approached the tent.

CHAPTER TWENTY-ONE

Three men were seated behind a skirted table. A tall trophy with a dark wooden base and a golden figure of guns and a target mounted atop it, gleamed on a side table. Harry stepped forward. "I'm Harry McKenzie."

"We just need to take a look at your weapon and ammunition, please," said the man in the middle.

Harry released the magazine and made sure the chamber was clear before setting it in front of him. She extracted the other magazine she had used from her vest and added it to the table.

He picked up the gun, along with the magazines, and looked them over before passing them to the other two judges. They nodded at each other.

"Is there a problem?" asked Harry, in a voice she hoped didn't reveal her irritation.

The judge in the middle slid the gun and magazines back to her. "No, no problem. It's just a technicality. We have to do a physical examination when anyone breaks a record." He grinned at her.

"Your time on the course beats the old record set over twenty years ago by over three seconds. That's quite impressive." He went on to explain that although the course setup varied each year, the length and number of targets was the same.

One of the other judges looked over at the announcer and nodded.

He picked up his microphone and said, "Folks, your attention please. Join me in congratulating Harry McKenzie. She's just broken the old record for the handgun stage of our event, beating the time set by Dusty Bailey over twenty years ago. How about a big round of applause for our newest shooter to join us and give such a spectacular performance. I'd say the Nolan brothers made a fine addition to their team this year. Rumor has it Harry could even be our next mayor."

She resisted the urge to throw something at the announcer. The crowd roared with hoots and whistles. Harry tried to smile as she re-holstered her gun, her cheeks blossoming. Feeling every eye watching her, she hurried across the pasture, back to where Clay and Heath waited.

They both beamed and pointed at the score sheet. Thanks to her record-breaking time, they had a comfortable lead over Team Ranchland. Heath put an arm around her shoulder. "Well done, Harry. That's some shooting."

She smiled. "I'm happy with the time. Could have done without the drama from the judges and that bit about being the mayor from the announcer."

Clay clamped his hand on her other shoulder. "You did an awesome job. Sorry, you became a spectacle. I know that's not your thing."

"Not your fault. I was just nervous I'd broken a rule or something."

Heath dropped his arm from her shoulder. "That's why they had to check your gun. Just to make sure you weren't pulling any funny business. They haven't seen a time like that in a long time."

Clay laughed. "I wish Dad was here. She beat his best time." He met Harry's eyes. "If we get that trophy back home where it belongs, you name it, Harry. Whatever you want, we'll make it happen. You deserve it after such a fine performance."

She arched her brows. "Oh, my. I'm going to have think about that."

They made their way back to the tent and helped themselves to coffee and cookies. As they snacked, people wandered by the table, congratulating Harry and shaking her hand, while whispering their hopes that she would run for mayor.

When the announcer's voice came through the speakers, inviting everyone to the buffet line for the barbecue, Harry breathed a sigh of relief. She extricated herself from the current conversation with the owner of the boutique near the Back Door Bistro.

By the time she and Clay reached the line, Harry was starving. She loaded her plate with meat and salads, and made her way back to the tent, where she helped herself to a bottle of iced tea.

Clay and Heath weren't far behind and joined her at the table, with their plates piled high. Every bite Harry took was scrumptious. Clay explained the ranch furnished the meat and manned the grill, and everyone else pitched in with side dishes to share.

Harry finished off the delicious baked beans with bacon, then took a bite of a grape salad, laced with nuts and a creamy dressing. "Well, it's all terrific."

"There's plenty, so take some leftovers home, if you want," offered Heath.

"Don't tempt me," she said with a grin.

As they finished the meal, the announcer invited everyone to the judges' tent, where in ten minutes the final results would be announced and the trophy awarded.

They bused their table and joined the other participants and spectators making their way to the judges' tent.

After thanking everyone for coming and praising Clay and Heath for hosting the event, the senior judge announced the top three teams, with Team Nolan as the winner. Applause and shouts of encouragement erupted from the crowd, and the three teammates walked toward the judge. He presented each of them with a medal and handed the tall trophy to Clay.

The crowd quieted down, and the judge continued, "We also have a special award for Harry McKenzie, who earns our Outstanding Shooter Award for her record-breaking performance." The crowd roared, and with a smile, Harry accepted the crystal paperweight and posed for a photo with the judges.

As soon as the photo was taken, the judge added. "We need to get your name engraved on it at the shop over in Medford. We'll get that done this week and get it back to you."

"Wonderful," said Harry. "Thanks again."

She joined Heath and Clay for another photo, this time for the newspaper, and Curt introduced himself. "My pleasure to meet you, Harry. I'm sure you've seen my articles mentioning you."

"Indeed, I have," said Harry. Her media training had taught her to be tight-lipped when it came to the press. "It's nice to meet you." She shook his hand, then walked between Heath and Clay as they made their way back to the tent.

Curt hollered out after her. "Can I quote you on anything, Harry?"

She turned and smiled. "It was a great day of shooting." She hurried after the two brothers, happy to have somewhere to go.

They finally got back to the tent, where celebratory cupcakes were scattered on the dessert table. Each had a bull's eye target on them, and Darcy beamed from behind the table when Harry complimented her.

"Thanks for delivering, Darcy. These look awesome," Clay said, taking two of the chocolate frosted confections.

Heath left them to enjoy their desserts and steaming mugs of fresh coffee to talk to someone across the tent. Clay breathed deep as he looked at the trophy he had placed in the middle of their table. "What a day, huh?"

Harry nodded. "It was intense, but fun." She squinted at the trophy. "Hey, how come they already have Team Nolan engraved on the little plaque for this year? He told me they'd have to add my name to the paperweight."

Clay chuckled. "Well, as you can see," he pointed at the gold plaques that filled all four sides of the wooden base. "It's statistically in our favor. They probably had one made up with our name and Ranchland's, just in case. It usually comes down to the two teams fighting it out for first place."

She nodded as she took in the decades worth of wins displayed on the trophy.

"The Most Valuable Shooter, that's a different story. They never know who that will be."

Several shooters and spectators came up to the table to congratulate Harry and Clay. Amid the many accolades, Harry had to endure their requests for her to run for mayor.

She thanked each of them but was steadfast in her decision to focus on the farm and stay out of politics.

As the day wound down, people began to leave. Staff members arrived to take down the tents and restore the pristine pasture to its former condition. Harry gathered her bag and cases, and walked over to the UTV. Clay and Heath met her as she loaded her things.

"Hey, you can take this back to the house if you want. Heath and I are going to stick around and help clean up," said Clay. "Keys are in it."

Heath added, "Also, Clara has some leftovers all boxed up for you, so be sure to grab those before you head home."

"Tomorrow, if you're up for it, we can take that horseback ride I promised you," said Clay.

Heath clapped his brother on the back. "And, I'll make dinner to celebrate our win."

"A girl would be foolish to pass up a horse and a meal. Count me in," said Harry, with a wide grin. "I had a fun today. Thanks again."

She climbed into the driver's seat and started the engine, giving the two brothers a wave as she made for the house. She was tired and ready for a quiet evening with the dogs and a fire.

CHAPTER TWENTY-TWO

Monday morning, Harry groaned as she got out of bed. She was sore everywhere. Yesterday's ride on Merlot had been fabulous. After breakfast at the ranch, Clay led them on a scenic ride of their property and then crossed over to Jewel's farm to show Harry the tree by the lake, where Jewel specified she wanted her ashes and those of Chuck to be interred.

They spent time there, taking in the beautiful view, which Harry knew would be even prettier in the spring and summer. That task weighed on her. It was important to celebrate Jewel's life and lay both her and Chuck to rest on the land they treasured. That, and so many other things, hinged on the decisions Olivia, Micki, Lydia, and Georgia would make.

After feeding the dogs breakfast, she took a long, hot shower, hoping the warm water would soothe her achy muscles. The dogs had been ignored this weekend, and looked at her hopefully with their gentle eyes. As soon as she got dressed, had some coffee, and swallowed a couple of pain relievers, she took them out for their morning walk.

She breathed in the fresh air, laced with the scent of woodsmoke, fresh grass, and pine. She only had two months before things would get beyond busy with the growing season.

Last night, after another of Heath's incredible meals, she'd voiced her concerns about the possibility of having to manage the farm and festival alone. Clay assured her he would help, and between them and everyone in Lavender Valley, they would pull together to staff the festival and make sure it went off without a hitch.

It had been a long time, perhaps all the way back to when she and Tim had been partners on the force since she felt like someone had her back and would mount any obstacle to help her. Jewel and Chuck always made her feel supported, but her career path had been a lonely one. Years of hard work, steadfast focus, and fierce independence.

Those were qualities that would get her through this next challenge. Jewel's words from her letter voiced themselves in Harry's mind. *I believe you're all at a point in your lives where you need your sisters and I often think of the five of you as sisters of the heart.*

Harry trusted Jewel, but she was losing patience waiting for a reply from the others. Now that her junk mail was arriving, she would give it a few more days and then get serious about reaching out to each of them again.

When she and the dogs arrived back at the house, the dogs took off at a sprint. Clay's truck was in the yard.

She caught up with them at the donkeys' pasture. Clay was leaning on the fence talking to Tyler, while the three dogs were busy spinning in circles.

She wandered over "You'd think those three hadn't seen each other in days."

Clay laughed. Tyler said his goodbyes as he loaded the golf cart with supplies to take care of a fence in need of mending.

When he drove away, Harry smiled up at Clay. "Coffee?" she asked.

Clay touched his fingers to the brim of his hat. "I could be persuaded." He followed her to the house, where she toweled off the dogs' paws and led the way inside.

Clay added a log to the fire, and the three dogs flopped down in front of it. He joined Harry in the kitchen, where she was retrieving the sugar and cream for him.

He stirred both into his cup and grinned at Harry. "How ya feeling this morning?"

She eyed him above the rim of her cup. "Great, how about you?"

"Oh, I thought you might be sore from the ride."

She would never divulge how much her thighs burned and her knees ached. She wasn't exactly out of shape, but wasn't accustomed to using those muscles as much as she had yesterday. "A little, but not bad."

"Anytime you want to ride, just let me know. You're welcome to take Merlot out whenever you want."

"That's kind of you. She's a beautiful horse, and very patient with me."

He took a sip from his cup. "Um, I was wondering if you're doing anything this weekend. Well, Saturday night to be specific."

She shook her head. "No, my calendar is wide open.

"Heath, he's on the volunteer fire department, and, well anyway, they have a Valentine's Dinner and Dance each year.

I wondered if you might want to go." He took another sip. "I mean, with me."

A flutter rippled through Harry's stomach. He was almost shy the way he was asking her. He was a friend and a neighbor – but if she removed the friendship and neighbor boxes, he was a handsome man. His eyes were enough to draw any woman into them. He was in good shape, polite, honest, and kind. She'd never been into Valentine's Day, but this wasn't about that. There was no question this time. He was asking her out. On a date. Should she go out with him? Her stomach fluttered again.

"Um, sure, but I have to warn you, I am no dancer."

Relief flooded his charming blue eyes. "Well, this is a little bit different type of dance. It's not high heels and tuxedos; it's boots and hats and line dancing."

"That beats high heels." She grinned and took another sip from her mug. "Still, don't expect much out of me."

"We could go to Rooster's on Thursday, just to practice a bit."

"Oh, that's right. You mentioned Tuesday Trivia. That sounded fun, too."

"I'll get Heath to get us a couple more team members, and we can plan on it."

"Great, so let me know what time, and I'll see you Tuesday and Thursday," she said, still feeling a little out of her element. She couldn't remember the last date she'd been on, but couldn't discount the admiration she felt for Clay. He was kind and such a help to everyone.

He slid off the chair and reached for his hat. "It's a date." His gaze dropped for a second. "Well, uh, not really a date, I guess. You know what I meant. We'll pick you up Tuesday for tacos and trivia. Does six work?"

"Perfect," Harry said, stifling a chuckle at his verbal

gymnastics. Apparently, he felt as strange about it being a date as she did.

Tuesday, Harry left Chief and Hope with a cookie when she hurried out to the door to Clay's pickup. She met him at the bottom of the porch steps.

"Heath's in the backseat. I cleaned it to get rid of the dog hair, but made him sit back there in case I missed a spot." He grinned as he opened the passenger door for her.

"Being around Chief, I've come to accept the stray hair or two. There's no getting around the shedding." She climbed into her seat and said hello to Heath.

"So, are you ready for another win tonight? One of my buddies from the fire department, Justin, and his wife Carolyn, are joining our team."

She fastened the buckle of her seatbelt. "You guys are so competitive. Remember, I've never been on a trivia team or played the game, so don't get your hopes up."

Clay put the truck in gear. "Yeah, we tend to overdo it on the competition stuff. We'll just have fun tonight, okay?" He glanced into the rearview mirror and found his brother's eyes.

"For sure. I just like the idea of winning."

"What's the prize?" asked Harry.

"Free burgers and drinks," said Heath.

Clay laughed. "The stakes are high."

When they were about halfway to town, Clay glanced over at Harry. "Oh, did you hear the news? You're off the hook for the interim mayor. They met this morning and appointed a retired judge to the spot."

"Oh, that's great news. I know everybody means well, but

I've been avoiding going to town because I'm so tired of saying I don't want the job."

In Rooster's, one side was filled with tables surrounding the bar. Neon signs, license plates, flags, military memorabilia, black and white photos, and humorous signs decorated the walls. The shiny wooden bar was inlaid with a copper stripe, and saddles were mounted on a few barstools.

The other side of the building was ringed with booths and a few tables. Clay pointed in that direction. "They empty that floor area for line dancing on Thursday."

"These tables by the bar are all reserved for trivia teams," He chose a table with six chairs, and Clay gestured for Harry to take the chair next to Heath. "I'll go put in our order. Tacos all around? And what are you drinking, Harry?"

"How about an Arnold Palmer or iced tea, if they don't offer that, and I've been dreaming of tacos since you told me about them." She reached for her pocket, where she had stashed some cash.

He waved his hand at her. "No, non-alcoholic drinks are free for trivia teams and tacos are a buck. My treat." He winked and turned toward the bar.

Heath rolled his eyes. "My brother is such a big spender. He really knows how to impress a gal. Might explain why he never dates."

Harry glanced over where Clay was waiting in line. "I think it gets harder to put yourself out there as you age. I'm sure it's even harder for Clay having lost his wife."

"I hear ya," he said. "Losing Karen and then our mom was really hard on him. I think he's sort of resolved to being alone for the rest of his life. And, if you haven't noticed, Lavender Valley is small, especially when it comes to available women. The ones that aren't attached…let's just say there's a reason." His eyes twinkled with amusement.

She laughed, then became thoughtful. "I'm sort of like Clay, I guess. My work consumed my life, so it didn't leave much time for dating, and I never had much luck in that department. Now, it scares the living daylights out of me. I don't trust easily, which makes it hard to meet new people."

Heath smiled. "Well, you trust us, so that's progress."

"Jury's still out," she said, as Clay arrived with their drinks.

"Uh, oh," he said, setting Heath's beer in front of him. "What's with jury talk? I thought you were retired."

Heath took a sip from the tall glass. "Harry says she doesn't trust people easily, but I pointed out she trusts us."

Clay grinned as he slid into the chair on the other side of Harry. "I'd say she's a wise woman."

Harry reached for the Arnold Palmer. "I'm joking, you two. Jewel vouched for you, and although I don't have any firm memories of either of you from my time at Jewel's, I know she adored your parents. From what I've seen, they raised two incredible sons."

Clay lifted his iced tea. "Here's to Jewel for bringing us together."

They clinked their glasses as a server arrived with a huge platter of tacos, plus an assortment of salsa, lime wedges, hot sauce, and plates for the table.

"Are your friends coming soon?" asked Harry, sliding two tacos onto her plate.

Heath added four tacos to his. "They'll be here in time for the game, but not for tacos."

As they munched on tacos, the tables filled with team members. When Clay boasted he had ordered a flight of thirty tacos, Harry couldn't imagine they could eat that many, but she was able to eat five of them herself. In her defense, they were small, more like a street taco size. Plus they were beyond delicious.

Several people stopped by the table to say hello to Clay and Heath, and they introduced Harry to some new faces. When they learned her name, most of their eyes would open wider, and many gushed on about how they read the article in the paper last week, and that she had their vote. She tried to explain she wasn't running for mayor and they had filled the interim position, but after a few failed attempts, she let it go.

Justin and Carolyn arrived, and Heath introduced Harry, who thankfully didn't have to field questions about the mayoral election. Clay went to the bar and came back with sodas for both of them.

A man with red hair stepped to the microphone and welcomed everyone. Clay leaned over to Harry and whispered, "That's Rooster. His actual name is Marco Gallo, but he's been Rooster forever."

Harry nodded. "Gallo is rooster in Italian and Spanish, right?"

His brows rose. "I'm impressed. I knew we were right to have you join Team Whiskeypedia."

"That's your team name?" She laughed, then focused again on Rooster, who was going over the rules. There would be five rounds of ten questions each, and the teams were required to write down their final answers on the sheets provided. They also had to place their cell phones into a lidded box on their table.

After the first round, they were in second place. The rounds continued with a short break after the third one. The servers were attentive and brought fresh drinks to the tables throughout the tournament.

Justin was a sports fanatic, and Heath proved himself to

be the master of all things related to music. Carolyn was an avid reader, so literature was her strength. Harry answered several of the history, geography, and medical questions correctly. Clay's knowledge was also well rounded, and he excelled in science and math.

At the end of the fourth round, they were tied with The Wise Quackers. Ten more questions, and Clay took their sheet up to the table where Rooster and his staff were scoring. Rooster announced ten points for them, and the crowd cheered. The Wise Quackers also received a perfect score.

Tie game.

With a dramatic flair, Rooster pulled a card from his stack of questions to serve as the tie breaker. The team had to provide the length of the underwater portion of the Chunnel between France and England. If neither team provided the correct answer, the team closest to the correct length would win.

The five teammates looked around the table at each other. None of them knew the answer. None had even been to England or France.

"I watched a detective series about a murder that took place halfway through the tunnel" Harry finally said. "They didn't say how long the tunnel was, but I remember it was about 15 miles to the scene of the murder. That would make it about 30 miles long, in total."

Clay nodded and wrote on a paper napkin. "I would say it's got to be close to 25 miles under the water, since part on each end is on land."

Heath hovered his pen over the paper. "Shall I say 25?"

Clay gritted his teeth. "Let's do an uneven number. That might give us a better chance. I doubt it is exact. How about 24.5 miles?"

The others nodded their head, and Heath hurried to get their answer down before the buzzer sounded.

He and the captain from The Wise Quackers took the score sheets to Rooster's table. Rooster checked both of them and addressed the crowd. "The correct answer is 23.6 miles."

He paused for dramatic effect, then said, "Neither team got the correct answer, but Whiskeypedia came up with 24.5 and was closest. Congratulations to our winners."

He came to the table and presented each of them with a coupon for a free burger, fries, and unlimited drinks during the visit. Clay led the way to the table with the six members of The Wise Quackers. "Good game, guys. That was close." He extended his hand to each of them, then introduced Harry to the table.

Harry shook hands with each of them, chuckling at the banter and jokes between the teams. One of the women went on and on about the wonderful job Harry did in catching the mayor. Clay ushered her away from the group and toward the exit.

Clay retrieved her jacket and held it for her. "We better get you out of here before more of your fans want to talk to you."

Heath laughed as they walked to the truck. "Having you around is like being with a celebrity."

She punched him in the shoulder, and he winced. "Ouch. You don't punch like a girl."

She climbed up into the passenger seat. "Obviously you don't know how hard girls can punch."

CHAPTER TWENTY-THREE

Late Thursday afternoon, Harry made her daily trip to the mailbox, taking the dogs with her in the golf cart. There was only one piece of mail, but Harry took one look at the return address and smiled.

The letter in the pink envelope was from Olivia Davis.

Harry drove back to the barn, parked the cart, and hurried the dogs into the house. She held the letter in her hand as she brewed a cup of tea. While she was anxious to know what Olivia had to say, part of her hesitated to open the letter. If she declined, Harry's hopes would be dashed, and she'd been living on hope that she wanted to keep alive for as long as possible.

She took her tea and settled in front of the fireplace, Jewel's throw blanket over her, and opened the envelope.

She scanned the handwritten page. Olivia apologized for her late reply, and said she'd been dealing with many challenges. She was retired from nursing, and her current circumstances were such that she was free to leave Spokane.

She needed time to get things organized, but promised Harry she would be in Lavender Valley by the end of March.

Her closing words brought Harry's hand to her chest. *Lavender Valley Farm was a place of great healing for me over forty years ago. I thought my worst days were behind me, but now the wounds are so much deeper. I'm trusting Jewel's wisdom and taking her invitation as a sign that there's something for me there. That hope is all I have left.*

Olivia provided her cell number and email address, and promised to be in touch when she had a firm date for her arrival.

Chief and Hope inched closer to Harry, resting their noses against her hand. She looked into their gentle eyes. That was the invitation Hope had been waiting for and crawled on top of Jewel's blanket. Chief moved to fill in the gap she left and placed his head next to Hope's.

"Soon, sweet ones. Olivia will be here soon, and it sounds like she needs us even more than we need her."

After she fed the dogs, Clay arrived to pick her up for line dancing at Rooster's. She made sure she had some money, her keys, and her cell phone in her pocket before she climbed into the truck.

"So," said Clay, turning the truck down the driveway. "What's new?"

"I received my first reply today." Harry smiled and added, "Olivia. She's from Spokane and will be here next month."

"That's good news. One down, three to go, right?"

She nodded. "I think I've been too impatient. It was easy for me to pick up and come down here. For one, I'm closer, and for another, I don't have a family to worry about or consult. It's a big decision. One that can't always be made quickly."

"Does that mean you're just going to wait instead of reaching out to the other three again?"

"I think I'll wait until March. I don't want to put any extra pressure on them. My personality tends to be one of action. So, I get a problem and I take immediate steps to solve it. Not everybody does that. Some people need time. I picked up on that in Olivia's letter. After reading it, I'm glad I didn't reach out again. The others may be dealing with challenges of their own."

Clay pulled into a parking spot. "That sounds very insightful. Like I said, no matter what happens, we can help you manage the farm and the lavender."

"Since we aren't exactly spring chickens, we'll probably need your help. I looked back at Jewel's journal, trying to get a feel for the ages of the women, and I think Olivia is about five years older than me. Georgia is older than that. Good thing Tyler's young. If Micki and Lydia come through, at least we'll have a couple in their forties." She chuckled as she walked with him toward the entrance.

They took a booth and opted to redeem their coupon for burgers before the dancing started. The waitress brought their soft drinks and promised to be back soon with their burgers.

"Where's Heath tonight?" asked Harry.

"Oh, he's having some friends over to play poker."

"He might be wiser than us. I warn you, I'm not a dancer."

He grinned. "Just think of it as exercise."

The burgers arrived, along with baskets overflowing with hot, salty fries. Harry raved about the juicy burger and finished off the mountain of fries just as a woman in cowboy boots, jeans, and a sequined blouse stepped to the microphone.

"Hey, everybody. Welcome to line dancing at Rooster's. I'm Sally and will be your leader tonight. We've got a few minutes, so finish your drinks and visit the powder room, and we'll be ready to go."

Clay took a swallow of his drink. "We need to get moving if we don't want to be stuck in the front row."

Sally started them off with basic steps, and as the evening progressed, added in more complicated moves. Despite Harry's worries, it proved to be fun. She and Clay had a position toward the back of the group, but not in the last row, which seemed to be perfect placement for blending in.

With only one break in two hours of dancing, Harry was tired and thirsty when the class ended. She and Clay finished two more glasses of iced tea before they headed back to the farm.

He pulled up to the porch and before he could open his door, Harry put up her hand. "I can manage and if your feet feel anything like mine, you need to limit your steps. Thanks for tonight. It was fun, and while I'm tired, I'm relaxed. Like you said, it's sort of like exercise you don't know you're doing."

He grinned. "That and all the laughter from our not so smooth moves." He took her hand in his and squeezed it gently. "I haven't had this much fun in a very long time. Thanks for that, Harry."

She tightened her fingers around his before reaching for the door handle. She had enjoyed herself and the tingle that traveled from her fingers to her toes when she touched his hand, told her there was more to this than she thought.

"You're sure I can't escort you to the door?"

She laughed and gestured toward the house, where Chief

and Hope pressed their noses against the glass door, their tails wagging in anticipation. "My two guards are waiting right there for me, but I truly appreciate the offer."

"See you tomorrow then. Sweet dreams, Harry," he said. He waited to leave until she was safely inside the house.

Harry gave both dogs an ear scratch as they watched Clay's taillights travel down the driveway. "I wasn't sure guys like Clay still existed. We're lucky we found him, aren't we?"

Their tails thumped against her legs in total agreement.

CHAPTER TWENTY-FOUR

Harry was in the habit of going to Clay's for dinner once or twice a week and they often went to the Grasshopper for breakfast at least once a week. Tuesday tacos and trivia won over line dancing and Harry was now a member of Whiskeypedia.

The Valentine's Dance proved to be very laid-back and fun. While the idea of dating or romance wasn't something she was seeking, she couldn't deny the flutter of butterflies when Clay took her hand or brushed against her shoulder. She'd written off the idea of finding a soulmate long ago, but Clay was the real deal. Honest, hardworking, kind, and easy to talk to.

There was something to be said for letting things happen naturally. What was budding between them was slow and steady. He felt like a friend the first time she met him and that friendship had only deepened. With both of them out of the dating game for so long, it made sense to start slow. She didn't want to jeopardize their close friendship.

Harry missed the excitement of her work in Salem, but

found great satisfaction in working in the fields and the slow pace of life in a small town. Despite the nonstop urging from everyone in town to run for mayor, Harry was happy to see a former city council member throw his hat in the ring. The special election would take place tomorrow and he was the only one on the ballot, so would be a shoo-in.

Over the last month, Harry found a rhythm to her days and while she filled her days with farm work, most evenings she spent cuddled with the dogs in front of a warm fire, watching something she enjoyed or reading a book.

The days became longer as March arrived. Harry and Tyler concentrated on prepping the lavender fields, weeding, and started the pruning process. The irrigation water would begin flowing the first week of April, and Harry intended to be ready for it.

Her muscles had adjusted to the strain of physical work, and rather than spending her time in an office or behind a desk, she was outside most of the day. Chief and Hope enjoyed their days, always beginning with a long walk around the fields. They were both off leash all day, and Chief's recall was now reliable, after spending so much time with Hope.

Olivia called that weekend, and she and Harry had a short, but friendly conversation. She planned to arrive the following week, and while Harry heard the tiredness in her voice, there was a lilt of hope when they talked about the animal sanctuary and the work needed to get Jewel's dog rescue functioning again.

Olivia was used to having a two-story house, so she was more than happy to take a bedroom upstairs. She had a bed she was bringing, and Harry promised to shuffle the furnishings to make room.

By the time Sunday evening came round, the fields were

ready for growing season, thanks to Tyler arranging a pruning party, and the kind help of the ranch hands from next door.

Harry cuddled the dogs on the couch as the evening's darkness settled in, then wondered what she should do – read a book or watch a show on television, as was her usual. She decided there was still too much to do, and reached for her cell phone, almost spilling the cup of tea she had on the side table. She tapped Clay's name, and he answered after the first ring.

"Hey, Harry, what's up?"

"I wondered if you would be up to helping remove the twin beds from upstairs? I think it's a two-man job and Tyler, of course, would help. Olivia will be here next week, and I need to make room for her things."

"Sure, no problem. Where are we taking them?"

"I'm not sure. Is there a thrift store or something like that in town? I need to find another full or queen-size bed for the third bedroom, too, but want to put Olivia in the largest room so it will be a game of musical furniture."

"Probably need to go to Medford to find a bed, but you can donate the others to the community thrift store. We can load them in my truck, and I can drop them off at the donation center downtown."

"That would be great. I need to make a trip to Medford and go to Costco anyway, so I'll look for a bed there."

"Most furniture places deliver to Lavender Valley, but if you need to borrow the truck, you're more than welcome."

"Thanks, I'll go check it out, and if I find something that can't be delivered, I'll take you up on that."

"Sounds good. Just make sure you're back in time for trivia tomorrow. We're on a winning streak."

"I promise," she said with a chuckle. "I'll see you there."

She disconnected with a smile and reached to pet the dogs. "I'm not sure what we'd do without Clay," she whispered.

Tuesday, Harry left Tyler in charge of Hope and Chief, and spent a long day in Medford. She loaded up on staples and groceries, and after looking at a couple of furniture stores, discovered the best deal was the bed she'd tried at Costco. She could get the entire bedroom set with a quality mattress delivered at a good price.

With her SUV loaded down with supplies, she made her way home in time to unload before tacos and trivia. She felt bad leaving the dogs again, but they were zonked on the floor, having traipsed around the property with Tyler all day.

Soon, she, Clay, and Heath were munching on tacos.

"Did you find a bed in Medford?" asked Clay, reaching for another taco already.

"Oh, yeah. I went all over town looking at furniture stores, but should have just saved the time. The best deal was at Costco. I ordered it online, and they'll ship it to me by the end of the week."

"Heath and I can move the twin beds tonight. I'm sure you'll want to clean before the new bed arrives."

"That would be great. It'll just take me a few minutes to strip the beds, and then I'll work on cleaning tomorrow."

Justin arrived just in time for the first round of trivia questions. "Carolyn is still working at the election, so I'm it."

Rooster announced the tournament would be a shorter

version, with only three rounds of questions. The Wise Quackers were on fire, and despite their best efforts, Whiskeypedia came in second.

Heath finished his beer, and Clay and Harry swallowed the last of their iced teas before the three made their way outside to Clay's truck. "We'll get them next week,," said Clay.

Harry nodded. "Yeah, there were too many questions about art and literature tonight, and Carolyn is the best at those."

Back at the farmhouse, Harry opened the front door, and the three of them were instantly mauled by the dogs, who acted like they hadn't seen a human for months. Once all the petting was done, the men followed Harry upstairs. She quickly removed the bedding and emptied the small dressers that matched the beds.

Heath and Clay made quick work of taking the twin beds apart in both rooms and transporting them downstairs to Clay's truck, where Heath used a couple of tie straps to secure their load. Clay gave Hope and Chief another scratch under the chin as he stood by the door, ready to leave. "Give me a call when you're ready to move the other bed and we can help you set up the new one, too."

"Thanks, guys. I appreciate the help. I'll be ready tomorrow. Just come at your convenience. I'd offer to cook you dinner, but that would really be more of a punishment rather than a reward. I'll treat you guys to dinner Friday to repay you."

Clay laughed. "You don't need to worry about it. We're happy to help." He tipped his hat and added, "Have a good evening, Harry."

She watched them drive away, then flicked the switch to turn out the porch light. With cleaning supplies gathered, she climbed the stairs to get a start on removing the layer of dust that was under the beds.

As she worked in the quiet house, the dogs snoozing in the corner, her thoughts drifted to Olivia's arrival. Harry remembered how when she'd lived with Jewel, she had fantasized about having a sibling. Since then, with her busy career, she'd hardly thought about not having a family or an extended family, even though she realized that being alone was part of the reason she chose to concentrate on her career and work holidays. It was easier to be doing something on the days others were surrounded by family.

But now Harry understood that as long as Jewel had been there for her, she hadn't felt completely alone. Jewel had been her anchor and her family – and with her gone, Harry felt… not exactly lost, but… adrift. That was it. Losing Jewel, combined with the end of her career, had left her rootless.

With Olivia coming in a few days and the hope of three others, Harry's spirits lifted. She might be used to being alone, but that was back in her own house, surrounding by everything she knew. Living in Jewel's house brought back memories, both good and bad, and along with those memories came the longing for something that was missing.

After working late, cleaning the two spare rooms until the floors gleamed and every speck of dust was removed from the baseboards and light fixtures, Harry slept later than usual.

The hot breath and thwack of two tails against the side of the bed finally prompted her to open her eyes. Two snouts and the gentle brown eyes of her faithful companions greeted her. She smiled at them, more aware than ever of the gift she had been given from Tim and then again from Jewel. With a dog by her side, she would never truly be alone.

Breakfast was late and they wanted to remind her. Gently, of course.

She rolled out of bed, fed the two dogs, and jumped in the shower.

After a cup of coffee, she took the two for their customary walk and returned to the house, hungry.

As she gathered ingredients from the refrigerator, the gate buzzed, and she glimpsed Clay's truck.

Minutes later, he was at her front door. She greeted him with a smile and gestured for him to come through to the kitchen. "I got a late start. Would you like some breakfast? Coffee?"

"Oh, I just came from the bakery, so I'm good." He tapped the newspaper he carried against his hand. "I just wanted to bring you this before you got ambushed."

She finished whisking her eggs, then walked over to the island counter, glanced at the headlines, and gasped.

CHAPTER TWENTY-FIVE

"I don't believe this," she said. "This can't be true."

She blinked and read the bold headline again. *WRITE IN CANDIDATE, HARRY MCKENZIE, WINS MAYOR'S RACE.* She met Clay's eyes. "Did you know about this?"

He shrugged. "I'd heard some rumblings, but didn't take it seriously."

"Now what?" she asked, frowning. "What a mess."

"Well," Clay said, as he pulled a bakery bag out from inside his jacket, "I brought you some donuts, so sit down and have one. The sugar might do you good." He retrieved a plate from her cupboard and placed the donuts on it. "You could always legally refuse the position, and then it would go to the other candidate. The problem is you won by like eighty percent of the vote. That's a huge message from the voters."

"Maybe I better go talk to Buck and get some legal advice." She sighed and pushed the bowl of eggs aside. "I've lost my appetite."

"Would you be willing to talk to my friend, Will? You met him at the shoot. With him being on the council, he might have some insight that could be valuable to your decision."

She shrugged. "Sure, I can talk to him. Honestly, this is not what I need right now. Olivia is coming and the growing season is upon us."

"Just talk to him. See what he has to say. It may not be as time consuming as you think."

She nodded. Her white knuckles straining as she gripped her cup. "Make it soon, if you can. I need to get this figured out."

He pushed the plate of donuts closer to her and pulled his phone out of his pocket. "I'll call him right now," he said, and wandered outside to the porch.

She eyed the chocolate donut sprinkled with walnuts, and though her appetite was long gone, still couldn't resist. She paced as she nibbled on it.

A few minutes later, Clay came through the door. "Will says he can meet you today. His family owns a food company and he's in his office there all day. I can take you out there."

"Great. The sooner the better." Still feeling discombobulated, she dashed into her bedroom to change clothes and make sure her hair was presentable.

Fifteen minutes later, they were on the road. Clay explained Will's mother had started a small organic food company in her kitchen and how it had grown over time. They now had a factory with an industrial kitchen operation in the middle of their farm, where they grew much of the food that they produced.

Harry listened, but only half-heartedly, as her mind tried to wrap itself around the election news. When Clay stopped the truck in front of a brick building, she was jostled from her thoughts.

When they entered Will's office, the tall man greeted Clay with a hearty handshake and tipped his hat when he stepped forward to offer his hand to Harry. "Nice to see you again, Harry."

"Thanks, Will. I appreciate you taking time."

He offered them chairs at a small table to the side of his desk, then offered them a beverage. Harry shook her head. "No, thank you. I'm fine."

Will tapped his fingers on the desk. "I understand you not wanting to take on the job of mayor. Clay explained you're trying to run Jewel's farm and make sure her Lavender Festival continues. I know all of that takes time and effort. I just wanted to explain more about the mayor's duties and the time it would take. I suspect you might think it's a full-time job, but it's much less than that."

Harry frowned as she listened to him explain that the major duties included the monthly council meetings, plus monthly work sessions where the mayor would review the budget, recommend budget items, and handle personnel, all with the help of the city manager.

"The biggest responsibility the mayor has is oversight of the police, which I think is why the community spoke with such a loud voice. Much of what the mayor does is ceremonial or limited, but historically, they've had a big hand in the police department."

Harry nodded. "Which is how Mayor Crawford was able to keep her scheme with Mayor Irwin running. She hampered the police."

Will nodded. "Exactly. The people want someone they can trust to manage the police, and you've proven yourself. I know you didn't do it to get the job, but I think you'd be wise to give it more consideration. Chief Phillips has been advocating for you. I think you could limit your time in the office and spend no more than twenty hours a week on the job, probably less."

Harry sighed. "I hear what you're saying. The idea of being a politician...it's just so not me. Not to mention, I'm not sure I'm staying after the end of the year. This term goes until next year. June or July, right?"

"That's right, and believe me, I understand. Maybe you need to reframe it as community service. Coming from Salem, I understand your disdain for politicians. I'm sure all of Lavender Valley feels the same way. We've got a great community of people, most of them willing to lend a hand to anyone in need. They love you and trust you. Frankly, that is every politician's dream."

Harry chuckled. "That would be great, if I was a politician."

"Small town politics isn't so much politics as it is building community and relationships, plus our new council is one that will work well together. We had one vocal proponent of Mayor Crawford, but he's gone now. And full disclosure, there's one council member left who followed his lead. She's a bit wishy-washy when it comes to taking a position and is easily led, but without her buddy on the council, I'm thinking she'll grow into her position. She's a bit high drama. Went to acting school originally and loves social media."

Harry wrinkled her nose. "You're not selling it," she said. "I know the type."

"Yeah, she's a follower, but the other members are good people, there to serve, so she won't have a bad influence. She's also up for reelection next year, and I doubt she stays. I think she thought it would be more fun and more of a status symbol. She and her husband moved here from somewhere outside of Portland. Rumor is they're looking to move again."

Harry shook her head. "I don't feel good about

committing to something I may not be able to deliver on. What if I decide to move at the end of the season?"

Clay cleared his throat. "In reality, if you decide to sell the farm, you're probably not going to have much luck during winter. Spring or summer are the most active times for real estate sales, and it will take time to find the right buyer. On the off chance you do end up selling, you can always stay at the ranch until your term is up."

Will smiled and added, "And you never know. You might end up staying in Lavender Valley for years to come. I'm old enough to know you can't outsmart the future, so I don't try."

Harry sighed. "You two aren't making this easy. I just don't know what to do. I definitely don't want to slight everyone who voted for me, but it's a big commitment. One I'm not sure I can make."

"Well, only you can decide. Just know I'm willing to help you as much as possible. Like I said, it's a position about community, built on trust and fostering a safe place where people want to stay and raise their families. It's not full time and would be less than twenty hours a week most of the time. I also think most everyone knows you're here because of Jewel's passing and that you're locked into running the farm this year. It means you'll get lots of community help and goodwill for the Lavender Festival. And if it does prove overwhelming, you could resign at the end of the year and the town could get by with an interim appointment."

Her jaw tensed. "I would really hate to do that. I like to finish what I start. Everything is just so up in the air right now."

Will nodded. "Well, I've given you my piece. The mayor is the chairperson and I'm the vice-chair, so the other members asked me to contact you to express our support and willingness to work with you. Our main goal is to reestablish trust and honesty in our city government, and we believe you are the best person to help us."

"Understood," said Harry, rising from her chair. "I appreciate the insight and will make a decision by tomorrow. I'm going to lay low until then."

She shook Will's hand and followed Clay to his truck.

"I guess stopping by the Grasshopper for lunch is a no, huh?" He chuckled as he slid behind the wheel.

She rolled her eyes. "Probably not today, but later this week would be great."

The ride home was quiet, with Harry lost in thought as she stared without seeing at the passing scenery.

When Clay pulled up to the gate, she hopped out and retrieved her mail. He drove her up to the house and before she got out, said, "I'll grab Heath after lunch, and we'll move that other bed for you. If you feel like it, come on over for dinner tonight."

"Thanks, Clay. I'm going to think a bit and I'll let you know for sure. I appreciate your help and advice."

He waved as he turned the truck to head back to his ranch.

She opened the door to swooshing tails and bright eyes. The dogs followed her happily to the kitchen, where they immediately lay underfoot as Harry took a tray of Costco prepared chicken enchiladas from the fridge, dished some out, and put it in the microwave.

As she waited, she rifled through the stack of mail. Mostly junk, but two handwritten envelopes stood out. She hurried to open the first, with a return address from Micki Armstrong.

Harry was still reading the letter when the microwave buzzed. Quickly, she removed the plate, poured some iced tea, and got back to reading as she ate.

Micki was sorry to hear about Jewel and had fond memories of her time at Lavender Valley. She was adjusting to an empty nest with her son and daughter at the University of Washington, and divulged that a fissure had developed between her and her daughter, Meg.

She didn't elaborate, but said that the idea of spending time at the farm, where she had enjoyed some of her happiest days helping plant lavender and sunflowers, would be a welcome escape. Working as a software programmer at home would enable her to move her workplace to the farm, so she would rent out her house and be arriving in April.

She provided her cell number and email, and promised to be in touch with an exact date.

Harry breathed a sigh of relief. Micki had the most experience with lavender, and having her come to help alleviated some of Harry's worries. She reached for the other letter.

It was from Georgia Moore with a return address in Boise, and her perfect penmanship reminded Harry of Jewel's letters. She scanned the paragraphs, feeling the grief in the words as Georgia described the loss of her husband, Lee.

She mentioned how much Jewel meant to her, what a treasure she had been in Georgia's life, and the happy years she had spent at the farm. She went on to explain she had worked in the school library and her husband had been a teacher. With Lee's passing, she could no longer stay in their home and had no idea what she was going to do. She'd sold her house and was in the midst of trying to find an inexpensive rental or apartment when she found Harry's letter among the many sympathy cards she was working through. The invitation to return to Lavender Valley provided the answer she so desperately needed, and she planned to be there by the end of April. She wondered if one of the cottages was available as storage, as she was planning to have a moving service deliver her belongings.

Harry put the letter down, her mind busy as she finished her lunch.

Perhaps the timing of the letters' arrival meant something. At a minimum she'd have three more helpers, which meant all the responsibility for the farm would not be on Harry's shoulders. Which meant she may have time for the Mayor position after all. But did she want the job?

She imagined Jewel, sitting in her chair, letting Harry talk through the pros and cons of accepting and rejecting the opportunity. Harry could almost hear her wise words, never pushy or authoritarian. Jewel's method had always consisted of asking Harry questions to guide her to consider all the possibilities.

Jewel would ask her what she feared about being mayor. Harry took great pride in doing excellent work and while she understood the policing aspect of the job and handled much of the budget back in Salem, she wasn't as familiar with the other departments under the mayor's purview. Jewel would have laughed and asked when did Harry ever let a challenge stop her.

Her old job dictated she be in the media spotlight at times, but they had a press officer and she was not the face of the department. Harry didn't like being the center of attention. She wasn't sure about dealing with the constant barrage of residents she would face on a daily basis. Jewel's bright eyes would have twinkled and she would remind Harry that Lavender Valley wasn't Salem. It wasn't full of politicians and bureaucrats looking for their next big job.

The people who lived here were content for the most part and weren't the type to whine about the small things. They expected the mayor to have other responsibilities, like running a business or farm. They didn't expect a politician. The old mayor had been in office for generations and was beloved by the community. Harry just needed to emulate what he had done. She was honest and hardworking and a born problem solver. She was perfect for such a calling.

Jewel would also point out that they had chosen her. They respected and admired her already. That was the biggest battle any mayor faced. She had their trust and she'd never failed at anything she set her mind on doing. She'd also remind Harry, with a gentle nudge, that personal growth didn't come without a little bit of pain and stretching herself, if that's what it took to overcome her aversion to the public part of the job, would only build her character.

In her heart, Harry knew Jewel would be overjoyed to see Harry as mayor of her beloved valley. Her smile, beaming with pride, the day Harry graduated from the police academy was an image seared in Harry's mind. Jewel would be bursting to think one of her daughters would be the mayor.

If Harry could believe Will, and she had no reason not to trust him, she would have the time to dedicate to the position and having a true servant's heart, Harry felt a duty to the people of Lavender Valley and a love for the town she thought of as her hometown. She had a true connection to this town and deep roots. She wanted to do her best for the people here.

In her mind, the pros outweighed the cons. She even found the idea of a new challenge exhilarating.

She texted Clay to thank him and accept his kind invitation to join them for dinner, then padded out to the deck to finish her tea, the dogs behind her. She had been so blessed by Clay's friendship, and it was no wonder that Jewel had thought the world of him and his family. He had become a constant friend to Harry. She felt like she had known him for much longer than the short time she had been in Lavender Valley. She'd even trusted him with her inner thoughts, and that was something new for her. Outside of Tim and Jewel, she'd never let people get too close to her.

Having Clay nearby and knowing he would do anything to help her was a comfort she welcomed. With his help and Heath's, along with the three women who would be her roommates, Harry was confident they could make Jewel proud.

The only sticking point was in staying until next summer. That would complicate her house rental back in Salem and leave her future up in the air. For the first time in her adult life, she might have to play things by ear come January and see what happened. It was scary and freeing at the same time. She was almost sure Cora would agree to extending her rental another six months, and like Clay said, if the farm had to be sold, he and Heath had plenty of room at the ranch. Worst case scenario, she'd end up staying there for six months, or if that felt uncomfortable, she could rent a small place in town

There was no way to predict what her sisters of the heart would decide after spending a season at the farm. It was a problem without a solution and a question that would only be answered in time.

Harry wasn't known for her patience, but in this situation, she had no choice but to wait and see.

CHAPTER TWENTY-SIX

Her phone chimed. Harry smiled as she read Clay's reply, telling her to bring the dogs and come now, if she wanted. He thought they had time to take the horses out before dinner. Then, he and Heath would follow her home tonight and move the bed for her.

It was a sunny day and perfect for a ride. She added a couple of layers under her jacket, in case it cooled off, and loaded the dogs in her SUV. Their tails were on nonstop wag as she drove next door and down the long driveway.

Clay welcomed the three of them inside and led the way to the kitchen, where Heath was prepping for dinner while Maverick and Ace watched.

"Heath is going to keep an eye on the dogs and whip up something delicious for us."

Heath smiled and caught his brother's eye. "Don't you kids stay out too late, now."

They made their way to the stables, where Merlot and Whiskey were saddled and ready. Clay made sure Harry was atop Merlot before he mounted Whiskey, then they rode side by side out of the barn and toward the open pasture.

They took a different route than their last ride, passing by the creek, which would soon start to flow from the runoff. Near a grove of trees, with a stunning view of the snow-topped mountains, Clay stopped Whiskey, and Merlot automatically stopped beside them. He dismounted and tied Whiskey to a hitching post near a wooden bench, then offered Harry a hand down.

When she stood beside him, he gestured to the bench. "This was my mom and dad's special place. They loved to come out here to enjoy the view and have a picnic."

Harry breathed deep as she gazed around. "It's stunning. Their own little slice of heaven."

"After we lost Mom, Dad spent lots of time out here. Both of their ashes are interred here, together, like they wanted." He reached for her hand and led her through the trees, where a large granite headstone was positioned with a perfect view of the vast pastures, and behind them, the mountains.

On the sides of the stone, two horses were carved in bas relief, and the Nolan name was near the top of the stone face, framed by a backdrop of trees and mountains. Below the family name, both names had been carved into the stone, with TOGETHER FOREVER BEYOND THE STARS, etched between them.

Harry knelt and traced the letters with her finger, and her eyes filled with tears. She looked up at Clay. "That's beautiful."

"They loved to stargaze and at the end, when Mom was so sick, Dad always promised her he'd meet her beyond the stars."

"A love story that lasts that long is rare these days. I'm sure you miss them terribly."

Clay nodded as he studied the stone. "Each and every day." He smiled sadly. "But I'm lucky enough to be here, surrounded by everything they loved. The home they built. Touching the things they touched, walking where they walked, seeing what they saw. It gives me comfort."

"It seems loss can do that. Or it can work the exact opposite and make people run away from all those memories." She took the hand he offered and stood. "I'm easing into that comfort stage now when I see Jewel's touch everywhere I look. At first, it made me sad, but I understand what you mean. It makes me feel safe, grounded."

He led her to the bench, and she noticed the engraving on the back commemorating his parents' twenty-fifth wedding anniversary. "Dad used to bring Mom out here all the time," Clay continued. "They often would sit in the back of his pickup and watch the stars. Heath and I made the bench for them, so they'd have a place to sit when they rode horses out here."

She ran her hand over the wood, smooth despite it being out in the weather for years. "I bet they loved it."

He nodded. "It was a hit. They weren't exactly easy to buy for." He gestured for her to have a seat, then joined her. Clay raised his brows. "So, I take it you made a decision about the mayor's office."

"I did. I received two more letters in the mail. Micki and Georgia are both coming and will be here in April. So, I'll have three people to help share the load. That will give me the time I need to dedicate to the job, if Will is right."

He grinned. "That's great news. I was really hoping you would say yes."

"Really?" she asked with a frown.

"Yeah, you'd be good at it. I know you aren't a politician but that's why people trust you. You're smart, logical, hardworking, and a problem solver. I think you'll be great at it, and whatever you need around the farm, we'll be there for you."

His words reminded her of the conversation she and Jewel would have had.

"That means a lot to me, Clay. Knowing I can count on you. Your offer to let me stay at the ranch if I need to helped me make the decision. Like I said, it's not something I went looking for, but I feel a strong sense of love for this town and a duty to the people here. I don't want to disappoint them or alienate them. And well, it's good to get out of your comfort zone sometimes. I've always enjoyed learning new things and the challenge of it is exciting."

"And you may decide to stay. Lavender Valley is filled with good people. Kind people. It's a great place to live, and although it's small and lacks a few amenities, I can't imagine ever leaving again."

They sat in silence for a few minutes, gazing at the peaceful landscape. Except for the tweet of a bird or two, the occasional shuffle from the horses, and the soft mooing of the cattle in the surrounding pastures, the day was quiet and still.

It was late afternoon when Clay helped her mount Merlot, and they headed back to the house.

By the time they took care of the horses and got them back in their stalls, Harry was ready for dinner. She and Clay made their way to the house and found Heath in the kitchen, amid the wonderful aroma of herbs and lemon.

After a quick trip to the powder room, Harry slid into her chair at the granite counter, where two roasted chickens waited to be sliced. Heath did the honors while Harry filled her plate with roasted veggies and a flaky roll, along with fruit salad. Heath added the juicy slices of chicken to each of their plates and then took his seat.

Heath looked between the two of them. "Okay, what's up? I can see it in your faces."

Clay tilted his head toward Harry. "Harry has news."

She smiled and said, "I've decided to accept the position of mayor."

"Well, that calls for a celebration," said Heath. "I think we have some bubbly in the fridge." He unearthed a bottle and popped the cork.

Clay raised his glass before they started to eat. "To our new mayor, Harry McKenzie."

Heath grinned. "Wonderful news, Harry. We're lucky to have you."

They clinked glasses and Harry took a quick sip. "That's very kind of you. Honestly, if not for you and Clay, I don't think I would have said yes. Not to mention that the three women are coming. Micki is the one with the most experience with lavender, so that's a huge relief."

Clay set his glass back on the counter. "Whatever you need, Harry, just ask. We're happy to help."

"It's been a long time since I had someone in my life I could count on, so it really means the world to me to know that." Harry took her first bite of chicken. "Wow, this is delicious, Heath."

He smiled as he took a forkful of vegetables.

Harry added butter to her roll. "I mean it, Heath. How are you still single? I can't believe some lady hasn't taken you off the market."

His cheeks reddened as he laughed off her comment. "I've been burned and have become much more discerning when it comes to women."

Clay glanced at Heath and added more to his plate.

Heath reached for another roll and added, "I'm also too busy, and Lavender Valley isn't exactly the dating capital of Oregon." He caught his brother's eye. "Besides, I'm not the only brother in this family who is available."

Harry collected the water pitcher to refill it, and went to the sink. The conversation continued behind her. Despite the sound of the water, she could still make out what the two were saying.

"I'm beyond out of practice and think that horse has left the barn. It might be too late for me to get a second chance."

Heath lowered his voice. "Right. You never know. Some smart, beautiful woman, who's a great shot, may move in next door..."

Clay cleared his throat, interrupting him. "What's for dessert?"

The water jug full again, Harry refilled all their glasses and returned the pitcher to the island, while Heath brought his napkin to his face to hide his laugh.

"How can you even think of dessert. Aren't you stuffed?" asked Harry.

Clay looked at his empty plate. "Well, yeah, I'm full, but just wondered what I had to look forward to."

Heath gestured to the counter. "I picked up a carrot cake from the bakery."

"Yum," said Harry. "The kind with that thick cream cheese frosting?"

"Is there any other kind?" Heath laughed and moved to collect the dishes.

Harry caught his hand and shook her head. "No, I'll do the clean-up. It's the least I can do after you worked so hard on dinner. You go relax."

Clay nodded. "I'll help Harry. Take a load off." He laughed

when the dogs followed Heath out of the kitchen. "He's like the pied piper with those dogs."

Clay rolled up his shirt sleeves and packed up the leftovers, while Harry rinsed the dishes and loaded the dishwasher. When Clay snapped the last lid shut and put the container in the fridge, he added, "You'll have to take some of that home. Heath made plenty so we have extra."

"You don't have to twist my arm. I wish now I'd paid more attention to Jewel when she was cooking."

"Our mom was a great cook too, and Heath spent quite a bit of time with her in the kitchen while I was always outside with Dad."

Harry washed and dried the knives before setting them on the counter and as Clay put them away, he said, "So, Curt from the paper has been blowing up my phone all day. You're lucky he doesn't have your number."

She sighed. "I half expected him to show up at my gate today. I'm sure he's itching for a comment or two."

"He begged me to have you call him."

"I'm going to call Will tomorrow and tell him I'll accept. I'm not sure of the protocol for how things roll out from there, but I'll make sure Curt is notified."

Clay added beans to the grinder and went about setting the coffee to brew. "Would you rather have tea or coffee?" he asked.

"Tea sounds great, thanks."

He added water to the electric kettle and unearthed his mom's tea chest. "I think it's warm enough to sit on the patio and enjoy the sunset."

She selected a tea, and when it was ready, took it outside to the table.

The lavender sky, a few purple clouds above, was lit by a warm glow of gold underneath, as the sun stretched to reach the horizon. The beauty caused Harry to suck in her breath.

The lights twinkling along the railing and the reflection of the sun's golden rays on the pond added to the jaw dropping sight. Clay joined her with a steaming cup of coffee and a warm throw blanket. "Just in case it cools off," he said, draping it across her back and shoulders.

He took the seat next to her and sighed. "This is my favorite time of the day. I also love a good sunrise, but I'm usually too busy to relax and enjoy them."

"Honestly, I haven't taken the time to enjoy either. My schedule was hectic, to say the least. Now, I know what I was missing." She took another sip from her mug. "Thank you for inviting me tonight. This is the perfect way to end the day."

He reached for her hand. "I'm glad you're here." He looked at the horizon and sighed before turning back to her. "I need to say something, Harry. I, uh…well, I'm out of practice when it comes to women, dating, anything in that realm. After losing Karen, I assumed that part of my life was over. I wasn't looking for anything, but then I met you. I value your friendship so much and would never want to jeopardize it, but if I'm honest, I think I'm falling for you."

He paused and added. "It's a little embarrassing, especially with Heath around to rib me and I've tried to dismiss everything and chalk it up to friendship, which it is for sure. That's part of the problem." He stammered and shook his head. "The more I talk, the less sense I make. I guess what I'm trying to say is—I like you, Harry. As a friend and more."

She smiled at him and found his fumbling endearing. "I have to admit, I've had a few fluttery feelings I haven't felt in a very long time. Maybe not since I had a crush on Donny Stevens in high school. Like you, I wasn't looking for anything close to romance, but I look forward to spending time with you. I find you easy to talk to, which is a huge deal for me. I heard Heath teasing you and you said you thought your chance was over. Do you really think that?"

He gave her a sheepish look. "I did, until now. I didn't want Heath pressuring me or making you feel weird. For years, he's tried to get me back in the game and I've resisted. I think he's noticed the change in my attitude and was just pointing it out in his seventh-grade boy way. I know I'm happier with you in my life."

His words warmed her heart. "I feel the same way. I'm not sure I noticed what I was missing until now. All those years in Salem, I threw myself into work and never had to face being alone or not having a true soulmate. Now, being older and not having the crutch of a demanding job, I've realized there is something missing. I think Jewel was right about coming back here to Lavender Valley. I'm not one hundred percent sure about this mayor gig, but being here at least until next summer is the right thing to do. I don't trust easily, but I feel like I've known you forever and am so thankful to have you here. I wanted to fulfill Jewel's wish, but wasn't sure how I could do it. And I couldn't without you."

As the sun disappeared and the first stars scattered across the sky, he squeezed her hand tighter. "Yeah, I think Jewel had more up her sleeve than we realized. Like you, I'm a bit of a loner, except for Heath, of course. You're different, Harry McKenzie. In a good way. I'm glad you're staying. The only concern I have is not being able to let you go next year."

Harry's heart did a little flip. She might not be a romantic, but his words awakened something deep inside her. "Meeting you, being with you, hearing you explain your feelings, it's the first time I've ever thought I might not always want to be alone."

He let go of her hand and slipped his arm around her

shoulders. "I feel the same way. I'm not sure where this will lead or what will come of it, but I like the idea of spending more time with you and finding out."

She leaned closer and rested her head against his shoulder. "I like the sound of that."

On Thursday afternoon, Harry chose her black pantsuit and a deep cranberry colored blouse, and made her way to town. Late that afternoon, in a standing-room only special meeting at City Hall, the justice of the peace swore in Harriet McKenzie as the mayor of Lavender Valley.

Harry took to the podium and gave a short speech, thanking the citizens for putting their trust in her, promising to do her very best for them, and letting them know she was ready to hit the ground running. The staff had already cleared out Mayor Crawford's office, and Harry had scheduled a meeting with all the department heads for Friday morning.

As soon as she finished greeting all her well-wishers and the hearing room was empty, she made her way down the hall to her office. It was in the corner on the first floor and consisted of the reception office overseen by her assistant, the mayor's roomy office, and an even larger conference room with a connecting door between the two. The window in her office looked out on a well-kept flower garden with a bench, while the conference room had a view of the street.

The two-story brick building was built in the late 1800's and had been fully restored and retrofitted for modern office use. Harry liked the glass cabinets and bookcases lining the walls, and the sound of the wooden floors under her feet. It reminded her of working in the old building in

Salem for all those years. There was something comforting about being where so many who had served before her had been.

She took a seat in the leather office chair behind the vintage wooden desk. Every surface in the room gleamed, as if the wood was freshly waxed. Except for the modern phone and computer, the office was like stepping back into time with all the mahogany and leather.

She stretched her hands across the glass atop her desk. She had to admit it felt good to be behind a desk again. She hadn't asked for this job, but now that it was hers, she was determined to do her best for the people of Lavender Valley.

She had already met with her assistant, Maxine. Harry was wise enough to understand that long-serving staff members usually had the most information and ideas. They knew about the unsaid rules and inner workings of an agency. Harry had asked what Maxine thought about the mayor hosting an informal meeting each month, where residents could air any concerns or ideas. From the short time she had been in Lavender Valley, Harry understood how much the citizens were looking for someone to listen to them and someone to care about their problems. She also knew the meeting could turn into a huge waste of time, but being new to the town, she wanted to make sure she stayed in touch with the people and understood their needs. If it proved to be useless, she could host the meeting less frequently.

Maxine, an older woman who favored print dresses and wore her gray hair in tight curls, liked the idea, and from talking to her, Harry learned the trusted assistant had been suspicious of Mayor Crawford and that there was no love lost for her old boss. Mayor Crawford had isolated Maxine and even locked her out of the mayor's office. By asking her opinion and valuing her experience, Harry had instantly made a loyal friend.

The creak of the floor drew Harry's attention, and a moment later, Clay walked through her door, smiling. "Hey, Madame Mayor. We've got a little celebration planned for you. I volunteered to escort you to the Riverside Grille."

Harry smiled as she shook her head and reached for her handbag. "I've had a really social day already, and I'm dreaming of hanging out at home with Hope and Chief. Hope is such a lap dog and I could use her cuddles."

"Well, you have to eat. And it's not a huge crowd, I promise. We just want to quietly celebrate and thank you. We got a private room in the back and it's a buffet. You won't have to stay long."

She laughed. "Who can say no to that."

"Just act surprised for me, okay?"

She took his arm as they made their way down the front steps. As they walked along the sidewalk, Clay looked at her appreciatively. "Happy looks good on you, Harry."

She grinned at him. "It's a new challenge. I just hope my best is good enough."

"Remember, like Will said, you only need to work at most half time. Maybe you can set up your office hours in the afternoon, since mornings are busiest at the farm. Then you can get in a routine. And, you don't have to do everything in a week. We like the slower pace around here. Our needs are simple. We just want an honest mayor who makes sure to keep Lavender Valley safe."

"That makes it sound easy," she said with a chuckle.

"I just don't want you working too hard. You need to leave time in your schedule for me." He stopped to face her, and their eyes locked, then he leaned close and brushed his lips against hers.

The little spark on her lips traveled all the way to her toes. It had been a very long time since she'd kissed a man. It was more exciting than she remembered. Or maybe Clay was more exciting than the last man, whose name she couldn't even remember now.

"I know you don't need rescuing, Harry," he added softly. "I admire your strength and character, and like you more than just a little. I want you to know I'll hold your hand and stand by your side through any storm, and I hope you'll do the same for me."

Harry's heart melted and her breath caught in her throat. No man had ever made her feel so strong and yet vulnerable at the same time. She wrapped her arms around his neck, and whispered, "Thank you."

As he led them around the back of the restaurant to the patio overlooking the river, she pressed her arm into him a little tighter. White lights glimmered in the planters and along the railings. Firepits provided a welcoming glow, and with Clay next to her, she was ready to face not only her adoring public, but whatever the future might bring, even if what was around the next corner in her path was completely unexpected.

EPILOGUE

As the first glow of light broke over the horizon, Olivia glanced in the rearview mirror. Leaving Spokane, the city she had called home since graduating college, broke her heart. Not that it wasn't already shattered. This was just the latest in a long string of losses. She struggled to remember the last time she had been happy, as tears streamed down her face. That she would have to leave her home was something she had never imagined.

The trailer that bounced behind her held the few material items she possessed. It hadn't taken long for the two college kids she'd hired to empty her small apartment and load the trailer. Her life with the big house with the white picket fence had slowly faded two years ago when Olivia thought the worst had come. Oh, how wrong she'd been.

Her son going to prison was just the first raindrop of a long and devastating storm. When he passed, just six months ago, she'd never felt such pain. In the aftermath, her already fragile marriage failed completely, and then came the end of her career. It all brought Olivia to her knees.

Literally.

She had turned to her faith and spent more time praying over the last six months than anything else, asking God for peace, for strength, for sanctuary. When Harry's letter arrived and she learned of Jewel's death, it was one more blow to her bruised soul.

As she came to terms with Jewel's passing on the heels of Simon's death, Olivia considered the invitation and took it as the answer to her prayers. Other than memories and heartache, there was nothing left for her in Spokane.

Well, there was Simon's grave.

Olivia couldn't bear to think about it.

To think about him.

The robotic voice coming from her GPS interrupted her musings. Olivia followed the instructions and turned into the parking lot of a burger place in Medford. She found a space for her SUV and small rented cargo trailer. Towing a trailer was outside her comfort zone, and she had white-knuckled most of the over five-hundred-mile trip.

After hours behind the wheel, she was ready to stretch her long legs and have a bite to eat. It didn't take her long to finish her meal, and when she went through the door to the parking lot, she locked eyes with a young man walking toward her. He had the same dark hair as Simon, the same dimples, but his eyes were bright and filled with hope.

She couldn't stop staring at him, remembering the happier years long gone. Longing for the time Simon had smiled like this young man, when his days ahead had been filled with promise. She forced herself to look away and focus on getting back to her SUV.

Tears welled in her eyes as she followed the road to Lavender Valley. Her GPS estimated she would be at the farm within thirty minutes. She needed to pull herself together before then.

The farm evoked warm and wonderful memories. Olivia had been in a horrible place when she first arrived all those decades ago, and Jewel had the patience to let Olivia rest and heal. The woman she thought of as a mother had seen something special in the downtrodden thirteen-year-old girl, and with her urging, Olivia discovered the happiness and satisfaction that came with helping others, especially animals.

Olivia hadn't had a dog in her life for a few years, and when Harry mentioned Jewel's dog rescue project and the animals at the farm, it had been the final tug she'd needed. She only hoped the magic she had found over forty years ago was still there.

She took the exit for Lavender Valley and slowed as she entered downtown. The brick buildings on Main Street gave her comfort. Almost like stepping back in time.

The store names may have changed, but for the most part, it looked the same as when she left. She drove through town and out into the rural area, where her GPS reminded her to turn right in one hundred feet.

She pulled up to the gate with Lavender Valley Farm lettered above it and hit the button on the intercom.

The first time she'd visited the farm, the same feeling she felt now had fluttered in her stomach. Scared and alone, terrified of the unknown.

Harry had told her she was the first of the other four invited women to respond. With her tendency to get overwhelmed in social situations with too many people, Olivia was happy to be the first. It would give her a chance to get settled and find a routine without the pressure of making small talk.

Harry's greeting came through the speaker and the gate swung open. Olivia eased her SUV through and down the driveway.

As the farmhouse that would forever hold a special place in her life came into view, Olivia said a little prayer that Jewel's wisdom in gathering her sisters of the heart would provide the sanctuary she was desperate to find.

Continue Olivia's story in SANCTUARY AT LAVENDER VALLEY, the next book in the series.

Don't miss a book in the SISTERS OF THE HEART SERIES.
Six women. Four decades. One long, unexpected reunion.

ACKNOWLEDGMENTS

Along with the gorgeous setting for this series, I had so much fun creating Harry. She was the first sister of the heart who came to me as I began creating this series. I loved adding in the bit of mystery in this one, which showcased some of Harry's strengths. As with all my books, this series is filled with furry friends, including some cute farm animals, who are some of my favorite characters.

My thanks to my editor, Angela, for finding my mistakes and helping me polish *Pathway to Lavender Valley*. She does an awesome job and I'm grateful for her. This gorgeous cover and all the covers in the series are the result of the talents of Elizabeth Mackey, who never disappoints. I'm fortunate to have such an incredible team helping me.

I so appreciate all of the readers who have taken the time to tell their friends about my work and provide reviews of my books. These reviews are especially important in promoting future books, so if you enjoy my novels, please consider leaving a review and sharing it on social media. I also encourage you to follow me on Amazon, Goodreads, and BookBub, where leaving a review is even easier, and you'll be the first to know about new releases and deals.

Remember to visit my website at http://www.tammylgrace.com and join my mailing list for my exclusive group of readers. I also have a fun Book Buddies Facebook Group. That's the best place to find me and get a chance to participate in my giveaways. Join my Facebook group at

https://www.facebook.com/groups/
AuthorTammyLGraceBookBuddies/
and keep in touch—I'd love to hear from you.

Enjoy Lavender Valley,

Tammy

FROM THE AUTHOR

Thank you for reading PATHWAY TO LAVENDER VALLEY. I love all the characters in this new SISTERS OF THE HEART SERIES and am excited for readers to get to each of them. I started this with a prequel book that gives readers a peek into the lives of all the women in the series. It's a great way to try it and see if the story appeals to you. Then, each subsequent book will feature each woman as the main character in her own story. Now that you've read Harry's story, I'm anxious to share Olivia's in SANCTUARY AT LAVENDER VALLEY. It focuses on Jewel's beloved dog rescue and animal sanctuary.

If you enjoy women's fiction and haven't yet read the entire HOMETOWN HARBOR SERIES, you can start the series with a free prequel that is in the form of excerpts from Sam's journal. She's the main character in the first book, FINDING HOME.

If you're a new reader and enjoy mysteries, I write a series that features a lovable private detective, Coop, and his faithful golden retriever, Gus. If you like whodunits that will keep you guessing until the end, you'll enjoy the COOPER HARRINGTON DETECTIVE NOVELS.

The two books I've written as Casey Wilson, A DOG'S HOPE and A DOG'S CHANCE have received enthusiastic support from my readers and if you're a dog lover, are must reads.

If you enjoy holiday stories, be sure and check out my CHRISTMAS IN SILVER FALLS SERIES and HOMETOWN CHRISTMAS SERIES. They are small-town Christmas stories of hope, friendship, and family. You won't want to miss any of the SOUL SISTERS AT CEDAR MOUNTAIN LODGE BOOKS, also featuring a foster sister theme. It's a connected Christmas series I wrote with four author friends. My contributions, CHRISTMAS WISHES, CHRISTMAS SURPRISES, and CHRISTMAS SHELTER. All heartwarming, small-town holiday stories that I'm sure you'll enjoy. The series kicks off with a free prequel novella, CHRISTMAS SISTERS, where you'll get a chance to meet the characters during their first Christmas together.

You won't want to miss THE WISHING TREE SERIES, set in Vermont. This series centers on a famed tree in the middle of the quaint town that is thought to grant wishes to those who tie them on her branches. Readers love this series and always comment how they are full of hope, which we all need more of right now.

I'd love to send you my exclusive interview with the canine companions in my Hometown Harbor Series as a thank-you for joining my exclusive group of readers. You can sign up www.tammylgrace.com by clicking this link: https://wp.me/P9umIy-e

ALSO BY TAMMY L. GRACE

COOPER HARRINGTON DETECTIVE NOVELS

Killer Music

Deadly Connection

Dead Wrong

Cold Killer

HOMETOWN HARBOR SERIES

Hometown Harbor: The Beginning (Prequel Novella)

Finding Home

Home Blooms

A Promise of Home

Pieces of Home

Finally Home

Forever Home

Follow Me Home

CHRISTMAS STORIES

A Season for Hope: Christmas in Silver Falls Book 1

The Magic of the Season: Christmas in Silver Falls Book 2

Christmas in Snow Valley: A Hometown Christmas Book 1

One Unforgettable Christmas: A Hometown Christmas Book 2

Christmas Wishes: Souls Sisters at Cedar Mountain Lodge

Christmas Surprises: Soul Sisters at Cedar Mountain Lodge

GLASS BEACH COTTAGE SERIES

Beach Haven

Moonlight Beach

Beach Dreams

WRITING AS CASEY WILSON

A Dog's Hope

A Dog's Chance

WISHING TREE SERIES

The Wishing Tree

Wish Again

Overdue Wishes

SISTERS OF THE HEART SERIES

Greetings from Lavender Valley

Pathway to Lavender Valley

Sanctuary at Lavender Valley

Blossoms at Lavender Valley

Comfort in Lavender Valley

Remember to subscribe to Tammy's exclusive group of readers for your gift, only available to readers on her mailing list. **Sign up at www.tammylgrace.com. Follow this link to subscribe at https:// wp.me/P9umIy-e** and you'll receive the exclusive interview she did with all the canine characters in her Hometown Harbor Series.

Follow Tammy on Facebook by liking her page. You may also follow Tammy on book retailers or at BookBub by clicking on the follow button.

ABOUT THE AUTHOR

Tammy L. Grace is the *USA Today* bestselling and award-winning author of the Cooper Harrington Detective Novels, the bestselling Hometown Harbor Series, and the Glass Beach Cottage Series, along with several sweet Christmas novellas. Tammy also writes under the pen name of Casey Wilson for Bookouture and Grand Central. You'll find Tammy online at www.tammylgrace.com where you can join her mailing list and be part of her exclusive group of readers. Connect with Tammy on Facebook at www.facebook.com/tammylgrace.books or Instagram at @authortammylgrace.

facebook.com/tammylgrace.books

twitter.com/TammyLGrace

instagram.com/authortammylgrace

bookbub.com/authors/tammy-l-grace

goodreads.com/tammylgrace

amazon.com/author/tammylgrace

Made in United States
Troutdale, OR
01/10/2024

16870827R00170